SAVING
grapes

Published by Emerald Book Company
Austin, TX
www.emeraldbookcompany.com

Distributed by Emerald Book Company

For ordering information or special discounts for bulk purchases, please contact Emerald Book Company at PO Box 91869, Austin, TX 78709, 512.891.6100.

Design and composition by Greenleaf Book Group
Cover design by Colleen Lanchester-Raynie
Cover image: ©shutterstock/iralu

Cataloging-in-Publication data is available.

ISBN 13: 978-1-937110-75-8

Part of the Tree Neutral® program, which offsets the number of trees consumed in the production and printing of this book by taking proactive steps, such as planting trees in direct proportion to the number of trees used: www.treeneutral.com

Tree Neutral

Printed in the United States of America on acid-free paper

14 15 16 17 18 19   10 9 8 7 6 5 4 3 2 1

First Edition

SAVING
grapes

A Romantic Comedy

J.T. LUNDY

EMERALD
BOOK CO.

CHAPTER 1

My ex-wife had been aiming for me all morning. Laura's old high school friends, Sheila and Erin, had been gunning for me, too. I wasn't bothered, though—not a bit. These three showed up every Wednesday at Eustace's Tees and slugged range balls my way as I drove the caged ball-picker back and forth, scooping up the evidence of golfers' frustration and glory. I ignored them, mostly, as they hit away and laughed. I'm good at ignoring things, which is probably one reason Laura left me in the first place. That, and she found some big-time bond trader whose lucrative career looked more attractive than my personality or prospects. No, they could shoot at me all they wanted.

Perfectly synchronized, Laura, Erin, and Sheila each took a mighty swing in my direction. I couldn't actually see the ball, or balls I should say, as they sailed, camouflaged through the gray Illinois sky, so I paid no mind and lazily cruised along. I was preparing to turn the picker around when the three white spinning projectiles arrived at once, pelting the wire cage with enough force to shake the coffee cup out of my non-steering hand.

"Hey," I shouted, knocked out of my self-control and faux nonchalance. Hot coffee spread on my green maintenance coveralls. I looked to the tees and saw Laura bent over laughing. Erin and Sheila high-fived. Laura straightened up and they all embraced, celebrating the miracle shots that had jolted a reaction out of me. The underside of my skin tingled.

I took a deep breath and tried to relax. Laura had deserted me, and I blamed her, but I guess logically I shouldn't have. Bond-trader-Tom was in the fast lane. Ball-picker-Jason was thirty-two and still mowing grass. For the most part, though, Laura and I had remained friends.

The happy threesome smiled and waved teasingly. So what, they got me. I should have waved back and shrugged it off, but there's only so much humiliation a man can take, and my range bucket was full. Week after week, all summer long, these three former prom queen wanabees took out their aging frustrations on me. It was fall and there were only a few weeks left in the season, but their affable taunting had finally gotten to me. I gripped the steering wheel and my arms trembled. I stared at Laura and tried to regain control, but then, in the parking lot behind the tees and jeering ladies, I saw a tow truck dangling my 1985 red Pontiac Fiero from its hook and chain.

The bank was finally calling my bluff. They were going to repossess my ride.

"Stop!" I steered the range picker toward the tees and raced for the parking lot. Laura, Erin, and Sheila grabbed their clubs and scattered. I hit the tees without a thought of braking. Ball baskets and tee mats went flying. A ball washer went down.

"Asshole!" Sheila cried.

I raced by the shocked women and headed for the tow truck. My Fiero moved toward the exit. The truck driver flipped me his middle finger out the open window. I couldn't catch up. The truck clanked out of the parking lot and dragged my sham sports car filled with memories, more bad than good these last years, down the road and out of my life.

"You're fired, Jason!"

I turned around. There he stood. Eustace Small, the miserly owner of Eustace's Tees and my former stepbrother. He was in front of the white wood-sided office in a very un-golf-like suit, his hands smugly on his hips. If there was a person who could get my ire up more than Laura, it was Eustace, and he was an easier target. I don't know why I did what I did—years of frustration I guess.

I whipped the picker around and back over the tee boxes toward Eustace. He looked at me in horror. I drove straight at him. Eustace ran, and I chased. The ladies whooped and clapped and cheered on my destruction.

I only wanted to scare him, and I was about to turn away when Eustace picked up the high-pressure water hose and pointed. A jet of water flooded onto my head. I instinctively lifted my hands to protect my face and the picker veered, slamming into an aluminum fence post. I pulled the picker back and stopped.

A metal creaking sound filled the air.

The top of the post teetered, and then it fell, pulling the fence with it. The post and fence crashed into the next post, and a giant chain reaction began. Posts toppled like dominoes, and the one hundred-foot-high mesh that encased the range tumbled to the ground.

The water barrage ended, and I regained control of the picker. I looked at Eustace. His hair was a straggly mess. Water dripped from his suit. He threw a golf ball at me, but it bounced harmlessly off the cage. He ran to the one hundred-yard marker, removed the flagpole, and threw it at me like a javelin. It darted through the cage's steel mesh, zipped by my nose, and hit the back roll bar where it stopped.

I tried to push the flagpole, but it had bent and wouldn't slide out. Eustace ran and grabbed a flagpole at the fifty-yard marker. He held his new weapon like a spear and charged. I kicked the accelerator and dashed across the range. I looked back. Eustace chased, but he couldn't keep up. In a final effort he launched his flagpole javelin high into the air, but it landed harmlessly behind me.

The one hundred-yard marker protruded out the cage's front as I crossed Route 57 and drove into Brentwood Estates, the city of Kankakee's most exclusive subdivision.

What to do? Stumpy. I'd go to Stumpy. Generally he was an idiot, but sometimes he gave me good advice. I hugged the street's side, half the picker on the road, half on the parkway.

An old man walked from his house toward the street. I smiled and waved and unintentionally ran over the newspaper at the end of his drive, mangling it beyond saving as it flipped into the hopper.

The old man shook his fist. "Criminal!"

I rounded a corner and turned onto Chicago Avenue, a busy strip mall mecca. Cars honked and people yelled. I drove two blocks and then bounced over the curb and came to a stop in Little Caesar's parking lot.

Inside Little Caesar's the air was thick with heat and the yeasty smell of dough.

"Jason!" Stumpy, short and squat with bowl-cut straight hair, stood next to a stainless steel counter in the back tossing pepperonis onto a pizza.

"Stumpy," I called. "You're the pizza master."

Stumpy laughed and overshot a pepperoni to the floor.

"That pizza for me?"

"If you want."

"For both of us. Throw that pie in the oven."

Stumpy looked at the oven uncertainly. "I'm not supposed to go near the oven anymore."

"Okay, well, come ring me up, then. Five ninety-nine, right?" I shoved my hand into my coverall's leg pocket. I was pretty sure I had a ten folded up down there somewhere.

Stumpy just stood there looking embarrassed, somewhat guilty even. "I'm not allowed to use the cash register anymore either."

"Hey," I shouted toward the back. "Can I get some service here?"

"Jason, please."

"Don't worry, man, just keep tossing them pepperonis on our pizza. I want extra, extra, pepperonis."

The nineteen-year-old string bean of a manager came out of the back office scowling at me. "Stumpy breaks in five minutes. You can wait outside."

"I'm a customer. One pepperoni pizza, good sir." I plopped down my coffee-soaked, crumpled up, ten-dollar bill.

Stringbean reluctantly rang up the total on the register.

"Are you hiring?"

He opened and closed his eyes slowly and shook his head. "We tried that already." He turned his head toward Stumpy with a disgruntled employer's glare, which quickly turned to shock. "What are you doing?"

Stumpy stopped humming and looked up. He stood before a pizza piled high with well over a hundred pepperonis.

I laughed. "Yeah. Pepperoni paradise!" I looked back to Stringbean. "Could you put our pizza in the oven?"

He was ready to cook us both, but I did some fast talking and negotiated our extra, extra pepperoni pizza price to my entire ten dollars, which he was not very happy with, but what choice did he have?

When the pizza was done, Stumpy took his break and we sat on the sidewalk curb, stretching our feet into the parking lot in front of the ball-picker.

I told Stumpy about my Fiero, and the ball-picker joyride. "What am I going to do?"

"You know what I think?"

"What?"

Stumpy shoved a whole gob of the pepperoni glacier into his mouth until his cheeks bulged. He looked at me with serious wide eyes and garble-talked insensibly as he chewed on the mouthful of pizza.

I laughed. This was an old tactic Stumpy and I utilized whenever we had something important to discuss. I shoved the meaty dough into my mouth until I could barely breathe and then gurgled an appropriate response to Stumpy's remarks.

We started laughing until our eyes watered. My breathing became dangerously stifled. I stood up and began spitting chewed pepperonis onto the pavement.

Just then, a siren wailed and the sheriff's car whipped into the lot. No great escape for the J-man. The ball-picker bandit was run down in under an hour. Just fabulous. Aunt Clara, Eustace, even Laura, all the pissed-off people in my pissed-off life would have something to say about this. Did it matter? Really, after all, did it matter any more?

The sheriff stepped his large frame out of the car and stood before us in his tan uniform. "Your brother, Eustace. He's real pissed off."

"You mean his stepbrother," Stumpy said.

"Former stepbrother," I said.

I stood up, cheese dripping down my chin, and put my hands together in front of me. The sheriff looked almost bored as he removed a pair of handcuffs from his belt and latched them over my wrists.

CHAPTER 2

Eustace was droning on. "The season's almost over. I need money. Jason has to pay."

So I sat, later that night, discussing my fate with Aunt Clara, Eustace, and Aunt Clara's attorney, William Hammersmith III, at a Denny's, because it was Aunt Clara's favorite.

Aunt Clara looked upon us with authority. She spoke in her thick French accent. "Let me tell you what's going to happen." Since the three of us were indebted to Aunt Clara in one way or another, she was pretty much calling the shots.

"Eustace. You will not press charges."

"I'm a grown man, Ms. Clara."

"You're a grown ass," I said.

Eustace grabbed his fork and raised it up my way like he was going to skewer me.

"Boys!" Aunt Clara slapped Eustace's hand down. "Stop it."

"Yeah. Stop it, you forker," I said.

Aunt Clara pinched the skin between her eyes, and I thought for a second she might be trying to stop herself from crying. "Boys, I was mother to you both for a short time. It ended badly between Eustace's father and me, but I like to think we were a nice little family for at least a while."

Mother. Ha. A mother that made me call her Aunt Clara, so as I wouldn't forget I was not her son. And the Eustace era was all a terrible time the way I remember it. I don't think Eustace's father, the philandering rat, ever loved Aunt Clara, but she, nevertheless, fawned all over Eustace, as if proving her worth would help the situation.

Eustace put his hand on Aunt Clara's shoulder. "Living in your house was the best time of my life."

Aunt Clara looked kindly at Eustace. "If only your father was as sweet as you."

Oh, please! What nonsense. I slapped my hand on the table. "You always liked Eustace better than me. Is that what we are here for? To compare me to Eustace?"

Aunt Clara grabbed her spoon and smacked my knuckles. "Have some gratitude. This is about us saving you from jail—and for the last time! Next time you'll simply be cut out of everything. I've already put it in writing."

Aunt Clara nodded to Hammersmith, who nodded pompously back. "Mr. Hammersmith and I just finalized my last will and testament." Aunt Clara's eyes never left mine, even as I looked around. "I love you, Jason, but this is your last chance."

Aunt Clara had raised me since I was a baby, but the only time I ever heard her talk about love, it was always followed by a threat.

She looked us over. "Jason you can move back into the house and I'll provide you room and board. You will then work for free and help Eustace rebuild the fence. I will loan Eustace some money to tide him over."

I had to stifle a groan.

"Mr. Hammersmith will write up an agreement, and we will all behave amicably and present it to the judge tomorrow and hope he lets Jason off."

Hammersmith looked back and forth at Eustace and me. "Agreed?"

Eustace and I nodded.

"Then shake hands," Aunt Clara said.

I shook Eustace's clammy hand as hard and friendly as I could. He smiled and squeezed back with less enthusiasm.

William Hammersmith III stood across the aisle and talked chummy-like with Eustace.

I sat at a wooden table before an ornate judge's bench in Kankakee's one hundred and fifty year old county courthouse. High ceilings and lacquered wooden tables, seats, and rails brought a gravity and sense of weighty tradition to the room. It smelled of plaster and looked like a country lawyer's dream.

Eustace stepped across the aisle and shook my hand. "Good luck."

Good luck? What did I need luck for? "I thought everything was set?"

"Things change." Eustace looked at Hammersmith and then to me, like what he was about to say was rehearsed. "I'm sorry, Jason, but sometimes life doesn't work out the way we plan." Eustace looked almost sad for me. Now I was really scared.

The bailiff bellowed, "All rise for the honorable Judge Landon Crawford." The old judge walked in with his black choir-like robe, stood behind the bench like a preacher in a pulpit, and locked eyes with me. I was looking up at the same old guy whose newspaper I had destroyed yesterday with the ball-picker.

"Would the parties approach the bench," Judge Crawford said.

Hammersmith stood between Eustace and me as we all looked up to the judge. "The facts are not in dispute in this case," Judge Crawford said. "Mr. Barnes admits guilt and my sentence is one year in the county jail."

I went numb. "One year?"

"Vehicle theft, driving an unlicensed vehicle, and damaging property." The judge looked at his notes. "One year is a light sentence, but still, I'm willing to listen to alternatives."

"We had an agreement!" I looked at the judge, then at Eustace, then at Hammersmith. "We had an agreement."

"Eustace has changed his mind," Hammersmith said.

I looked around for Aunt Clara, but I couldn't find her.

"I understand the parties are related?" The judge said.

I regained some feeling and tried to be hopeful.

"Stepbrothers," Eustace said.

"Former stepbrothers," I said.

The judge arched his eyebrows in confusion.

"My aunt was my guardian," I said. "My parents died in a car accident when I was a baby."

"My dad was married to his aunt for six months when Jason and I were ten," Eustace added.

"It was six months of hell," I said.

The judge pounded his gavel. "To the point." He looked at Eustace. "You insist on pressing charges?"

Eustace looked deadpan at me. "Absolutely."

"What are your damages?" The judge asked.

"Sixty thousand dollars."

"Wait, what?" My head jerked around and I looked wide-eyed at Eustace. "Sixty thousand!"

Eustace opened up a folder. "I have all the estimates, plus legal fees, and the standard add on for pain and suffering."

"We'll see what Aunt Clara says about that." I bit the inside of my lip, lest I strangle him right there. "Okay, fine. I'll work it off. I'll pay him back. That's what we agreed."

"That's an interesting idea," The judge said. "What if Mr. Barnes were to repay the damages?"

Eustace slapped his folder shut. He ran his hand through his thinning black hair. "He deserves a lesson. I'm pressing charges."

"We agreed. We shook hands." I put my hands together as if in prayer. "Eustace, we're brothers."

"*Former* stepbrothers."

"Mere semantics. Perhaps we haven't been the best of pals, but family should help each other out in times of need."

Eustace smiled. "Not this time."

I spread my hands wide. "Why the hell not?"

He pointed at me. "I'll tell you why." He pressed his hand against his suit. "I've worked hard all my life and watched you slide by. I'm pressing charges."

Damn. Why was Eustace being such a jerk? That is, why was he being an even bigger jerk than he usually was? "Please, Eustace. Have some mercy. I don't want to go to jail. I'm sorry for all the bad things I've ever said or done to you."

Eustace pursed his lips and shook his head resolutely.

"Don't do this, Eustace," I pleaded. "I'll tell Aunt Clara. This is not what she wanted. She's not going to be happy." I looked around. Still no Aunt Clara.

"I agree Mr. Barnes deserves a lesson." Judge Crawford grimaced. "And I'm still ticked off about my newspaper." He closed his eyes and opened them slowly, considering my fate. "But even so, I'm a fair man and I will give him a chance. If Mr. Barnes can repay the damages, that's enough for me." The judge pounded the gavel. "Mr. Barnes you have thirty days to pay sixty thousand dollars to this court or the conviction stands and you shall report to jail. The court will record any funds collected and distribute them to Mr. Small."

I couldn't grow that kind of money. I was going to be in the slammer for a year.

I stood outside on the court steps, leaning against a limestone column that felt smooth and solid, unlike me. I looked downtown to Rosewald Drugs and the vacant movie theater. St. John's steeple rose high into the air. Stumpy always tried to drag me to that old Baptist church, but I had been raised Catholic. I had given up on that kind of stuff anyway. People walked past the church and shops unhurriedly, with freedom, without a thought of going to prison. I envied them.

Hammersmith came walking out with an irritatingly cheesy grin on his face. "For sixty grand you're free and clear."

"Wait till my Aunt hears about this."

Hammersmith smiled proudly, as if he had done me a favor. Had Aunt Clara turned on me, too? Was this all her idea? I tried to think of the other things I had done that could really set her off.

"The court wants your passport. The judge thinks you're a flight risk."

"Like I'm going anywhere."

"You brought your passport, right?"

I pulled my passport out of my back jean pocket and handed it to him. I turned and walked down the steps to the sidewalk, thinking about spending a year in jail.

I had to find Aunt Clara. Something told me she was behind all this. I bet she was trying to teach me a lesson. Perhaps she had the judge in on it, and it was all a big ploy to scare me.

A white Range Rover pulled up along the curb. The window rolled down and Laura looked at me, concerned for a change.

"You're too late if you want to testify against me."

She acted like she hadn't heard me. "The hospital called. They still had me as a contact. I'm sorry, Jason, Aunt Clara had a stroke. She's passed away."

I stared at Laura, my senses deadened. I had wished for Aunt Clara to die probably a thousand times over the years. I felt queasy. Now I wasn't so certain. I tried to breathe to stop myself from throwing up. That's why Aunt Clara hadn't shown up for court. She hadn't turned on me. Oh, Jesus. Aunt Clara had her faults, but she was the only family I'd ever had—the only mother I'd known.

"Jason? Are you all right? Get in. I'll give you a ride."

I didn't know what to do. I stared at Laura. She now had blond hair and extra hips, but she was still as cute as ever. I climbed into the Range Rover and shut the door, natural, like Laura picking me up from court happened every day.

I sat silent, bewildered and dumfounded from the events in court and the news that Aunt Clara had died. Laura prattled on. "What happened? Are you guilty? Eustace is such an ass. I'm sorry about Aunt Clara. She didn't like me much, but I am sorry. Are you all right? Should we stop?"

I waved my hand to keep going.

"Father Roger will visit you to take care of the funeral details. Did she have a burial plot?"

I shrugged.

"I wonder what she left you? I bet she had money stashed away." Laura looked at me like money could solve all unpleasantness.

I stayed silent and we continued on until reaching my apartment.

I skipped the funeral service at the church. I'm not sure why. Was I mad that she had left me? Aunt Clara was all about obligation, and even though she was dead, I could still feel her controlling influence. Maybe that's why I didn't go; it was my last act of defiance. I wasn't supposed to be a pallbearer or anything, but my absence would be noted, another mark against the uncaring, disrespectful Jason Barnes.

I put on a Thelonious Monk album from an old collection of jazz records Aunt Clara had given me. Jazz was the one interest we had in common that we could speak about without arguing. I listened to the music and paced. I stopped and looked at the one photograph I had of my parents, taken a week before they had died. In the faded color photo my frighteningly young parents seemed awkward together. They stood close, their hands inches apart, like they wanted to hold each other, but were afraid to. My mother cradled a mass of blanket that was supposedly me.

Did they love me? Of course they loved me, but would they love me now? Would I have turned out different if they had lived? Would they have approved of how Aunt Clara had raised me—stern with unreasonable expectations? I'd always imagined my parents would have been perfect, loving, and kind, but maybe not. My mother was Aunt Clara's younger sister, maybe she would have been worse. I stared at my parents, and I knew what I should do. I hopped on my Trek mountain bike and headed for the cemetery. Everyone, even Aunt Clara, deserves a final farewell.

I rode through the cemetery gates and followed the curvy asphalt road to the back. I leaned my bike against a grand tombstone and walked toward a somber group surrounding Aunt Clara's freshly dug grave. I could hear Father Roger mumbling some words through the strong breeze. The sky was gray and the leaves rustled as the old trees in the cemetery swayed.

I made my way up and stood by Stumpy in the front. His eyes were red from crying and he was in his best, but still sloppy, suit. I wore jeans and a T-shirt.

"Where were you?" Stumpy hissed.

I shrugged.

"Jesus. Your aunt may have been mean, but she at least raised you."

Aunt Clara never attended a school play or a sporting event. She'd yell at any child who even thought of walking on our grass, and was so intimidating no kid but Stumpy was willing to play at my house. Yeah, she had raised me.

They lowered the casket into the grave. I stared into the pit. It didn't seem real. Stumpy sobbed.

"Jason?" Father Roger asked. "Would you like to say a word?"

I tried to say *no*, but I weakened. Father Roger calling me out felt like a cork had been popped from my gut. "I, I." I was going to cry. Damn it. I didn't want to give the old biddy the satisfaction. I fought to stay stoic, as Aunt Clara would have expected, as she would have wanted. I recovered. "No, Father. Thank you." I picked up some dirt, tossed it into the grave and walked away.

CHAPTER 3

Sheila played a golf game on her computer as I walked into the reception room at Hammersmith's office. Paintings of English fox hunts and tall mast warships hung from the deep blue walls. Oriental rugs covered the floor. The dark wood trim and carefully placed antique lamps created an old men's club feel to the office.

"Hole in one?"

Sheila looked at me with disgust and then motioned to an office door down a hall. "He's waiting."

I walked by Sheila. "Swanky joint for you to work in."

"Have fun picking balls in prison."

I walked into Hammersmith's office and slouched on a leather couch. Hammersmith, our "family" attorney, looked across his clutter-free mahogany desk, oversized to intimidate, and cleared his throat. "Jason, the unfortunate day you have been waiting for has arrived."

"Yes. I mean no, sir."

Hammersmith grimaced. "For the matter at hand, Ms. Barnes's last will and testament."

I sat up straight.

Hammersmith adjusted his power red tie and pressed a button on a remote control. A wall-mounted flat screen TV came to life. Aunt Clara stared down at me with vengeance. She wore her special occasion blue polyester dress she bought back in '79 and her pointy black glasses I imagined she was born with.

She spoke with her ever-present accent. *"I'm dead and gone. You can wipe that smile off your face, Jason Anthony. I've raised you since you were a baby, but I've made no secret of the fact that you've been a great disappointment."*

"Psh," I said, rolling my eyes. Like I hadn't heard that one before.

Aunt Clara smacked her lips, looked left, and then right as though she were considering. *"You need to learn what it's like to work."*

I shook my head and looked at Hammersmith. "I've worked my butt off at Eustace's for three years."

"And driving golf carts is not work," Aunt Clara said angrily. *"When I was young . . . "* I said the words along with Aunt Clara. *"I hoed weeds and picked grapes from sunrise to sunset."*

I laughed. Aunt Clara was dead, and I still had to hear the same spiel.

"Don't you mock me, Jason Anthony. It's time you grew up and became a man. It's time you learned how to make a woman happy."

I jumped up. "Wait, what?" Aunt Clara had always viciously blamed Laura for our divorce. She had never insulted me like this, and I must say, it hurt. I sat back down as Aunt Clara continued. Her voice softened. *"Mon petit garcon. Tu as besoin de profiter de la vie. I'm going to give you a chance to redeem yourself, Jason. That vineyard I've always told you about that I grew up on—well, I own it—and if you are willing to work like a man for a change then it is yours."* Aunt Clara then raised her voice and pointed her finger and spoke to me again as she was accustomed. *"But if you turn out a bum . . . if you go to jail . . . I'm giving it all to Eustace."*

The screen went blank. Hammersmith looked at me with disapprobation over his spectacles, uncannily like Aunt Clara would have done.

I stood up and put my hands on the desk. "I'll show her. I'll work like a man. What about her money? Do I get any cash or not?"

Hammersmith leered at me. He seemed almost happy. "No. No money. Clara generously donated her portfolio to charity."

To charity! I thought Aunt Clara dying would be my ace card out of jail. This generosity stunt designed to rile me was just like her. In second grade she made me give all my first communion money to the church. I was supposed to learn the power of giving, but all I learned was resentment—and that I craved money even more. She had done it to me again, but perhaps this vineyard was a way out of my troubles. "What about this vineyard?" I asked.

Hammersmith pulled out a photograph. An old stone house with blue shutters and red roman tile roof overlooked a sunny, unbelievably gorgeous vine laden landscape.

"Your aunt left you this."

I clapped my hands. "It must be worth millions. How do I sell it?"

"The inheritance is not final yet."

I pointed at Hammersmith. "Well, finalize it."

He was annoyed with my impertinence. "That can only take place in France."

"Wait, what?"

Hammersmith took off his glasses, and I thought he might have made a slight smirk. "To inherit the vineyard, you must personally have it notarized in France."

"I've got twenty-seven days to pay the court." I stood up. "If you don't mind, I'll be on my way to France."

Hammersmith stood up as well. "Sit down. You can't leave. The court has your passport."

Damn, he was right. I sat back down. "Does this vineyard make any money?"

"Plenty," Hammersmith said. "Clara split the profits with the vineyard farmers."

"Do I get the profits now?"

There was that little smirk again. "That's the work part."

"I have to work?"

"As your aunt said, 'to become a man,' if you remember."

"I am a man."

"Well, yes, but implicitly I think she meant, *better* man. In any case, to receive any profits you must help the farmers work the vineyard."

"The grapes of wrath! Work? In France?" I was so stupid. I finally realized my predicament. "Will Eustace really get this place if I go to jail?"

Hammersmith patted a stack of papers. "That's what the will says."

"But, but, not this time, right? Aunt Clara said 'the next time I went to jail' when we were at Denny's. We had an agreement for this time, right? You heard her."

"Uh." Hammersmith looked nervous. "Technically, no. Eustace changed his mind the next day, well within the three days legally allowed to break a contract, and nothing was in writing."

I should have hired my own lawyer, but the thought never occurred to me. I didn't have the funds anyway. My vision blurred, and Hammersmith's head seemed to balloon. "Eustace knew! You both knew that Aunt Clara had died before court started."

"I can't discuss Eustace's business," he said matter-of-factly.

"Was this crazy will all your idea, Hammerhead?"

Hammersmith put his hands up. He was flustered and defensive. "Not at all! I'm just doing my job." He then regained his composure and tried to appear forthcoming. "I must admit I find it amusing, but the caveats of the will were all Ms. Barnes's idea. I put in the standard

Good Character Clause she refers to when speaking of jail. Your aunt wanted the clause to be effective forever, but legally once you inherit the vineyard it's yours to keep whether you are incarcerated in the future or not."

I sat down in defeat. "Aunt Clara and her damn character building."

CHAPTER 4

Stumpy waved at me from our regular booth near the end of the bar, happier now that the funeral business was over. He smiled at me with more friendliness than I deserved. Stumpy and I had been best buds since second grade. I had treated him bad off and on, I admit, dropping him for long stretches of time to hang out with the more popular crowd and things like that; but from helping me deal with my Aunt Clara, to holding my hand through the divorce, Stumpy had always stuck with me.

I made my way through Lucky Mike's, an Irish pub in the heart of corn-fed Kankakee. The place served beer and hard liquor and made a terrible mojito. Classic rock thumped and the bartenders didn't hurry. Neon Coors and Old Style signs reflected off the mirror-backed shelves, the only bright lights in the dark room. A group of lecherous men and observant women crowded the bar, talking and drinking and clamoring for attention.

Stumpy stood up to greet me. I was five-foot ten and I had at least six inches on him.

"What's up, Jason?"

The lack of couples reminded me it was the first Tuesday of the month, unofficially, divorce night. The typical woman in the bar had a husbandless subdivision castle, two or three activity-prone kids, not enough income to support it all alone, and worked out like crazy in hopes of attracting someone who could help.

The men were either looking for love or looking to get laid. Some women had difficulty discerning the difference. Others didn't care.

I sat down across from him. "I hate divorce night."

The place smelled of perfume, beer, cologne, and desperation.

"It's okay. Changes the scene at least. Hey, look, I'm really sorry about your aunt."

Stumpy had endured Aunt Clara's unrelenting wrath ever since we started hanging out in the second grade. The guy never did anyone harm. I don't know what Aunt Clara had against him, other than that he was my friend.

"It was nice that you made it to the funeral."

"She would have wanted me there."

I laughed.

Stumpy laughed, too. "But I'm serious." He touched his chest. "Deep down I think she liked me."

"Man, you are an optimist. She used to call you Frumpy! And remember when she said you were fatter than fois grois?"

"At least I learned what fois grois was. Talking with Aunt Clara made me feel wordelly."

"Do you mean *wordy* or *worldly*?"

"The second one."

Lucky Mike slid two Miller Lites across the table to us. He had black hair and blue eyes like me, but wore a beard wild enough to intimidate anyone. Mike went to high school with us and was good about letting me have credit when I was low on funds.

"Well? What did Mr. Hammersmith say?" Stumpy asked.

I pulled out the vineyard photograph and slapped it on the table. "Aunt Clara left me a French vineyard. Hammersmith says it might be worth millions."

"Millions? Like dollars?"

"Euros? Dollars? It's all mud until I sell. Can you help me?"

"What do you mean help?"

I looked at Stumpy, disappointed. I had already told him what happened in court. "I have twenty-seven days to deliver the court sixty grand or I go to jail and Eustace gets the vineyard. Now, you've saved some money."

Stumpy closed one eye and looked at the ceiling with the other. "I've only saved about five grand."

"Five grand. We can go to France with five grand."

"You can't leave the country."

"Lucky Mike says he'll help out with a passport."

Stumpy frowned. He didn't like it when I started scheming. "That'll never work. They, like, computer-check those passports now."

"They scan them, and only to see if they've been reported stolen or if the person is on some bad list."

"How do you know?"

"I googled it, and stolen passports are the problem. I'll be using a legitimate passport, so as long as I look like Lucky Mike, getting into France should be quiche."

A raucous laugh came from the bar. Stumpy and I looked and saw Laura, Sheila, and Erin standing with a crowd enjoying a drink.

"I heard those French girls are sophisticated, and classy." Stumpy tilted his beer at me to accentuate his point. "Or chic. That's the word."

I was surprised Stumpy was hip on French women, though he does read a lot of magazines at Wal-Mart during his spare time.

Laura caught me looking at her. She smiled and waved her arms wide and I could tell her preferred Captain Morgan rum had gotten a hold of her. She walked through the crowd toward us.

"Shit. Look who's coming."

Stumpy looked up and waved to Laura.

I pointed at him. "Not a word."

He nodded. "Not a word."

Laura slid into the booth next to me. "Buy me a drink?"

Laura became obnoxious after a few drinks. "I don't want the responsibility."

"Typical." She laughed and touched my arm. "What are you doing here?"

Looking for what you frittered away, I wanted to say. "Me? I'm always here. And I'm still divorced in case you forgot." Our hearts had gotten along fine, but the world's demands and pressures and expectations, like the need for a job, for example, or the ability not to embarrass yourself at a cocktail party, got to her. I liked to think that if we could've stayed in a safe place like college, we'd still be together. "What are *you* doing here?"

"Girls night out." She nodded to the bar. "Sheila and I are trying to usher Erin back into the game." Laura rubbed her chin. "What do you think, Jason? You and Erin might hit it off."

Typical of Laura to look out for me, as if seeing me happy with someone would erase her guilt. But Erin was a disaster, an emotional wreck and over the top on the high-maintenance meter. And I was still a mess from the divorce. I'd only gone on two dates in the five years since. "No thanks."

"Jason needs to meet some sophisticated ladies," Stumpy said.

Laura picked an ice cube out of her rum and coke and threw it at Stumpy. "Sophisticated? Like those girls you hang out with, Stumpy?"

"I was talking about Jason."

"Ha!" Laura slapped her hand on the table. "That's too funny."

"Wait, what? You don't think I'd have a chance with a more refined, say, international woman?"

Laura sat up straight, pursed her lips, and gave me a good looking over. "You're still reasonably fit, but your job sucks. I mean, really. You pick up golf balls for a living."

"Used to pick up golf balls, and not everyone can be a *Master of the Universe*."

Laura looked at her Rocky-Mountain-sized diamond ring. "That's true, though Tom's job is stressful."

Stumpy coughed into his hands and mumbled, "Masturbator of the universe."

"Fine." Laura stood up. "You two clods discuss how you're going to meet sophisticated," she made air quotation marks, "international women. Ha!" Laura walked back to her friends.

Lucky Mike walked by and dropped off two more beers.

"Stumpy, we've been best friends for a long time, right?"

"Since always."

Stumpy had forever stood behind me. That's something I've come to appreciate now that I'm older, especially after Laura gave me the heave ho. I waved my hand. "Come on. Help me sell this France property and our days of begging the man for scrap jobs are over."

"It hasn't been so bad."

"Are you kidding me?" I looked at Stumpy, shocked. "You could use some serious cash. Come on. Just pay for the airfare and food and stuff and I'll give you ten percent."

"Ten percent of what?"

"Of the vineyard! Of millions!"

"And we get to meet French women?"

"Of course, you can meet all the chic French women you want."

"I meant you, too," he said. "I'll do it if you at least promise to try and have some fun for a change."

Typical. I don't think "millions" even registered with the guy. He was going to pay our way to France just to help me forget about Laura.

"I promise. I'll try."

"No. Really try. Like Six Flags try." One summer in high school Stumpy got a job being Tweety Bird at Six Flags. One day he snagged me a Bugs Bunny costume and we followed these girls we were hot on, the Menendez twins, around the park, flirting and entertaining them with improvised pantomime routines.

I pointed at him. "We held their hands on the Demonic Dragon."

"And the Gold Gusher Falls."

"And the Tornado Tower!"

Our faces became solemn as we finished our remembrance, and we both said, "The Cyclone Crunch."

After the Cyclone Crunch, Stumpy threw up his lunch and had to take off his Tweety Bird helmet. One of the Menendez twins ripped off my helmet and, not too pleased to recognize us, punched me in the stomach.

"It was fun, though," I said.

"That's the kind of fun I want to have in France," Stumpy said, a hopeful glint in his eye.

I lifted my beer up. "Okay. Six Flags try." We clinked bottles and then shook hands.

"We're going to France!" I said.

Stumpy smiled.

CHAPTER 5

Stumpy and I sat together on a wide-body directed toward Paris. It was a quick exit from Kankakee, but that's how we rolled once our heads were put together. We hadn't told a soul and probably wouldn't be missed, as dropping out of a job and skulking off the radar wasn't that unusual for either of us. Course, this time we wouldn't be man cavin' with the Xbox and Doritos, but jet-setting into "le gai Paris" for an extra culture kick.

I had given the old chops a break from the razor and I had enough scruff to impress a lumberjack, or at least to confuse the airport folks that I was a somewhat cleaned up version of Lucky Mike McCreedy. Besides the beard and mustache, Mike's passport photo pretty much had the same dog-eared features as yours truly. It had already worked on the airline desk agent and the TSA security guards, and I hoped it would fool a blasé French customs officer.

We bumped through channels and turbulence and enjoyed the private screen and video choices. And wouldn't you know it, the beverage cart rolled by, pushed by a lovely lady flight attendant. She was so short that from our angle we could barely see her over the diet soda cans, but Stumpy saw all that he needed.

Stumpy loved a woman shorter than him. "Jason." Stumpy pulled on my shirtsleeve and whispered. "Jason, Jason, did you see?"

"I saw. I saw."

I could feel Stumpy scheming up a love plan to full court press. He squirmed and fidgeted in his seat until a brainy idea must have clicked in his noggin and he calmed. He reached up to push the call button, but I had already anticipated this angle. I slapped his arm down before the ball could be checked.

"Hey."

"Forget about her. We can't risk your bumbling overtures."

Stumpy looked offended. "I never overtured anyone."

"I should hope not." I pointed at him. "But you've got a knack for chaos as far as women are concerned and we don't need the attention."

Stumpy sighed.

"Calm down, man. Once we're in France and take care of this vineyard business, your game will be unstoppable. You'll be ripe on the vine and flush with the juice."

"And you, too." Stumpy smiled and gave a contemplative laugh, which was good because it meant that I had diverted his attention. "Women sure do light up when you mention France and vineyard in the same sentence."

I felt my right eye twitching. "What women? You didn't tell anyone about our mission, did you?"

Stumpy looked down to his round belly and I could tell he had spilled the beans. "Who'd you tell?"

"Well, not really tell. I saw Laura at the gas station. She knew Aunt Clara had a will."

"But I'm not supposed to leave the country. Laura will tell everyone."

Stumpy rubbed at the mustard splotch that stained his white shirt. "She talked it out of me before I knew."

I had to forgive him. Laura's multi-directional chatter could crack you even if you were prepared and focused.

"Don't worry. Laura promised to keep mum. But she was sure interested to hear you had inherited a vineyard."

I shook my head and rolled my eyes. "I bet. All those old loving feelings she claimed to have had for me probably bubbled right up again." No matter what Laura had said about us having different interests, or friends, or outlooks on life, it was difficult for me not to think that she had left me for money.

"Laura's always had feelings for you, Jason. I can see it in her eyes." Stumpy was good at picking up those little cues.

"Really? You really think so?"

"Really. I don't mean feelings like you think I mean. But she does care for you."

The beverage cart rolled back down the aisle and Stumpy shut up and became transfixed. The flight attendant had blond hair cut short into a bob. She had a natural smile and appeared at ease when she served the passengers. She had dark mascara and triple-pierced ears that rebelled against the simple appearances of her stiff coworkers. And yet, there was something sweet about her. She seemed to like the passengers. She was trying to do a good job.

"Not a word," I said.

"Please, Jason? Can I at least give her my card?"

"You have a card?"

He shrugged his shoulders like it was no big deal. "Yeah, I had some made up for our trip."

I hated being a spoiler. "Okay. But let me take care of it." I back-handed his shoulder. "Let me see this card."

The flight attendant leaned into our row and smiled with what I thought was a slight smirk as she took us in. "Something to drink, gentleman?"

"None for me, thank you," I said. "But if I may speak for my friend?" I nodded at Stumpy and then spoke to her conspiratorially. "He's a little awestruck and having a speech situation at the moment." Stumpy smiled dumbly. "He was wondering if you wouldn't mind meeting up with him for a drink at a café in Paris during your layover?"

Stumpy handed me his card. I read it as I passed it over. "*Neil Hammond*," it said. "*Winer in France.*"

Before I could pull the card back, her quick fingers snatched it out of my hand. She grinned as she read it. "You're a winer?"

I slapped my thigh and looked unbelievable-like at Stumpy. *A winer?*

He shrugged, and his face turned spelling-bee red. "You know, someone who makes wine."

She looked at the card again and then burst out laughing. "This is the best." She rolled her cart away, shaking her head with a grin.

Stumpy was beside himself. "She said it was the best."

"I hate to say it, dude. But I think she was just brushing you off."

He touched his finger to his chin. He had a determined, far-away look that had me worried. "There's always a chance."

The plane landed early morning in Paris. We stood in the long immigration line. A family with three kids and a crying baby stood behind us. Stumpy and I approached the glass-encased customs station. The man on duty held up his hand and motioned Stumpy back. "One at a time." Stumpy took a step behind me. The customs official swiped my passport. The baby screamed louder. The official glanced at me and down at the passport. I gave my best Mike McCreedy deadpan look. I heard Stumpy gasp. I looked over and saw the cute flight attendant passing by unmolested in the employee express line. Stumpy waved to her with exuberance. She smiled and waved politely at us. I smiled and waved. The customs officer watched her saunter by. He looked at me, winked, stamped my passport and motioned me into France.

I waited for Stumpy to come through and we walked to the baggage claim. My shoulder muscles relaxed. I had been more worried about the fake passport than I liked to admit, but no worries now.

Our bags came and we headed for the taxi line. There was no wait and we slid into a taxi and were off.

"Jason, look!"

The flight attendant was getting into a small hotel van with the rest of the flight crew.

Stumpy's eyes narrowed and locked onto that van like he was Inspector Clouseau. "Follow that bus."

The taxi driver looked at us with confusion. "*Où allez-vous?*"

"We have to nab a train," I said.

"Not till this afternoon, you said."

"We can't stalk a girl we don't know through Paris," I said.

"I'm following my heart, not stalking. And you promised."

I gave Stumpy an I-don't-know-what-you're-talking-about look.

The hotel van started pulling away.

"You promised to try like Six-Flags-try."

I had promised, and I now slightly regretted it. How many times on this trip would Stumpy call me on the Six Flags promise?

"*Où allez-vous?*" the driver said.

I pointed at the bus. "*Le bus, s'il-vous-plaît.*" I had picked up a few phrases from Aunt Clara, mostly when I was younger and we conversed more.

Stumpy pointed frantically. "The bus. The bus."

The taxi driver touched the top of his head. "*Le bus. Oui, porquoi pas?*"

We followed the hotel van into Paris. Stumpy and I smacked our mugs against the glass as we took in our first glimpse of Paris through the early morning light. "The Eiffel Tower." Stumpy tapped on the window as *la tour Eiffel* fleeted in and out of view. "Jason, Jason, the Eiffel Tower."

I must admit, I too felt that spring of hope from seeing something grand for the first time. "It's like, like . . . majestic."

We craned our heads to keep an eye on the tower as our taxi followed the van into the heart of Paris. Chic people sat sipping their morning coffees at swank cafes in front of old buildings like I had only seen in movies. The lampposts were even fancy.

"This is better than Six Flags," Stumpy said.

The taxi double-parked on a small side street as we watched the flight crew exit the van and enter a small boutique hotel. When we felt it safe, Stumpy and I paid the driver and tumbled out onto the sidewalk.

We were in the St. Germain neighborhood, and it smelled like a warm baguette. I looked down winding café-lined lanes.

Stumpy breathed in deep and looked content. "Isn't it romantic?"

Hmm. The scene was cool, but given my history I was still suspicious. "I suppose."

"This is a place to fall in love." Stumpy looked at a young couple walking arm in arm. "Really in love."

I don't think Stumpy realized that we were looking for different kinds of love. "I don't know," I said. "Maybe for a day or two."

"Aw, Jason. You're so bitter."

Laura and I had first held hands walking through a carnival as seniors in high school. I looked at the stylish people of Paris and at the enchanted buildings. I wish back then I could have brought Laura to Paris and held her hand while walking down these streets. Money again. She left me for money. Big muscles worked for cavemen. Big money works for modern men. Money is what I needed, and with this vineyard, money is what I was going to get.

I looked at Stumpy. He didn't care about money. He was an endless romantic, believing in love, always looking for love.

"Yeah, well." I was about to ramble on to the dream pumpkin about how the world really works, but in a rare moment of restraint I clenched the jawbone shut. We were in Paris—I would let Stumpy hold on to that optimism as long as he could. "If it could happen, I suppose it would be here."

Stumpy grabbed my shoulder affectionately. "That's the spirit."

I smiled and felt numb. Jet lag cried for my body to sleep. "Now what do we do?"

"Be like Persians," Stumpy said.

"Parisians you mean."

"That's it. We need to blend in like the locals."

"We have suitcases." I noticed three very attractive women crossing the street. "Ooh, la, la."

"Ooh, ya, ya," Stumpy said as we watched the women walk into a shop with a window bursting with chocolate confectionaries. He read the store's sign. "Jacque's chocolate tire. I like that. It's fun. Can you imagine eating a whole chocolate tire?"

"That's *chocolatier.*" I slapped him on the back. "It means chocolate shop, Sherlock."

"We should buy the vineyard farmers a present," Stumpy said. "What were their names again?"

I looked at a scrap piece of paper in my pocket. "Claudette and Lucia Morceau. They're sisters."

"We can sit by the window and watch for the flight attendant."

It was a hopeless quest. The flight attendant was probably sound asleep by now, but I'd let Stumpy figure that out on his own.

We jostled into the chocolatier and were engulfed in a rich cocoa aroma dense enough to eat. People and bright chocolate and French words swirled around us, and after shouts and mime signals and a paycheck worth of Euros, we were seated at a small table with a rect-angular copper-foil-wrapped box and a couple of thick-as-pudding hot chocolates.

I took a sip of the hot cocoa and felt an instant endorphin rush and a warm affection for Paris. "That's the stuff."

Stumpy locked the cup to his lips. "Mmm hmm."

I touched the box of chocolates. "Do you think the vineyard farm-ers will like it?"

"Who knows?" Stumpy said.

"Who knows?" I said.

"Who knows?" Stumpy said.

And then I couldn't believe it. The flight attendant walked through the door. She went to the counter and bought a cup of some-thing hot and pieces of chocolate. She paid and sat at a table next to us, oblivious to our presence.

I pulled the cup off Stumpy's face and gave him a kick and a nod and an eye roll to the left until he comprehended my wireless signals and took a stop-breath stare. He closed his eyes psyching himself up. After a moment, he was ready. He leaned over and said with perfect debonair, *"Bonjour, Mademoiselle."*

The flight attendant had changed into jeans and a blouse and did not look as intimidating, but I was still surprised at Stumpy's cool.

She laughed. "Following me?" Her face hinted at a touch of seriousness.

"I should ask you the same," Stumpy said, "being we've been here a half hour now."

Good one, Stumpy. I nodded in agreement. "Sippin' the molten cocoa."

"I thought you'd be wining by now." She raised an eyebrow and smiled slightly.

Stumpy shifted, embarrassed. "We won't reach the vineyard until tonight. And I've since learned it's a vintner. My card should have said vintner."

"Your card should have said bullshitter." She laughed. "You're funny, though, and kind of cute." She looked at Stumpy affectionately. "My name's Betsy."

Stumpy's eyes lit up and I could tell that he and Betsy had made a connection. "I might not know anything about vintning, but it's true, we're going to work at a vineyard in Bordeaux."

"Sell a vineyard," I said.

Her head tilted and her smiled disappeared. She believed us. "You really own a vineyard?"

I held my hand toward Stumpy. "Straight up. We're partners. This vineyard has been an investment for us."

"It's outside Bordeaux in the Dordogne region," Stumpy said.

"Really?"

"Really!" we said in unison.

"You should visit us," Stumpy said.

"Maybe." She took a sip. She reached into her pocket and handed Stumpy a card without looking at him.

"*Betsy*," it said above a website, login phrase, and password.

Stumpy was transfixed by the card. He stared, seeming unable to speak anymore.

"What's that?" I asked.

"Have your semi-mute winer log in and fill out the questionnaire. If we're a match, I'll give him a call."

"I'll do that," I said.

Stumpy looked up. "I'll do that."

"Yes. You should do that." Betsy stood up to leave. "I want to call you, but we should take care of those online formalities first." She smiled at him with a smile that willed Stumpy to fill out those online forms.

Stumpy and I stood up as well.

"Do you live here?" Stumpy asked.

Betsy didn't answer, but pointed at Stumpy and said, "Online form."

"Of course," Stumpy said. We shook hands and said goodbye.

Stumpy and I descended into the metro, punched the billet machine a few times, and knocked against some Parisians until we figured it all out. After taking two trains in the wrong direction, we solved the Metro Maze and ended up at the Gare du Nord train station. We hopped on the last express to Bordeaux. Stumpy hugged the window like a terrier on a Sunday drive. The TGV skimmed over the land. Small towns and endless fields of grain blurred by.

Stumpy had an old phone, but it could still connect to the Internet. He struggled with the archaic interface and eventually logged onto Betsy's website and online dating form.

"Do you think I have a sense of humor, Jason?"

"Yes."

The cool cabin air smelled like carpet and leather and lemon air freshener. The window fan hum and vibrating train made me sleepy.

"On a scale of one to ten, how would you rate my intelligence?"

"Ten."

"Jason!"

"Okay, nine."

"That'd be fudging the truth and you know it."

"Everyone fudges the truth. Do you want this girl or not?"

"Okay—eight then." Stumpy laughed. "This is fun. I could fill it out any way I want."

"Yes! That's what online dating is all about."

Stumpy smiled and continued his project. I looked out the window and drifted off to sleep.

"Jason, Jason." Stumpy nudged me as the train slowed into Bordeaux. I don't think he'd missed a moment; such was his excitement.

The setting sun dimmed the light on the sleepy town. The grand palace-like buildings spoke to livelier times gone by. I had peaked in college, so I could relate. Bordeaux made me feel sad in that way.

Stumpy's credit card procured us a rental car, but the tiny Toyota was a stick shift. We got in the car and Stumpy whiplashed us down the middle of the street toward a roundabout. He turned left directly into oncoming traffic. Horns honked. Cars veered left and right. We lurched and swerved down another street.

"Other side," I cried.

Stumpy was on the left side of the road heading directly into a truck. He veered us right. We missed the truck. Stumpy popped the clutch and we stalled next to the curb. "They drive crazy here," he said.

I slapped him on the shoulder. "You're the crazy one. Why do you keep running into traffic?"

"Don't they drive on the left side here?"

"No! That's England." I got out of the car and walked around and opened his door. "Out. I'm driving."

We headed east, destination Duras, a small town in south central Dordogne. Stumpy put his face in the map and sniffed out the directions.

After many wrong turns we only had correct ones left and we were soon in the vicinity. I was excited, I admit. "Let's go by the vineyard. We can check into the hotel later."

Stumpy had X'ed the spot about eight kilometers outside Duras. The night was complete now as we drove over the rolling landscape; only starlight graced the fields, hinting at the rows and rows of grapes.

"We should be there," Stumpy said. "This could be your land."

It was beautiful even in the dark and I felt myself wondering about the people who lived here. Was their life better than mine? More relaxed? More purposeful? "Cash. Think cash, my man. Cash is king."

A six-foot-high rock barrier fence arose along the road next to us.

I stopped in front of a spear-pointed double wrought-iron gate.

Stumpy folded up the map. "This is it. This has to be it."

We stepped out of the car and put our hands on the gate's bars— cool and moist like the night—and peered into the dark. A large stone structure loomed before us. A dim porch light revealed two massive wooden doors above three stone steps. A cross hung on the exterior wall above the transom.

"It's a mansion," Stumpy said. "The Morceau sisters are living large."

Convincing the Morceau sisters to sell might not be as pie as I had hoped.

I heard a huff, huff, pitter-patter, and then barks. Fang-like teeth chomped and snarled at us through the gate, barely missing a Stump and Chump meal.

Stumpy and I backed away. "Sh, sh. *Bonsoir, Bonsoir.* Doggy, doggy."

A woman spoke in rapid French from the dark. The ferocious dogs quieted and disappeared toward the voice. More French.

"Madame Morceau? It's Jason Barnes, Clara's nephew. I sent you a letter."

A shadow walked up the stone steps, opened the door, and then before entering the house, held up one finger toward us.

"She wants us to wait," Stumpy said.

"Nothing escapes you, man."

The double iron gates swung inward.

The double wooden doors opened outward.

Two nuns stood in the doorway.

CHAPTER 6

One of the nuns motioned us forward. Stumpy and I stood at the bottom of the stone steps and after a *bonsoir* or two, a bow, and some clumsy hand gestures, we settled on English as the best way to communicate.

The nun on the left spoke. "I am Claudette Morceau. This is my sister, Lucia Morceau. Lucia is in a state of silence and will not speak this evening." Sister Claudette stared at me for a moment, like she recognized me but wasn't sure.

"You're sisters," I said.

"Yes, we are sisters."

"Really Sisters."

"Yes, we are really Sisters."

"Sisters and sisters."

"Yes. Sisters and sisters."

I felt uneasy. "How many Sisters are there?"

"We are the nuns of St. Sebastian." Both the sisters spread their arms wide as Sister Claudette spoke. Their robes hung like banners from their arms and they looked like dark angels in the night, welcoming and formidable at the same time. "We are eighty-two sisters strong, doing God's work and humbly harvesting the land to make wine." The sisters bowed their heads and lowered their arms, clasping their hands in front of them.

"Like Jesus," Sister Lucia whispered.

My head spun as my plans for an easy sale seemed to be floating away. "Eighty-two Sisters?"

Sister Claudette nodded. "Now you know us. Who, good sirs, are you? We are rarely disturbed this way in the evening. Sister Anne said you wrote us a letter?"

A nun appeared in the entryway and handed Sister Claudette a letter. Sister Claudette stood taller than Sister Lucia. She had a long nose and a stern face. She looked at the return address and then at me and I saw a look of understanding cross her brow. "I had not seen this letter yet."

"I'm Jason Barnes. My Aunt Clara was—"

Sister Claudette held up her hand to stop me. She made a great show of opening my letter. She put on a pair of black oval reading glasses and inspected the blue airmail paper like it was a lost scroll. "You didn't give us much warning."

"Well, I, er, I was—"

Sister Claudette held her hand up again and I shut up. She looked over her glasses accusingly. "Telephone? Email?"

I dropped my head. "I'm sorry, Sister. We shouldn't have disturbed you. We'll return in the morning."

"No, no. Come inside where we can get a look at you two. Leave the dogs." The sisters left the door open and disappeared into the convent.

The beasts sniffed at our heels, and we both flinched. I laughed. The dogs were small fluffy white poodles and looked like little snowballs. "The devil's got a hold of those two, I tell ya."

"Aw, come on, Jason. They're nice."

"Nice? Did you see their fangs? Their incisors were like a sabertooth tiger's."

Stumpy and I stepped inside. I shooed the dogs away and shut the doors.

"I don't know about their teeth. I didn't see either one of them smile," Stumpy said.

I socked him in the arm. "I'm talking about the dogs, you dodo."

"Oh, of course. The dogs." Stumpy laughed. "Geez. I wondered. Even for you those comments were insensitive."

We walked down the dimly lit arched stone hallway. It smelled like cold concrete. We made our way until we stood outside a main office door.

"I don't know," I whispered. "Dogs or nuns—they all looked ready to bite."

We entered the office and sat in two wooden chairs. Fluorescent lights illuminated the modern office. Modern, that is, as opposed to the ancient abbey. The office was 1950's modern with dull white tile and metal cabinets. Paintings of Jesus and Mary hung on the olive-colored plaster wall. Black and white photographs of unsmiling nuns lined another wall. The sisters sat behind desks in front of us. A color photograph of Mother Teresa sat on Sister Lucia's steel desk. A photograph of Pope John Paul II sat on Sister Claudette's desk. Sister Claudette looked severe. She had a nameplate that proclaimed her mother of the place and her demeanor exuded superiority. Sister Lucia had a round, kindly face. She couldn't stop smiling at us. I felt like she wanted to hug me.

I whispered in Stumpy's ear. "Be smooth. Keep it cool."

"And you must be Neil," Sister Claudette said. "Better known as Stumpy?"

Stumpy sat up straight at being called out. "Yes, Sister." He looked like a miracle had been performed in front of him. "Amazing, Sister."

Sister Claudette opened an expandable legal-sized folder. "Oh, we know all about you two." She pulled out a stack of letters and a couple dozen photos. "These items are mostly about Jason, though Clara kept us well informed."

She spread the photos in a line across the desk and I saw all the stages of my life before me.

"You sure were a smiley kid," Stumpy said.

"So full of hope and promise," Sister Claudette said.

I squirmed in my seat.

"But you haven't aged well," she said.

"I'm only thirty-two."

"Yet filled with an old man's contempt."

Aunt Clara had obviously confessed my sins and shortcomings to these two penguins in the pile of letters. If she had wanted me to own and work this vineyard why did she sell me so short to these nuns? It was always fifty-fifty with Aunt Clara. She had to make it tough for me—a present with a problem. "Jesus," I said.

Sister Claudette shot me a wolfhound look, and if Sister Lucia hadn't patted her hand I think she would have clamored across the desk and clamped my neck.

"I can see the degradation of your soul in the photos, and I can see it before me," Sister Claudette said.

"I'll admit to a little weakening, but degradation is a little over the barrel."

Stumpy touched a photo of the two of us standing arm in arm at a water park. We must have been seventeen. "You'll notice the stark contrast between this photo . . ." Stumpy pointed to another photo. " . . . and this sad photo." In the second photo I was smoking a cigarette leaning over the Brunswick lane's Galaxy Bar. It was right after Laura had dumped me, and I don't know who took the picture, but I did look horrible. "The spirit has clearly left the man," Stumpy concluded.

The sisters frowned and nodded.

I stood up angrily. "What is this—an intervention?"

"Should it be?" Sister Claudette said.

"No." I slapped Stumpy in the back of his head. "What are you doing?"

Stumpy shrugged his shoulders sheepishly. "Just talking. Just saying what I feel."

"Well keep your feelings to yourself." I looked at the sister Sisters. "And save your soul saving for the next drifter, cause we're here on business. Now I was going to wait a few days until we got to know each other, but seeing as you all are so personal with me already, we may as well discuss business now. I'm here to sell the vineyard. This place is worth millions and that will help my soul out plenty." I sat down. "Now let's talk."

Everyone stared at me like I was Mephistopheles.

"Real cool," Stumpy said. "Real smooth."

Sister Claudette stood up. She placed her fists on the desk and leaned over. "The St. Sebastian Sisters have worshipped the Lord, harvested the grapes, and made wine—"

"Like Jesus," Sister Lucia whispered.

"Like Jesus," Sister Claudette said. "For nigh four hundred years now."

I sat back down, as did Sister Claudette. I clasped my hands together. "I understand your attachments are deep—"

"Like the vine roots in the soil. We own the convent and a small parcel within the vineyard you have inherited." She put her palms together as if in prayer. "And I'm sure you are aware that our approval is necessary if you want to sell the vineyard." Sister Claudette looked at me with steadfastness. "But never will we sell."

"Wait, what?" I had to have their approval to sell? I took a moment to digest this troubling information. I smiled. "You're coming in strong Sisters, and I respect that. But at least we're negotiating."

"We are doing no such thing."

"I'm willing to offer you a higher market value for your portion. Did you have a figure in mind?"

Sister Claudette waved her hand back and forth like she was trying to swat me away. "You are not listening. We don't care about market values or negotiating. We are not selling."

"But Sisters. Why don't you let me sell? We can stipulate that the new owners keep the same agreements, and the St. Sebastian nuns can make wine here for the next four hundred years."

"Like Jesus," Sister Lucia whispered.

Sister Claudette glared irritably at Sister Lucia. "Whispering is not silence."

Sister Claudette then stared at me with a solemnity that weighed me down. I felt immobilized as her eyes pierced into mine. "Jason." She made a tsk, tsk sound. "It is all much deeper than you think." She stood up. "It is late. There is a guest room you can use."

"We have reservations at the hotel in town," I said.

"Nonsense. This is your land. It will be right for you to stay here. We shall clean up the vintner's house tomorrow; it has remained empty for twenty years now." Sister Claudette continued to stare at me. I felt unraveled, but I stared back as forcefully as I could.

A nun led us down a dimly lit, stone-walled, marble hallway to a sparsely furnished dorm-like room.

Stumpy and I lay side by side in twin beds, exhausted.

"They're tough," Stumpy said.

"Like French Foreign Legion tough."

"I don't think they're going to sell."

"I'll think of something," I said. "There's gotta be a way."

"I don't know, Jason. She said it goes deeper than we think."

"Yeah, what the hell?" I looked around remembering I was in a convent. "Sorry, heck. What the heck was that all about?"

"The way she said it . . . It feels powerful." Stumpy rolled away from me and drifted off to sleep.

Stumpy was right. Something did feel powerful. Cashing in on this vineyard might be tougher than I thought.

Game on, Sister.

CHAPTER 7

I awoke late in the morning feeling fresh—jet lag in the bag. Stumpy, however, was having trouble with the time change and was a bit of a groggy mess. He wore a nice shirt to impress the nuns, but had buttoned it one off. It was classic Stumpy, and I thought it so funny I couldn't bring myself to tell him.

We toured the convent and met many nuns, but caught on quick that a long conversation was the last of their intents. The rectangular abbey enclosed a large courtyard where square plots separated by pebbled paths contained purple, yellow, and white flowers that I could admire but not name. A cloister walkway with Roman arches and columns lined the perimeter. In the courtyard center, Sister Lucia pointed to a large circular basin fountain that contained a statue of a robed and bearded man. "Saint Sebastian," she said.

"He looks a little stiff," I said.

Stumpy elbowed me in the side. "Respect, Jason."

"Respect, Stumpy." I slapped him in the belly. "Try buttoning your shirt again."

We left the courtyard and stood outside in the shade and looked up to the gargoyle-protected church that formed the west wall. A cross sat atop the steeple, the tallest structure in the vicinity. A rectangular stone winery barn for making and storing wine stood close to the east wall.

Beyond the abbey the sun beat down through the pure-smelling air and filled the endless grape rows with life. The abbey sat atop a small hill. On the church side, the land swept into a yellow valley and rose again to a plateau where the vintner's house rested.

We drove the rental car over with our suitcases and pulled into the house's pebbled driveway. Stumpy struggled to re-button his shirt. Lilacs outlined a stone patio and buzzed with honeybees and tiny white and yellow butterflies. Birds chirped; grasshoppers jumped and made helicopter noises. Other insects sang a low hum. There were no man-made sounds to be found here.

The house and the surroundings were so beautiful and peaceful. I felt relaxed and safe. It was like I was meditating on a happy place to go, but was actually there. Stumpy must have felt the same. He spun slowly around—a look of wonder on his face.

A squadron of nuns had been silently attacking the dust in the house all morning. Now they stood outside the front door, smiling and welcoming Stumpy and I as we approached. The dogs stood with the nuns as if they were part of the work crew, and as we passed they fell in and trotted next to Stumpy like guards.

Stumpy looked at it all in awe. "This is for us?"

The simple two-story rectangular farmhouse was made of sand colored stone and had a faded red Roman tile roof. Light blue shutters accentuated the windows, and the place looked, I dare say, romantic.

"Temporary," I said. "Don't get too comfortable."

The house's thick walls were cool on the inside, the same as the floor. We inspected the kitchen and main room, which had a fireplace. Upstairs, three bedrooms sat close together. A loft with railing overlooked the main room. Simple French country furnishings decorated the house throughout.

Stumpy and I thanked the nuns profusely for their labor until they became embarrassed. The nuns left us alone, and we sat down on the patio and took in the view.

"The nuns are nice," Stumpy said.

"Most people are when they first meet us," I said.

The abbey sat majestically about four soccer fields away and slightly above us. The church steeple and cross reached high into the crisp, cloudless sky.

I sat on the concrete patio and tried to understand it all.

"It sure is beautiful," Stumpy said. "I could get used to this."

"Don't. Think cash. Cash is—"

"Cash is king," Stumpy said without enthusiasm.

"Today we are vintners," I said, trying to bring him around.

Stumpy smiled. "I like that. I like being a vintner. But we don't know anything about vintning."

"Exactly." I slapped my hands and laughed. "We're going to be the worst vintners ever."

"But we could learn."

"Rubbish. If those sisters won't let us sell and are so keen on having us as 'deep' land partners then God forgive their ignorance."

Stumpy looked worried. "Jason you're not going to sabotage the wining and vintning, are you?"

"No. Of course not. Well, not on purpose, anyhow. But just think of all the jobs we've had, Stumpy, and think of how many times we've been personnel department fodder. Dereliction of duties could be on the top of our resumes. Those nuns have no idea what they're up against." I stood up, spread my hands apart, and laughed. "All we have to do is be ourselves. Those sisters will be begging us to sell in no time."

I walked with Sister Claudette down a row of grape vines. Stumpy had gone with Sister Lucia to do some chores.

"We mow between the rows," Sister Claudette explained, "to keep weeds and other growth under control."

I cupped a grape bunch.

"In a few weeks they will be ready." Sister Claudette picked a grape and rubbed it between her fingers. "When the skin is velvety smooth . . ." she plopped the grape into her mouth and I saw her face relax for the first time, ". . . and the sweetness is at its peak, that is when we harvest."

I put a couple of the purple gushers inside the old muzzle, swirled them around, and did a crush. "Mighty fine. They taste about right to me."

Sister Claudette held up one finger. "Not quite. The most important thing is that we harvest the grapes when they are sweetest. It will take many harvests for you to fully taste the changing grape stages and know when the time is perfect. Jason, you must learn to understand your grapes, their vines, roots, and soil." She scooped up some sandy earth and dropped the pebbles into my hands.

I sifted my hands and let the rocks and silt fall through my fingers. I felt powerful. This was my land. I imagined the grape roots pulling at my feet—inviting me to be a part of their world. I felt that if I concentrated hard enough I could help them grow. *Nonsense.*

"The soil provides the true essence and flavor to the grape." Sister Claudette waved her hand. "This ridge we are standing on has the gravelly earth necessary to produce our best wine."

The way Sister Claudette talked about the land it all sounded so good, so right. I looked further out and forced myself to think about the millions this place could be worth, and the fast times I could have with all that moola, and then felt like myself again. I had twenty-three days to pay the court. I needed to stick to the plan. "What about those slopes?"

Sister Claudette shook her head. "Those vines are shaded too long from the ridge across the vintner's house. No, only this spot has the perfect terroir for our wine."

"Terror wine?"

"Terroir, Jason. Terroir is the soil, the sun, the wind—all the natural elements that go into the grape."

"What about all the other grapes?" I was trying to get a good assessment of the place, but Sister Claudette had a kinder interpretation of my question.

"You show an interest. That is good." Sister Claudette gave me a nod as if it were a blessing, a stern show of approval much like Aunt Clara would have given.

"Most of our grapes we press ourselves, and then we sell the juice to Chateaux Dubois Winery. We only use the very best grapes to make St. Sebastian wine."

I picked another grape, chewed, and swallowed. Man it sure tasted good. I couldn't imagine the berries any sweeter. "I don't know, Sister. They seem good enough to harvest now."

Sister Claudette laughed. "You will see."

We walked further. She stepped and clipped a growth from a vine. "We prune the suckers and pull any extra weeds by hand." She handed me the pinchers. "That is something you can do. Walk the rows, pruning and weeding—communing with the fruit." Sister Claudette spread her hands. "Go now, Jason. Walk the land. Care for the land. Understand and come to know the land. Constantly taste the grapes. Taste how they change through the vineyard. Taste how they change as we approach the harvest."

It was quite a stirring speech. Sister Claudette was trying to sell me on this place, but I had been raised on infomercials, and I wasn't buying. I'll admit, the way she explained things—the way she connected it all—had an attractiveness to it, an attractiveness I had difficulty understanding. I had to remember that cashing in this vineyard would solve my current problems. "I'll do my best, Sister."

She turned to walk away. "I will leave you to the vineyard."

I could hear a distant tractor putt-putting down a row. The dry air smelled like dusty leaves and rich soil. *All right*, I'd give myself a lonely tour. I'd had tougher jobs, and this land-walking seemed about my speed. I stopped after a few meters and took a clip off a sucker, assuming I had done it right, but not caring a frog's leg either way, as was my normal vocational inclination.

A high-pitched screech rose up from the field. "No!"

I looked up. Four rows over, the vines rustled and then collapsed. I could hear the tractor chugging and dogs barking. Another section of vines fell like dominos. I heard a scream.

Stumpy! I thought.

I looked down my lane and saw Sister Claudette dive through the vines and head toward the victimized row. I did the same, and we arrived at the same time. The vines had swiped her black veil and white coif, and her gray hair spread like a peacock.

Sister Claudette ran after the rogue tractor. I sprinted and passed her. Stumpy was gripping the tractor's steering wheel, his head bent low, his eyes closed, and his face grimacing. Grapes and vines and leaves flew in all directions. The poodles ran alongside, yapping all the while.

Suddenly, Sister Lucia appeared, and ran next to the tractor shouting directions. She hopped on the side wheel well, reached across Stumpy, and pulled on his arm to turn the tractor, but his grip and confusion were too strong. The tractor bounced and Sister Lucia fell to the ground.

I jumped on the tractor and then on top of Stumpy. I headlocked the sweaty brute with my left arm to immobilize him, and reached with my right hand to turn off the ignition. The tractor stopped, and all was quiet.

I released Stumpy and jumped off. Sister Lucia lay on her side in the grass. Sister Claudette attended to her.

The dogs yipped at my heels, circled around me, and then barked into the air like it was all my fault. "Is she all right?" I said.

Sister Claudette helped Sister Lucia up to a sitting position. "*Pas de problèm. Ça va*," Sister Lucia said.

Stumpy wobbled to my side. Cuts and scrapes covered his skin. Grape juice splotches filled the gaps. He picked up a dog in each arm and they licked his face. Stumpy held a dog out to me. "This is Matthew. The other is Mark."

I backed away. "Pontius Pilate and Judas, more like."

Sister Claudette glared at us. "You must be careful. You must respect your work. Respect and care for the wine and the creation process." She helped Sister Lucia stand. "Otherwise, careless accidents like this happen and people get hurt."

Stumpy was nervous. "I don't know what happened."

"Someone could have been hurt badly," Sister Claudette said. "Sloppiness causes injuries. And injuries or not, sloppiness is reflected in the character of the wine. You must care to work here."

Stumpy and I had heard that quality-control speech before, but this time Stumpy dropped his head, loyal to management. "I'm sorry, Sister."

Other nuns had arrived, and they were picking up the mess—carefully repositioning the vines that were still intact.

54 J.T. LUNDY

I picked up an errant grape and inspected it like it might hold a clue. "How much money is this accident going to cost, Sister?"

Sister Claudette's wild gray hair and steel pupils were Medusa-like as she looked intently at me. It was like she was trying to understand my soul. I averted my eyes.

Later in the day, I sat in the abbey courtyard under the shade of a plum tree with Sister Claudette and Sister Lucia and listened to more smashing grape facts. The air smelled full of flowers. White butterflies air-danced around the fountain like mini angels, landing but a moment on Saint Sebastian for a water sip before rejoining the ball again. The bubbling fountain made me sleepy.

A nun walked into the courtyard followed by another woman who sported a fashionable charcoal business suit and walked with an authoritarian air. She had silky black hair pulled tight into a ponytail. Her suit skirt held tight against her thin waist and stopped conservatively sexy above her knees. She had—oh, forget it. I'll cut right to the chase. She was awesome, and I was dumbstruck.

The sisters greeted her coldly and failed to introduce me, but she stuck her hand out my way and spoke rapid French. I touched her smooth white skin and said, "*Enchanté. Je m'appelle Jason Barnes.*"

Her eyes lit up and she switched to English. "Oh, Mr. Barnes. I have desired to meet you. I am Jacqueline Thibodaux." She had a thick but lovely accent.

My eyes widened, and I might have made a humming noise.

Sister Claudette and Sister Lucia stood stone-faced.

I gathered my courage and squeaked, "What do you desire? I mean, why do you desire me?"

She paused and looked at me a moment in assessment. When a woman does this, it's usually a signal for me to move on, but Jacqueline

Thibodaux had her intentions. She handed me a business card. "I represent France's Ministry of Energy."

From Sister Claudette's attitude, I figured the government folks were intent on meddling, as governments like to do. "I assure you, Madame, the vineyard's energy facilities are up to date."

Jacqueline laughed and then quickly composed herself. "I'm sorry for the disturbance." She glanced nervously at Sister Claudette. "Monsieur Barnes, I was wondering if I could talk privately with you?" When she asked, her voice became quiet and her eye twitched. I could tell Sister Claudette intimidated her. Or perhaps I made her nervous? Was she attracted to me?

I nodded for what felt like a long time before I spoke. "I'd like to talk privately with you, too."

"We could have lunch," she said with a friendly smile.

"At a French café, perhaps?" I said eagerly and suavely like a true idiot. Why did I say 'French?'

"*Mais oui,*" Jacqueline said with an enthusiasm that made me feel at ease.

"*Mais non,*" Sister Claudette barked. "If there is any lunch to be had it can be right here in the convent, with all of us, in the presence of God where there are no secrets."

Wait, what? Sister Claudette just put a vintage crush on what I thought was a little flirtation I had going with Jacqueline. I couldn't believe it. She was pulling an Aunt Clara on me. No girl was good enough for Aunt Clara. She treated them all with a vengeance, like they were all out to ruin my life. To think of all the fantastic dates I could have had if Aunt Clara was not around. "Goddamn it!" I blurted out.

Jacqueline's eyes went wide, and she covered the rest of her face with her hands.

Sister Claudette's face turned red, and her lips moved around like she was chewing on marbles.

Jacqueline removed her hands from her face, and I wasn't sure, but I think she was trying to stifle a smile as she spoke. "Thank you, Sister, but I think it best I leave." She gave a slight nod to us. "*Bonne journée.*" She turned and walked out of the courtyard.

I looked to Sister Claudette. She was fuming. I looked to where Jacqueline had been standing. I looked left, right, left, right.

Sister Lucia put her hand on Sister Claudette's arm. "The Lord our God is merciful and forgiving."

"Please forgive me," I said in probably the least contrite voice they had ever heard.

Sister Claudette calmed, but stayed stoic.

Sister Lucia smiled at me and nodded. I took that as forgiveness and permission to leave. I ran into the convent, through the long hall, and out the front steps.

Jacqueline was about to get into her car. "Oh, Mademoiselle?" I looked at the card in my hand. "Ms. Thibodaux."

She turned to face me as I approached. "I've dealt with the Sisters before. *Est-ce-que vous êtes fou?*"

"Absolutely," I said, not understanding. "Can we still have lunch?"

She laughed. "*Oui.* I would very much like to have lunch and discuss an important matter with you. I am staying at the Hotel Duras. They have a very nice *French* café." She laughed. "Shall we meet there tomorrow?"

"*Mais oui,*" I said, concentrating so as to not say anything else stupid. "Until tomorrow."

CHAPTER 8

Jacqueline and I sat across from each other at a small table outside of the Hotel Duras. I was wearing jeans and a polo shirt. A short, wrought-iron fence separated us from a lightly traveled sidewalk. We had exchanged pleasantries and Jacqueline was talking about how she had missed a train connection coming to Duras yesterday, or something. I don't know; I just couldn't stop staring at her. I didn't mean to say anything, but the words just came out. "You are so lovely."

Jacqueline was as surprised as I. She looked taken aback and may have even blushed. She opened her mouth to say something, but then stopped. She reached her hand out and I thought she might touch mine, but then she set it on the table and regained her composure, smiling demurely.

The warm, fresh air was scented with a hint of the red flowers that hung down in pots from a green awning. Waiters bustled around the crowded tables where people talked quietly, clinking their plates with silverware.

"It is lovely here, Monsieur Barnes, but my interest in speaking to you is strictly professional."

Jacqueline was not as intimidating as when we'd first met. She wore a light blue skirt and a white sleeveless blouse. Her black hair waved down onto her shoulders.

"Yes, of course," I said. "I assure you. My interest in speaking to you is strictly professional."

"A professional lunch between two business people." She said this like she was convincing herself.

I tried to look solemn. "A professional lunch between two business people."

"Are you always so repetitive?"

"Repetitive?"

"There you go again."

"Go again?"

"You're repeating everything I say."

"I'm repeating . . ." Good god, why was I such a dork? She had me so flustered. "I'm sorry. Sometimes I'm a repeater. Would you like to have some wine?"

"Yes, I was going to ask you if you'd like some wine."

"Now you're repeating me."

"Monsieur Barnes—"

"Jason, please, just Jason."

She smiled. "Thank you for meeting me, Jason."

There was an awkward pause for a moment. I looked to a sidewalk chalkboard easel, which sat before the café: *Plat du jour—Tête de veau.* I realized I should probably say something. Jacqueline had waited long enough for me, though, and we spoke at the same time. "The reason I want to speak with you—" she said. "This area of France is gorgeous—" I said. We laughed. We each started again. "I—" she said. "I—" I said. We laughed. Things were going good.

Jacqueline looked at me with a kindness I had not seen from a woman in a long while. She was beautiful, and I felt drawn to her—but it was more than that. She had confidence and ambition, and seemed to know what she wanted in life. And I imagined she had a plan on how to get it. All these characteristics and energy that I lacked wrapped up in a beautiful woman intoxicated me. I wanted to learn more about her and keep the conversation personal. "Where do you live?"

"I live in Paris." She pulled a strand of hair behind her ear and I skipped a breath.

"Oh, Paris. Lovely," I said, like I knew the place intimately. "I adore Jacque's Chocolatier."

Jacqueline's face beamed. She touched my hand. "The croissants and coffee are superb."

"The best," I agreed.

"And you are from K—K,—"

"Kankakee—the heart of Illinois. How did you know?"

"I did my research. Do you have a favorite café in Kanky?"

"Lucky Mike's," I said enthusiastically. "Two buck drafts and the best brats around."

She smiled and raised an eyebrow. "What are a buckdraft and a brat?"

"Cheap beer and you know, brats. Bratwurst."

"Oh, yes. Bratwurst.

"And free popcorn." I had a pang of homesickness.

"Americans and corn. Why do you eat so much? Corn is for animals, no?"

"Mostly, but sweet corn is a delicacy you should try." I became animated. "Roasted sweet corn, yellow or white . . ." I circled my fists. ". . . or a jumble of both kernels with butter and salt right off the cobb, its like America's buttery baguette."

I don't think I convinced her, but she smiled. "You make it sound like a party."

"It can be. You should see my buddy Stumpy devour a dozen ears in under a minute at the county fair."

She laughed.

"He's not so bad at mud wrestling pigs either."

"You are joking me."

I held up my hand. "God's honest truth."

"I want to meet this Stoompy."

"You will, soon enough." We were getting along pretty well, I thought. I took a drink of wine to congratulate myself, but the husk was, I wasn't even trying. I was at ease. I felt a comfortableness talking with her that I found soothing.

An older waiter took our order. He had lanky limbs, black hair, and deep set eyes—common features in this area—features not unlike my own.

"I'll have *tête de veau*," I said.

Jacqueline's eyes went wide and she looked at me with respect. "*Tu es un brave Amêricain.*"

"Wait, what?"

She smiled. "You enjoy cow brains?"

I looked at the waiter. "Changed my mind—*croque monsieur, s'il-vous-plaît.*" Aunt Clara used to make me the French ham and cheese sandwich, and it was my favorite.

Jacqueline ordered and became serious. "Are you going to live here now that you own the vineyard? Or do you plan to return to your corn?"

Was I a long-term or short-term candidate? Is that what she was asking? I hoped so. My answer had to be money. "I'm weighing my options." I looked around. People held hands and ate their lunch slowly. Others sat alone, reading a book or paper, sipping coffee. Nobody appeared in a hurry to be anywhere other than here. "I certainly could see myself living in France, but I have to be honest. I'm no farmer. What I'd really like to do is sell the vineyard and buy a house or flat somewhere." I opened my hand toward her. "Perhaps Paris."

She smiled her biggest smile yet, a Pyrenees-sized grin, and her eyes sparkled. "Paris is wonderful—the food, the art . . ."

"Good brats?"

"Certainly, no, but there is excellent food, and wine, and if you like music, there is always jazz."

"Jazz? I love jazz!"

Jacqueline's face lit up. "Do you like John Coltrane?"

"Yes! Thelonious Monk?"

"Of course! But my all time favorite . . ."

"Louis Armstrong!" We both said together and then laughed.

We stared at each other a moment and smiled. I was in heaven. I couldn't believe what I did next, but I started singing in my best Louis Armstrong voice. *"When you're smilin' keep on smilin' the whole world smiles with you."*

Jacqueline laughed and looked around. "Stop it. You can't sing here." Her eyes and smile said something different, though. She might have been embarrassed, but I felt that part of her thought my singing in public was fun.

I had started, so—true to my nature—I couldn't stop. I sang louder with more enthusiasm. *"And when you're laughin' oh when you're laughin' the sun comes shinin' through."* I started to trail off, feeling embarrassed. What was I doing? And then, to my utter amazement Jacqueline joined in and sang with me. *"But when you're crying you bring on the rain. So stop your sighing baby and be happy again. Yes and keep on smiling, keep on smiling. And the whole world smiles with you!"*

We stopped singing and burst into laughter. A few patrons clapped. The lanky waiter walked by and patted my head. Jacqueline couldn't stop smiling at me. Oh my, she was a dork just like me. At that moment, I fell in love. I reached out my hand and clasped her fingers.

She squeezed my fingers back. "How do you do it?"

"Do what?"

"Use foul language against nuns. Sing in cafés. You do what you want, ignore the unspoken rules, and get away with it. You really know how to live life, don't you, Jason?"

Wait, what? Wow! Most people just thought I was a trouble-making jerk. Jacqueline actually appreciated my talents. "Sure enough," I said.

I thought it was a good time to order more wine, and I looked around for the waiter, but Jacqueline's phone buzzed. She removed her fingers from my gentle hold and read a text. She looked to the sky, and sighed. "I envy your freedom. I must leave for Paris."

"No problem." I took a bite of my croque monsieur and half the ham fell out onto the table in a cheesy glob. Jacqueline sat back, a hint of concern twinged in her eyes. Perhaps I was too uncouth for her. She stood up to leave, and luckily her smile returned. "I've never had a singing lunch before. Perhaps we could see each other again?"

"For absolutely!" I tried to think of an idea for a date, but Jacqueline was ahead of me.

"Why not here?" she said.

"Why not?"

"Same time five days?"

"Same time five days," I said.

I went back to the vineyard elated, calculating the minutes until I would see Jacqueline again. I breathed in and tried to remember her smell. I tried to picture her face but it would move fleetingly in and out of my mind. I had been like a rock since my divorce and I had planned on staying that way. Damn. This woman had gotten to me. I mummed up around Stumpy, though. I didn't want him to know. It was weird. It was like I was embarrassed to fall in love again, and I was mad that I had broken my own oath not to. And I didn't want to see Stumpy gloating about how he had predicted I'd find someone some day.

Instead, I tried to talk to Stumpy about our plan to annoy the sisters.

"I like the sisters. I like this place," he said.

"I like the sisters, too, but in twenty-one days I'm heading to the slammer. We came for the cash, remember?"

"I don't want to anger them on purpose. They're doing God's work, Jason."

"They're making wine."

"But the profits go to good causes."

My scheme had lost Stumpy, but only in spirit. Regardless of his intentions, I knew I could count on his bumbling. Of course, I didn't want anyone to get hurt, but I was sure, based on our history of being bad employees, that the sisters would come to abhor us as partners in a short time.

The harvest approached. Whenever Sister Claudette's taste buds signaled the grapes were sweet, the picking party would begin. In preparation for the great grape gathering fest, the sisters put out the call and imported some other good Sisters until the abbey swelled with farm laboring nuns ready to pick for Jesus.

The next afternoon, after a lackadaisical stroll pruning and telling stories to the grapes, I rounded an outbuilding and saw Stumpy demonstrating to one of the new immigrant nuns how to put on a plastic backpack crate for when picking time came.

"Oh, hey there, Jason." Stumpy had a big grin. Stars were sparkling in his eyes. "This is Sister Melanie."

Oh no. Sister Melanie had a dimpled smile and round face and was cute as a hummingbird. And, you guessed it, she was a good two inches shorter than Stumpy. "Nice to meet you, Sister Melanie."

"Nice to meet you." She looked toward the abbey.

"Get this. Melanie spent a year as an exchange student in Chicago. She's even been to Kankakee!" Stumpy was beyond excited. "She can speak good American."

Sister Melanie smiled. "I have to be in the chapel in five minutes." She flickered her fingers in a wave as she walked off.

Stumpy waved. "See you later, Sister Melanie."

I grabbed Stumpy by the shoulders and looked him in the eye. "Get a hold of yourself, my boy. She's a nun. There's no way."

His eyes spun like firecracker pinwheels. "She's cute and short and nice and—"

"And a nun. What about Betsy the flight attendant? I thought you loved her?"

Stumpy scrunched his face like he had sucked up a sour grape. "She doesn't like me."

"You don't know that for sure. She seemed interested when we were in Paris."

Stumpy had a faraway honeymoon look in his eye and had stopped listening to me.

I slapped him. "Melanie's a nun."

Stumpy shook his head and smiled. "She was flirting with me, I think. Did you think she was flirting with me?"

Actually, I think she was. Innocent nun-like flirting if there is such a thing. That's okay, right? No—probably not. And then it hit me. If Stumpy was let loose to harass this cute little nun, that surely would ruffle the old Morceau sister's ire. They'd see the evil in us then.

I smiled and patted Stumpy on the shoulder.

"Yeah, I think she was flirting with you."

"You think? For real?"

"For real."

"But like you said, she's a nun."

"Hmm, good point." I rubbed my chin. "But God's a big fan of true love, no? It's not like it's never happened."

"What's never happened?"

"A Sister leaving the convent for true love."

"It's never happened?"

"It happens all the time."

"For real?"

"For real."

Stumpy looked out toward the convent, and I could see the moral struggle on his face, but I knew love would always win Stumpy over. I was confident the romantic ringleader within the poor sap would gain complete control of him, and for once, I couldn't wait for the love circus to begin.

Matthew and Mark went running by barking and chasing birds away from the grapes. They had the run of the vineyard and were everywhere and nowhere at once.

"But I could go to hell for seducing a nun."

He was really worried. "Nonsense. Where does it say that?"

"I think it's implied."

"Pshaw. Did you ever take a vow not to love a nun?"

"No."

"What's the first thing you learned in Sunday school?"

Stumpy closed his eyes and pinched the skin on his forehead.

"God is . . ." I motioned my hand for him to complete the sentence. "God is . . ."

Stumpy spoke slowly. "God is. God is." He paused. "God is love." He smiled. "God is love."

I smiled and nodded reverently. "That's right. God is love. If you and Sister Melanie end up loving each other then I don't care what anyone or any book says, God wants you and Sister Melanie together."

Stumpy gave me a hug. "Yes, yes. Thank you, Jason." He tumbled out of the room like a wayward wrecking ball and ran down the hill into the vines.

The next day I meandered over to Stumpy's shed, thinking about Jacqueline the whole way. I think she liked me, a little, at least. I'd see her again in three days. She liked my spontaneity—my singing! Should I sing again? How can I be spontaneous if I'm trying to be? I'll have to concentrate really hard to mind my manners and be respectful—that was the only way. Still, I should have a song ready just in case. *It's a wonderful world* popped into my mind, probably because when I thought of Jacqueline I was starting to believe that was true. That song meant a lot to me. Aunt Clara used to sing it to me at bedtime when I was young and innocent enough for such nonsense.

I stopped and looked over the sun-drenched vineyard and suddenly felt choked up. Aunt Clara had been here as a child. She had tended these vines, picked their grapes. Aw, man. Aunt Clara was mean, but suddenly she didn't seem so. Damn it. I missed the old biddy. I pulled off a grape and rolled it through my fingers as I resumed my walk toward the shed.

Stumpy had taken over the job of plastic crate and backpack storage and repair technician. The backpack crate is exactly as its name suggests—a crate attached to shoulder straps to be carried like a backpack. During the harvest, the nuns would pick the grapes, set the clusters into the crates, and then carry them on their backs to a waiting trailer. I peeked through a dirty shed window and saw Sister Melanie and Stumpy standing innocently together.

Stumpy talked.

Sister Melanie talked.

They both smiled and looked at each other lovey-dovey like. Sister Melanie left the shed. Stumpy stared after her, starry-eyed.

I waited until Sister Melanie was halfway to the abbey. I scampered around the opposite way and into the shed. Stumpy looked deliriously happy.

"What happened?"

He looked past me like he was seeing Shangri-La. "She likes me, too."

We had been here a week. I had fallen for a girl, and Stumpy had now fallen for two—a flight attendant and a nun! Oh, la, la the Stumpy love bomb had struck. "Sister Melanie likes you, too?"

"Yes, but she has to think about it. I can't explain everything right now, Jason, but it's a big deal for her."

I shook his hand. "That's great." It was all coming together, a perfect scheme. We were indeed bad workers with bad attitudes, at least I was, but there was also about to be a scandal. I could feel it.

CHAPTER 9

"Take your pick. They all point back to me as Jason Barnes." I plopped down my Illinois vehicular license, GameStop credit card, Park District pool ID, Larry's Lawn Irrigation business card (old sales job), and AMC moviegoer card. I spread them out.

I sat with Sister Claudette and Sister Lucia and a gentle looking man in a lawyerly office. He ran his hands over a worn, but tasteful suit.

"He says only a passport will do," Sister Lucia explained.

The man was Picard Aceau, *avocat*. He looked old-school and had a patient countenance about him.

He spoke some English phrases I couldn't understand. He had a rough accent and Sister Lucia had to translate his English into English for me.

The French government had approved Aunt Clara's will to pass St. Sebastian vineyard on to me. A long document detailed all the members of the Barnes family that had tilled the land since grapes began. Sister Claudette had tried to enlighten me with the oral history of my ancestors, but I found it hard to keep straight, and I cared little, anyhow. These ancestors had done me no good in the states and would do me no good after I cashed in.

Aceau again asked something about verifying my identity.

I shrugged. I had nothing else. I explained how I must have misplaced my passport between Paris and here.

Aceau shook his head.

The sisters vouched for me. They offered to bring in old photos and described how my behavior matched Aunt Clara's description perfectly.

Old Aceau didn't care. An inheritance transferring to a non-French person required an official national-government-issued identification, i.e. only my passport would do.

"Contact the American consulate in Bordeaux," Aceau said. "They should be able to reissue a passport. Until then the property remains in the estate."

Seeing how my passport was with the Kankakee County Court, and I was officially supposed to be nearby, I anticipated some difficulty obtaining a reissued passport from the consulate.

I needed a passport to inherit the land. I needed the land to cash in on a few million. I needed sixty grand to maintain my non-felon status and bail out my passport, and I had only eighteen days to do it. I needed to have passed algebra to figure it all out. If they convicted me and Eustace snatched this vineyard, I'd suck down grapes until I fermented and they could bury me in an oak barrel.

Sister Claudette and Sister Lucia sat outside with me at a casual restaurant off Duras's town square.

"Cheer up, Jason," Sister Lucia said. "A new passport will arrive soon enough."

The greasy smell of frites drifted through the air. Pigeons fluttered in small flocks and raced between buildings in the cloudy sky.

I cut my *jambon* and *fromage* crepe into tiny pieces. I didn't feel like eating. I cut the tiny pieces into tinier pieces.

"What do you think of the vineyard, Jason?" Sister Claudette smiled with the friendliest face I had yet seen from her. "Have you enjoyed your property walks?"

Old men in berets sauntered by, their hands folded behind their backs. Shopkeepers stood outside their doors, chatting with passersby.

Click, click. I got it. Algebra be damned. "The profits," I said. "The vineyard profits. How, when, and where will I get them?"

Sister Claudette's smile evaporated into the cold wind that overcame her. "Tsk, tsk. Money, money. Can you think of nothing else?"

Plenty, I thought. But at that moment my brain jingled with Uncle Sam's coins and how to keep my mug out of the jail yard. "I'm sorry, Sisters. I've been favoring my own charity for a long time and circumstances preclude me from switching allegiances at the moment."

"You're in need of money, then?" Sister Lucia said with concern.

"Right, ho, Sisters." I smiled broadly at them.

Sister Claudette remained stoic. She arched an eyebrow. "For gambling debts or other nefarious purposes, no doubt?"

I sat up straight. "I assure you, Sister, my obligations are of the highest quality."

Her demeanor did not change. "Well, then, Mr. All-Business, back to your question. Profits are distributed twice a year."

"And the next distribution is?"

"After the harvest we will distribute profits."

Oh boy, the hamster was sprinting on the wheel now. "And will I be part of that distribution?"

Sister Claudette pursed her lips and nodded slightly.

"Even if I don't get my new passport by then? Even if technically I haven't yet inherited the estate?"

Sister Claudette mini-nodded again. "You've worked, or attempted to appear interested in the vineyard. Clara clearly wanted you to have the vineyard and the profits. I'm the executor of the estate, and I will adhere to her wishes. I can think of no good reason not to distribute your share of the profits." She paused. "Can you think of any reason?"

Eustace. Hammersmith. The judge. Eighteen days until jail! All these thoughts flashed through my mind. "No, Sister." I can't think of anything.

"Then you shall still receive your profits while we wait for the government's rubber stamp."

I raised my fist in the air. "Hallelujah."

Sister Lucia smiled.

Sister Claudette's eyes widened. "This is not a religious occasion."

"Of course not, Sister, but I felt joy."

"You felt the culmination of your greedy desires in an evil epiphany."

Whatever. Sister Claudette was getting on my nerves, but I pretended like I didn't notice her last uppercut. "So, you sell the wine right after the harvest?"

Sister Lucia laughed. "No, no, we sell the juice."

"The juice?"

"We don't have the capacity to make all our grapes into wine," Sister Lucia explained. "So we sell the juice."

"Eliminates some of the risk, evens out the cash flow," Sister Claudette said. "Make sense to you, Mr. Business?"

"Sure, sure. What kind of cash we talking about?"

"Profits," Sister Claudette said. "That is what we distribute, if any."

"What do you mean—if any?"

The sisters looked at each other.

"Some years there are losses," Sister Claudette said, her jaws clenched. She looked like she took losses as a personal failure, as if she and the nuns hadn't worked hard enough, as if failure was a sin.

I wasn't so hip on the idea of losses either, especially for this harvest. I rubbed my temples. "Oh, jeez. Losses?"

"But if the harvest is as good as last year the juice profits should be sufficient."

"Sufficient for what?" I said. "How sufficient are we talking here?"

"Lucia?"

"After last year's juice sales, Clara's share was forty thousand Euros. Based on todays exchange rate, that would be—"

"Fifty-six thousand dollars," I said. With fifty-six Gs I'd be reaching for the champagne on the victory stand. I could borrow the extra four grand from Lucky Mike or maybe even Laura, and I could pop the cork. "But it's possible the profits could be even more, right?"

"Or less, or nothing," Sister Claudette said.

"Prices are high," Sister Lucia said.

"But profits depend on how many quality grapes we can harvest," Sister Claudette said.

I could feel that old beginning-of-semester drive—when all looked hopeful before the distractions prevailed. I stood up. "Why are we wasting time here? We have work to do. We have to be ready for the harvest."

The sisters looked at me with kindly surprise, like a bad pupil they couldn't help but like, and then they laughed.

I dropped the sisters off after our lunch and hurried over to the vintner's house. Stumpy and I had to get serious. The sisters weren't going to let me sell, but they were going to let me have the profits. I could work on the selling part later, right now the profits were the key—the key to keeping out of jail.

We had to make sure all the equipment was ready to go for the harvest. The hoses and the sorting conveyor had to be cleaned. The hopper and crusher had to be cleaned and tested. Everything had to be perfect. Not a grape could go to waste.

I burst into the vintner's house with rah rah vigor. I rounded the hall into the main room, and lo and behold, Stumpy and Melanie stood together holding hands with their eyes locked.

"Holy . . ." I was at a loss for a second word. "Holy hand holders," I finally said.

Stumpy and Melanie stepped apart. Stumpy shifted his feet, embarrassed. Sister Melanie stared at me, oddly composed.

Due to my passport difficulties and Sister Claudette's promise to distribute harvest profits, Stumpy's nun seduction plan had to change. Or, ideally, be completely reversed. If the sisters found out about this wayward nun and Stumpy's and my part in the process, the Champagne victory would be toast.

"You two should be ashamed of yourselves."

"Jason, say what?"

I pointed at Stumpy. "You, an honest churchgoing Baptist messing with a nun—a married woman!"

"Married woman?"

"Jesus!" I pointed at Sister Melanie. "She's married to Jesus. Have you forgotten your vows, Sister?"

Sister Melanie put her hands on her hips. "Now wait just a minute."

I grabbed her arm and pulled her toward the door. "I don't want to see your dimpled cheeks or fluttering eyes anywhere near this house or Stumpy again."

Stumpy grabbed my shoulder, but I had too much momentum. I whipsawed Sister Melanie out the door.

"Have you gone mad, Jason? We're in love. It's right like you said."

"I said no such thing." I shooed Sister Melanie away. "Go pray, Sister. Pray on the sanctity of your vows. Pray to save your soul."

Sister Melanie gave me a venomous look. She opened her mouth and looked ready to let loose a tirade, but then her jaw clamped shut and she exhaled a deep breath from her nose. She breathed in deep and scrunched her little face, closed her eyes, and then relaxed. She turned and left. I had thought she might have been a tad more contrite, considering the circumstances.

Damage control with Stumpy would be difficult.

Stumpy's chest heaved. His eyes averted my eyes and focused on my torso. His nostrils flared, and his ears twitched. One foot stepped back, and he charged.

"Stumpy, wait. Listen." He was beyond hearing, much less reasoning. Stumpy had attacked me once before, back in grade school after I had called him fatso or something. Teasing each other was not unusual, but Stumpy and I at this particular moment had been crushing on the same girl, sweet Carol Jenner. As we waited in the cafeteria line Stumpy was showing his R2D2 pin to Carol when I flipped my teasing comment Stumpy's way. All the kids, including Carol, laughed, and the next thing I knew Coach Williams, the lunchroom monitor that day, was pulling Stumpy off me to save my life. I ended up in the nurse's office with a bloody nose and bruised eye and got a free pass home to cry over my wounds.

I stood in the vintner's house paralyzed with fear. Coach Williams was nowhere around and probably too old to help anyway. Stumpy's red face and wide body barreled toward me. Time slowed down. His fists pumped. The clock said 2:35. I noticed because I thought I might die and it seemed important, like I needed to record it or something. Crazy. A fly flew out of the room.

I snapped to. I dodged left, right, spun around and tried to run, but Stumpy had eyes on me like a bull to a matador's cape. His head dropped and hit me square in the chest. I landed on my back on the Oriental rug. Stumpy sat on my solar plexus and pinned my arms with his knees in a classic playground maneuver. He had no intention of tickling me.

"Stumpy. I have a new plan."

He slapped me. "I don't care about your stupid plans."

"But—"

He slapped me twice more. "You said I should love her."

"I—"

Slap, slap

"Okay, okay, I did. I told you to love her."

Stumpy stood up and walked away.

"Stumpy, wait. I can explain."

He turned angrily. "I'm tired of you, Jason. I don't want your money. I don't want to be your stooge anymore. I want Melanie, and nobody is going to stop me."

CHAPTER 10

I figured Stumpy would get over Sister Melanie soon enough, and the syndicate would be back together. Sister? Surely Stumpy would realize his mistake and wake up soon.

Now that I was in on the harvest profits, I was all business. I covered the vineyard, pruning, weeding, and loving them grapes. I was the big boss with the big heart. I waved and smiled to the nun workers, encouraged them on, and reminded them they were working for the good Lord.

The way Sister Claudette explained the old picking process was that once them purple berries sang sweet we needed to pick and haul 'em in as fast and careful as the nuns were able. I tested the crusher every morning and made sure it was ready. I had the two tractors tuned up, fueled up, and their trailers in working order. I had the nuns assigned to different crews prepared to work at any time. A mid-sized tanker truck was reserved and ready to go in Bordeaux.

The day after our wrestling match, I went down to see Stumpy in the shed. Light shone through the cloudy windows, but Stumpy worked at a bench in the dark shadows. Even though I gave a friendly 'hello,' Stumpy responded with the backside silent treatment as he worked on the crates.

"Now, Stumpy. I realize you're still a little miffed over Sister Melanie, and I'm not saying you don't have a point or two, but, Stumpy, a job has got to be done here and we're still partners and all, and I'd appreciate it if you'd listen to my ideas."

Silence.

"Okay, then. What I'm thinking is a two-crate backpack. All we need to do is lengthen the straps and add connectors and we could stack one crate on top of the other and cut our hauling time in half."

Silence.

I walked across the dusty wood floor to Stumpy. I took hold of a crate. "Let me show you." I reached across him to fetch a buckle and he grabbed my arm. He looked at me with sad droopy eyes and I felt the guilt gorilla squeezing my heart. I tried to move my arm but Stumpy held on. "All right. All right, all right, all right." He let go and I threw my hands into the air. "All right." I sat down on a crate. "God help me, but if you like that cute nun I'm not going to stop you."

"Her name is Melanie."

"Yes, Melanie." I spun my finger to signal a home run. "You and Melanie have at it."

A huge smile spread across Stumpy's love-struck face.

I stood up and opened my palms to him. "But can you wait a couple of weeks, or at least keep it under wraps until after the harvest?"

Stumpy put his arms around me and lifted me up. He set me down and tenderly patted my cheek. "Thank you, Jason. Of course. Nobody will know until after the harvest." He ran out of the shed, undoubtedly in search of Melanie.

I picked up a backpack and went to work figuring out how to double it up. They stacked on top of each other easy enough. I found a couple clamps and screwed them on the bottom crate so it was easy to latch the top crate secure by hand. I weaved the straps from the backpack through the top crate, and the double backpack was complete. I strapped it on and walked proudly around the shed.

I wanted to show Jacqueline—see what I can do! I'd have to wait until tomorrow. Could I wear a double-crate backpack to the café? Naw, probably too contrived.

I walked out the door and marched with the backpack over to the convent to show off for the good sisters. I found Sister Claudette reflecting at the fountain in the center courtyard. The sun shone through the cloudless sky, and the courtyard was hot. The air smelled of dust, kicked up by silent nuns who crisscrossed on the pebble paths.

"You call it a double what?"

Sister Claudette had trouble grasping the name. "Double-hauler," I said. I held up one finger and my thumb to signal two, French-like. "Twice as much. We can cut our grape-processing time dramatically."

"But it will be too heavy for many of the nuns."

"But not all of them. And they don't have to fill both crates. Whatever extra each nun can carry will help."

Sister Claudette rubbed her chin, intrigued. "We might not have to have so many visiting nuns."

"I was more concerned about the processing time."

"With the increased rate . . ." Sister Claudette looked at the fountain as if asking Saint Sebastian to help her calculate. ". . . The crusher will reach maximum capacity . . ." She rattled off a bunch of productivity rates and capacity algorithms and such until I had that old feeling I would flunk again.

Sister Claudette smiled at me, which took me off guard. "The *dooble holer* might work. We could increase processing speed and eliminate laborers."

I was excited. "You're all business, Sister."

Her smile disappeared. "I do manage a convent. And there are a lot of mouths to feed." She touched my shoulder. "But good work, Jason. Clara would have been proud."

Yeah, I thought. Aunt Clara would have been proud. It felt good. Sister Claudette's fingers gently clenched me. Warmness radiated through me like a blessing. I thought she might give me a hug, but she straightened up and removed her hand. I wished she hadn't.

I used to crave Aunt Clara's approval, her love, her touch, but it never came. No matter how I tried, I could never get over the feeling that I was a nuisance. And maybe I was, but how did Eustace do it? She loved that Boy Scout with his straight A's, expertly-made bed, and clean room. That neatnik won Aunt Clara's affection in the few months he lived with us, and his perfection overshadowed my faults for the years to come.

The day had finally arrived. Noon—the Hotel Duras café. Jacqueline and I collided at the maître d's stand. On cue, we greeted each other at the exact same time. "Bonjour," I said. "Hi," she said. We laughed and did the European hat-trick cheek kiss.

The warm air smelled like bread, wine, and garlic. Jacqueline's face radiated happiness and anticipation. We caught each other's eye, and then I saw the look. That was the moment. She gave me the look, whether she wanted to or not. It was the look that said she liked me. I might screw it up in the next hour, or week, but at that moment, the bobber was sunk. Be cool, Jason, be cool. Don't sing. Don't say anything.

I held out my hand, and she took it. Absolutely electric! Her eyes were springing with affection. I led her, and we floated over to our table. I sat down without bumping into anything.

We ordered some wine, exchanged pleasantries, and recapped our past four days. I sat, mesmerized—basking in her words, her aura, and her smile.

"What do you do for fun in Kanka—Kankakee?" Jacqueline looked at me, wondering if she had pronounced it right.

"You got it. Kankakee." I tried to think. What did I like to do?

"Do you surf? Americans surf, right?"

I laughed. "Not me. I like to mountain bike. I have a Trek mountain bike that I ride all over the place."

Jacqueline smiled, eager. "I love to mountain bike. I bike in the Alps every summer. What mountains do you ride in Kankakee?"

I thought of the hundreds of miles of flat cornfields. "None. I've never seen a real mountain in my life. A curb is the highest thing my mountain bike has gone over." I felt guilty. I wasn't a true mountain biker.

She smiled, though, and was still enthusiastic. "You should try the Alps, then. They are only a few hours from here."

The blue sky and a cool breeze made the day refreshing. The café was crowded with people sitting close together. Waiters weaved their way through with trays piled high. Jacqueline and I laughed and talked about different things, but then our lunch came and the enchanted woman became all business.

"Back to your plans here in France," Jacqueline said.

I thought she was still worried the J-man might pull the old kiss and split. "Like I said. I want to sell the vineyard and buy a smaller place—maybe in Paris." I emphasized Paris, but she ignored the reference.

It turned out Jacqueline was all stirred up over the selling part. She looked into my eyes all serious-like. "I want to buy your vineyard."

"Wait, what?"

Jacqueline gave a hearty, friendly laugh. "I mean the government does. France wants to buy St. Sebastian vineyard."

My head snapped backward. "How much?"

"We are prepared to pay you seven million Euros."

The golden grapes were ripe. The cash was at hand. If I could sell the vineyard, I wouldn't have to work. It wouldn't matter what the harvest profits turned out to be. Seven million Euros! That was ten million dollars! The French government was a legitimate buyer—able to pay actual cash. A potential sale seemed more possible now. If I could only convince the sisters.

I took a healthy, very un-French-like, gulp of wine. "I'm more than ready to make a deal, but there's a stipulation: The Morceau sisters must agree to the new buyer. From the way they reacted to you, I don't think they would like the government as a partner."

The waiter took Jacqueline's plate, and she placed her hands delicately on the table. "We know about the stipulation, and we don't want to be partners with the nuns. We want to buy them out, too."

She looked intently into my eyes. "We've found another vineyard—a more profitable one in Provence—with a castle that will make an excellent abbey. The owner is retiring and moving. The nuns could have the same arrangement as they do now. I think they would be very happy there."

It sounded perfect. The sisters might reject the sale, citing tradition and all that crap, but at least this was a new angle, and an attractive angle at that. I mean, Provence!

The passport! Before I could sell, I needed my passport to inherit the vineyard. I might have to find a quicker way to pay off the court than waiting for harvest profits.

Jacqueline reached across the table and touched the top of my hand affectionately, bringing me out of my thoughts of money. She smiled, and I was all hers.

"This is very serious, Jason."

"Very serious," I said.

She didn't smile. She did look serious. "Negotiations can be tough. I can't reveal all the details now, but I want you to know I'm just doing my job."

I pounded my chest. "I can be tough."

Her face look conflicted, like something between sympathy and admiration. "I wish I could be like you sometimes—relaxed and care-free, everything a game."

She was wrong, though; I didn't feel relaxed and carefree. I was so excited to be talking to her that my stomach sizzled like it was full of Pop Rocks. I'd do anything for this woman. "Don't you worry; I'll convince the Morceau sisters to sell."

"You really think so?"

"Absolutely!" I thought back to all the schemes I had hoodwinked Aunt Clara on. A new Abbey in Provence. I could sell that. It was all coming together. I was getting confident, and my mouth got ahead of the weak self-monitoring sensor in my brain. "No problem. If there's one thing I'm good at, it's bullshitting old ladies."

Jacqueline didn't blink. She seemed encouraged. "Bullshitting? That's good, right?"

"Yes, yes. The sisters will sell for sure." I could feel my body and face radiating with excitement. "And then we can celebrate—with champagne!"

Jacqueline laughed and relaxed. "*Oui*, we can celebrate with champagne."

I stood up. "I have to go." I was going to cash in on millions and be Jacqueline's hero in one stroke. "I have to find the sisters."

I drove in a fever, battling the thin country road back to the convent like a true Frenchman, excited to tell the sisters about the French government's plan. I had sixteen days left, and I was beginning to think I could actually pull this off.

The abbey's hallways teemed with busy nuns quietly heading to prayers or other such nun-ish events. I made my way tank-like toward the Morceau sister's office.

"Jason, what's wrong?"

I stood in the doorway and looked at a group of nuns sitting at a long table. Sister Claudette and Sister Lucia sat together at one end. "We need to talk."

They stood up and came to me, their faces concerned. Sister Claudette wrapped her arm around my shoulder and led me down a short side hallway. "There's a small private chapel where we won't be bothered."

She opened the door and turned on the lights. Six wooden pews lined up behind a small altar. In the last pew, Stumpy and Sister Melanie sat sucking lips like they needed to breathe each other to live.

Sister Claudette gasped.

Sister Lucia said, "Ooh."

Sister Melanie screeched and stood up.

Stumpy turned red and smiled guiltily.

Sister Claudette did not control her anger. She lashed out at Stumpy, Sister Melanie, and me at once. "You are a visiting nun. That does not mean you are on vacation from your obligations." She spun to Stumpy. "And you, you chubby little Baptist. I thought you were a good Christian, nonetheless."

Sister Melanie straightened her habit. "But, Sister—"

Sister Claudette's wrath bore down on Sister Melanie. "Don't you, 'but Sister,' me." She pointed her finger right at Sister Melanie's heart. "You are to be silent for the remainder of your stay. And you are confined to the convent with kitchen duty sunup to sundown."

Her anger revved higher, I feared for the devil himself if he were so unlucky to meet Sister Claudette. She poked Stumpy in the chest with her index finger. "You are banned."

Stumpy had lots of abuse-taking experience. He put on his dumb, innocent look which only enraged Sister Claudette more.

"Don't give me that. You try to seduce a nun in a convent—in a chapel, no less? I hereby ban you from St. Sebastian."

Before I knew it, Sister Claudette was in front of me. All I could see was black and white and her enraged eyes. "I'm sure you've played your part in this. Have you no respect for the sanctity of this place?"

"Tell her, Jason," Stumpy said. "Tell her how God is love. Tell her how Melanie and I are meant to be."

"I knew it." Sister Claudette glared into my eyes. "God is love to those who deserve it." She spread her hands out. "God's love is a gift to those who obey his laws and to those who honor their vows." She looked at Sister Melanie. "God's love is not cheap."

"Ah, Sister," I said. "I don't think you understand. You're being a bit tough."

She looked around at all of us. "I understand perfectly well. Thank God we've stopped this before it went any further." And then her pointy finger pounded me in the chest. "I'll show you tough. You are banned, as well. I want you and your friend off this land by tomorrow. I'll honor Clara's will, but you will enjoy no profits until you are the official owner."

I threw up my hands. "But, Sister!"

"No more *buts*. Now everyone out. Sister Melanie and I have a lot of praying to do."

Sister Lucia covered her eyes and cried.

CHAPTER 11

"Now what are we going to do?"

Stumpy did not respond.

It was the next morning, and we had to vacate. Stumpy and I moped around the house and slowly packed our belongings. Acting like ourselves had worked—unfortunately too well, and too soon—and we found ourselves back in our sad old problems: no job, no money, and no prospects.

"Where are we going to come up with sixty grand?"

Stumpy still did not respond.

I sat down at the kitchen table and plopped a grape into my mouth from a deep purple bunch that sat in a bowl. I couldn't think of anyone who would loan me that kind of cash, and with court problems and a missing passport, no bank would be willing to lend me the money—no matter how solid my possible inheritance looked. I couldn't even get back into the US without a hassle. Perhaps being a fugitive in Europe was my best hope.

"Where are we going to go?" I asked.

Nothing. Stumpy continued to fold his underwear, taking five minutes per garment.

"Hello? Hello! Hello! Hey, thong-man. We've got a serious problem here."

Stumpy used his thumbs to slingshot a blue-striped brief at me. "I don't care."

Disgusted, I pinched the tiniest amount of elastic band and flipped the oversized underwear back to him. "What is that, a flag?"

"Vertical stripes are slimming." He was serious, but at least he was talking, and with Stumpy that usually signaled his shorts were becoming unbunched.

"So," I said. "On the hundred to one shot your jockey wins the trifecta . . ." I counted with my fingers. "One, you get a girl alone. Two, you take your clothes off. And three, she doesn't bolt. You're going to impress her by slimming down the old horse with striped skivvies?"

"Well, I hadn't thought of it that way."

I pulled up my whitey tighties above my jeans. "White, see? The standard—fattens up the package."

Stumpy started laughing. "Man, Jason, you're fucked up."

I popped another grape into my mouth and stood up. I spread my hands apart and talked as I chewed. "I'm fucked up? Dude, we're standing on ten million grape skins and all you can think about is baggin' a nun." I held my hands to my chest. "I'm fucked up?"

"It's not that way and you know it."

"I know. I'm sorry, I know." I closed my eyes and sighed. "But, Jesus, Stumpy."

Stumpy zipped up his suitcase. "Jesus, you, Jason. All you can think about is the cash."

Okay, so what. All I could think about was the cash. I'd been accused of being greedy and selfish before. Well, who the hell isn't? "Like that's a big surprise to you, Stumpy. Don't give me that altruistic

bullshit. Every poor sap buys a lottery ticket once in a while hoping for
the good stuff. Greed is in us all; I'm just not afraid to admit it."

Stumpy grabbed a handful of grapes and shoved them into his
mouth. He garble-talked worse than I did around the purple pearls.
"What about the vineyard? What about the sisters? What about love?"
He swallowed and spoke clearly. "What about Jacqueline?"

"Psh—just a girl."

"Psh, right. I saw how goose-bumpy you were after that lunch. It's
been a long time, but I know the old J-man-flip-o-rama over a girl when
I see it."

I tried to gather the gumption to confound his insight with
some macho bullshit, but I thought of Jacqueline and couldn't help
but smile. I couldn't wait to see her again. She was so beautiful, and
funny, and kind, and I was pretty sure she liked me. It was like she
saw right inside of me—into who I really was. She saw the good and
the bad—and thought it all good! She was really worried about her
job, though. I had to help her. I had to figure out a way to convince
the sisters to sell—for Jacqueline and me. If I didn't, I'd be sent to the
slammer in the states and probably never see Jacqueline again. Damn
Eustace! Why did he have to be such a snake? Aunt Clara and I were
true family—Eustace was only a nasty blip in our lives. Couldn't he see
that? Did he have to try and steal the vineyard in such an underhanded
way? We had an agreement! We shook hands in front of Aunt Clara.
"You bastard!"

"Say what?"

"Sorry, Stumpy. I was thinking about Eustace."

I didn't have to explain further. "Oh."

I had to come clean with Stumpy. "All right, you got me."

"Where?"

"Jacqueline, you dope. You were right. I think I love her. I think I
love her more than I thought I'd ever be able to love again."

He looked surprised. "Really?"

"What do you mean, really? You're the one who brought it up."

Stumpy looked thoughtful. He rubbed his chin. "Yes. I know, but I'm surprised you admitted it. You've taken a big step, Jason. I'm happy for you. Maybe this isn't such a bad day after all."

How could Stumpy always see the bright side of everything? "Great day? Stumpy, this day is the beginning of the end. The end of our chances of cashing in on ten million."

Stumpy sat my suitcase upright for me. We were ready to go. "You're right. Everyone's selfish and greedy, but look around you." Stumpy did a three-quarter spin around and then back like a sprinkler. "You have to balance that with what's important in life. Otherwise, where are we?"

"Where are we? Where are we going to go?" Stumpy had some points. I give him that. I laughed. "You should have your own talk show, man."

"Where will you go?" Sister Lucia stood in the doorway. How long she was there, I didn't know.

"There's a gypsy river camp by Beynac we got our eye on, Sister."

"Like in *Chocolat*," Stumpy said.

Sister Lucia walked into the room. "Why don't you hold off for now."

The gumball machine spun, and I hoped for a good one. "We've been forgiven?"

Sister Lucia smiled. "I forgive you."

Stumpy ran to her, and they held hands. "Thank you, Sister."

"But—"

"But, Sister Claudette," I said.

"But, Sister Claudette," she said. "You must understand she is very protective over her nuns—and the vineyard, for that matter."

Stumpy looked at me. "Things that are important to her."
Stumpy offered Sister Lucia the grapes. She tasted one and her face
puckered. "Sour."

"Like Sister Claudette," I said.

They both frowned at me and looked disappointed, though not
unexpectedly so.

"Sister Claudette cares about you, Jason. Both of you boys are
important to her." Sister Lucia put a hand on each of our shoulders.
"More important than you know. Still, even though she has calmed
down, she is far from forgiving you two."

"There's a club she could join," I said. It was all more Aunt Clara-
like talk. You are important to me—but a "grave disappointment."
I felt bad Sister Claudette had too high of expectations concerning
yours truly, but what could I do—stop being me?

Sister Lucia looked at me confused and then continued. "Sister
Claudette has agreed to a meeting to more calmly discuss the situation."

"Oh, that's great," Stumpy said.

"But not with you," she replied to Stumpy. He looked to the
ground, disappointed. Stumpy was always the last guy picked, always
left out, but there was nothing I could do this time. Sister Lucia looked
at me. "Would you join me and Sister Claudette this afternoon?"

"Of course. In your office?"

"We will pick you up. We are going to go for a drive."

A 1957 classic Citroen DS pulled up after the noon hour. A wooden
rosary was hung from the rear-view-mirror. Sister Claudette drove.
Sister Lucia smiled from the passenger seat, her hands folded in her
lap. The car had flat black paint and white leather interior and looked
like an extension of the sisters.

I sat in back and was chauffeured—destination heaven or hell, both seemed likely enough. We drove around the vineyard, our windows rolled down. The air was cool and still smelled of the Atlantic, one hundred kilometers away. We drove over the hillcrest that landscaped our patio view, and down the dusty road to the very back valley of the vineyard. If it were anyone else besides the Sisters driving me to this unknown destination I would have been terrified. It felt like I was in a movie being driven out to some secret mafia burial ground. The car climbed another large hill that marked the property's boundary. A small stone chapel sat at the very top. I had walked into this valley before, but had yet to climb this hill. The car lurched over rocks as it struggled up the incline. Halfway up, we pulled off to a grassy outcropping.

I exited the car with the sisters, and we walked over to some gravesites and an above ground burial vault. Matthew and Mark were next to the vault, lazing on the grass, panting easily. They gave me a break and paid me no mind. I swallowed. "Barnes" was inscribed on the vault's side. A list of names was etched on a tarnished copper plaque. Encased photographs surrounded it.

Sister Lucia bowed her head and prayed silently.

Sister Claudette pointed to a picture of a man and woman standing together. "Your grandparents." The couple was fiftyish. They were tan, their clothes loose over their slim frames and taut skin. The man's nose was long and could have been mine. Sister Claudette pointed out more pictures and more names, but it became a jumble to me.

I continued to stare at my grandparents. In the photograph they stood next to the vintner's house where the patio began. The vineyard, dusty looking in black and white, stretched behind them. The vines were younger, but the house and view were the same as I had come to know. I became oddly nostalgic. It was like this mystical past that Aunt Clara always rambled on about suddenly became real. I felt heavy in my bones. Aunt Clara and I shared this. I felt guilty. We shouldn't have become so estranged.

"And my parents? Is there a photograph of my parents?" I thought of the photograph I had of my parents that hung in my apartment. When I was old enough to understand, Aunt Clara had explained that I was an illegitimate child. My parents had escaped their parents' wrath and public humiliation by running away to the United States to live with my mother's sister, Aunt Clara. They planned to elope after they gave birth to me, but a month before the marriage they were killed in the car crash. Aunt Clara took me in out of obligation and gave me her and my mother's last name, Barnes.

"Your parents are not buried here," Sister Claudette said.

Sister Lucia put her hand on my back. She must have seen that I was confused. "The photographs encased here are only of people buried in this tomb."

The vault looked only big enough for one coffin. "All these people are buried in there?"

"No." Sister Lucia snickered. "When the sun beats down on the vault it can reach over four hundred degrees inside and eventually the corpse incinerates."

"Like a magic-cleaning oven," I said.

Sister Claudette scowled. "Let's move on."

The car climbed further up the hill until we pulled off onto the hard-packed ground next to the chapel. Square sand-colored stone of different sizes were mortared together to form the rectangular chapel. A thin cross stood atop a crumbling, aged steeple. A small iron bell hung from a window below the cross. A red Roman tile roof, patched with gray stones, sheltered the top. A small stained glass window was on each chapel side.

Inside the chapel, sunlight streamed through the stained glass windows. Pedestals with lit candles surrounded a small altar. It smelled of wax and incense. Two nuns sat in the front pew, their heads bowed in prayer. The sisters gave me a short tour, stopping at a small glass cabinet. "Our relics," Sister Lucia said. Inside the cabinet, small pieces of cloth were strewn over a rosary and wooden crosses. On the middle shelves, small brown pieces that looked like bones rested on each other. A row of silver and gold chalices lined the bottom shelf. I wondered how much they were worth. Probably a pretty penny. Should I add that in when figuring out the sale price? Naw, they probably would stay with the Sisters and the church. I wanted to ask, but I figured it was impolite, and kept my mouth shut for a change.

Sister Claudette led us outside. She looked around and waved her palm slowly across the grand view. The breeze picked up, and soft white clouds hurried overhead; their shadows, like dark green zeppelins, floated across the valley floor. The air smelled different here. It was thin and crisp and had not yet touched the richness of St. Sebastian Vineyard. The opposite hill blocked the vintner's house, but to the left stood St. Sebastian abbey watching over the chapel like a parent over a small child.

"This vineyard. This place is your history," Sister Claudette said.

I was beginning to understand, although it was difficult. I had felt out of place most of my life. This land was beautiful. I could appreciate that on a different level now after seeing the tomb and all my ancestors. "I'm sorry, Sister Claudette, Sister Lucia. I did not mean to disrespect you, nor the St. Sebastian nuns. I was only trying to help Stumpy."

Sister Lucia nodded. Sister Claudette remained stern, but she may have nodded, perhaps imperceptibly so.

"I have the reputation of St. Sebastian and all the nuns to uphold," Sister Claudette said.

"I know that now," I said.

"Good."

"I want to apologize for my behavior."

The sisters looked at me, patient.

"You were right. I did encourage Stumpy. I—I made him believe pursuing Sister Melanie was the right thing to do, but I see now I have disrespected you and the convent, and I'm sorry."

"Very good," Sister Lucia said.

Sister Claudette pursed her lips. She spoke with reluctance. "I must admit I am still angry with you, Jason, but I appreciate your honesty."

"Thank you." I looked down and ground my shoe into the pebbles as I used to do as a child when Aunt Clara scolded me. "It's just that . . . I saw them together and they looked so happy, like they were truly in love."

"It happens sometimes," Sister Claudette said. "But the results are never good. Every nun is tempted sooner or later, and it is our job, our mission, to honor our vows."

Sister Lucia didn't say anything, but she looked like she might cry. I guessed she had inherited the emotions for both of them.

It might have been a bad time to toss the subject, but seeing as it felt we were all opening up the lockers for inspection, I gave it a shot. "Remember Jacqueline, the government lady?"

The sisters did not respond, but their heads twitched like alert owls.

"Please hear me out." I talked quickly. "The government wants to buy the vineyard, the abbey—everything. They'll move you to a new place in Provence by the sea. You'd be very—"

Sister Claudette held up her hand before I could whistle it all out. "You would bury all this?"

I didn't know what she meant, but I didn't let that stop me. "The new place is just as beautiful and more profitable. You could always come back here and visit. I'll come back to see the cemetery, now that I know about it."

Sister Claudette smiled with indignation. "In a submarine?"

"Wait, what?"

"Or are you a scuba diver?"

"A scuba diver, what?"

Sister Lucia put her hand on my shoulder. "The government, they want to build a dam." She paused and swallowed to contain her emotion. "They want to flood our land."

Sister Claudette panned her hand out across the vineyard like she was trying to capture all its essence for us to feel at once. "Everything would be gone. The convent, the vineyard, hundreds of years of memories." She turned to me and placed her hand on my chest, like she was imparting the history of the vineyard into my heart. "Your family, Jason—your ancestors—would all be gone."

It felt like the ground shuddered. A cloud raced overhead, and as the shadow passed the hill appeared to move. The vine leaves shook, and I steadied myself. The vineyard. The land. My ancestors. I felt like they were all judging me.

"We found out from some of our sources. And it might not matter if we want to sell or not. By law, they can force us to sell."

"Flood the land? Force us to sell?"

"Yes. Didn't you know from your meeting with that woman?" Sister Claudette said.

I shook my head, embarrassed. Jacqueline hadn't said anything about flooding the land. She had set me up. I was a fool. Was she conniving like Laura, too? Were all women? I should have never let my guard down. I couldn't believe it. I thought we had made a connection. I thought she actually liked me for me—dumb old Jason Barnes.

We turned to look at the view again.

"I can't imagine the vineyard under water," Sister Lucia said. "It would be horrible."

As much as I wanted the money, I still had to agree. "You're right, Sister. It would be a shame."

We were silent as we imagined the vine-covered valleys, the forest patches, and the rock outcroppings from the hills all vanishing from the view. "All my ancestors. I feel like I just met them."

The sisters nodded.

"Would the chapel and abbey be underwater, too?"

No one answered. The question was too difficult to consider. Sister Claudette folded her arms across her chest.

Sister Lucia touched my arm. "What should we do, Jason?"

There was a man in my brain with a Gucci suit and slicked back hair that had been saying, *sell, sell, sell. Sell the land, take the cash and run,* but he was growing smaller. I thought on what Stumpy had said about balancing out what was really important in life. After seeing the cemetery, I finally felt I might have a place—a special place to connect me to this world—and the government wanted to drown it all. "They're not going to force me to sell. We should fight them with everything we've got."

The Sisters' eyes opened wide, and they stood up straighter.

"Do you speak the truth?" Sister Claudette asked.

I did. At least I thought I did. "Sisters, I know now you'll never agree to sell the abbey or the land, no matter the price, and you shouldn't, especially in this case. So my best option is to help you maximize vineyard profits. To do that we need to be a happy team, and I'm willing to help out all I can."

Sister Claudette looked almost kindly.

Sister Lucia clapped her hands together prayer-like. "But what can we do? How can we fight the government?"

"In court, for one. And for two . . ." I raised my finger into the air. ". . . Publicity! The public needs to know about our plight. This is not just our fight, Sisters. Our fight should be the fight of all the people in this area. Our fight is France's fight." I threw my arms toward the surrounding countryside. "This gorgeous land should not drown."

Sister Lucia clapped her hands.

Sister Claudette reached her hand to shake mine. "Okay, Jason, we're a team. I like your attitude, even if all you think about is money. We can work on that later, but for now you are welcome to stay and share in the harvest profits."

"And hopefully many more to come," I said.

She pulled me in and wrapped her arms around me and hugged me tight. The last time Aunt Clara had hugged me I had just graduated high school. That was a long time ago. I hugged Sister Claudette back. Her embrace felt so good I wanted to cry.

Sister Claudette pulled away from me and finger-pointed into my chest. "But keep your friend, Stumpy, away from the convent."

CHAPTER 12

Stumpy and I rode on an ancient tandem bike toward Duras. I steered.

"Are you pedaling?"

The sisters had encouraged us to take their tandem (single speed, fat tires, solid steel "woman's frame") into town for the weekly market day. Stumpy powered up on the idea, but I was less than juiced. The rusty black monolithic bike had gigantic wire baskets on the front and sides. We looked like dorks, but the scenery was beautiful, the air fresh, and the activity would keep Stumpy from brooding over Sister Melanie.

"We're lucky the sisters let us stay," I said.

"*You're* lucky. *I've* been banned from Melanie."

Stumpy kept coasting when he talked. I breathed hard as I hammered on the pedals. "We've got to reap the cash on this harvest. I don't want to lose the vineyard. Are you pedaling?"

"Worry about yourself—you're good at that."

I ignored the dig. "I thought Jacqueline liked me. I can't believe she didn't tell me about the dam and the flooding of our land."

"Women!" Stumpy said.

The tires kicked up small stones and crackled against the road. "You think she was just playing me all along? Are you pedaling?"

"Are *you* pedaling?" Stumpy asked. "Jacqueline might like you, but she has her job. Either way you've been a sap."

"Wait, what?"

"No respect. You need respect."

"What are you talking about? Are you going to pedal?"

"Let's coast."

"Coast? We're going uphill!"

Stumpy looked behind him to check my assertion. "Holy tires, it's the Tour de France."

It wasn't the Tour de France, but a group of cyclists decked out in full regalia on aero-jet-like bikes. They overtook us easily and whistled and hollered as they passed. One guy shouted, *"Petites filles!"* and blew kisses.

All of a sudden, our bike surged. I thought we might have been banged from behind by a car, but I looked over my shoulder and only saw Stumpy. He was red faced, flexed up, and pumping the pedals in a rage. I tried to match the pedaling madman, and together we Lance Armstrong-ed our way up to the cyclists.

Stumpy picked out the quadricep of a man who had flicked the "little girls" comment our way. He shook his fist at him. "Petite *this*, spandex-boy!"

The man sat up and rode no-handed. *"Qu'est-ce-que vous faites?"*

"Fay you, too, buddy," Stumpy shouted and gasped for air.

The cyclist reached into his back jersey pocket and produced an energy bar of some sort. He handed it to Stumpy as a peace offering. Stumpy never stayed riled up for long, and free food was just the stick to make him genial. *"Merci,"* he said as he unwrapped the bar and stopped pedaling.

The cyclist raced ahead of us. *"Bonne journée,"* he called.

"Bonne journée," I said.

"That's how you do it," Stumpy said.

Sweat dripped off my nose. "Pedal." I breathed. "Do what? Scare energy bars out of cyclists?"

"Respect. You're too timid, Jason. Sometimes you first have to rile these French people up for them to listen to you."

"Start the engine back there again, would ya? And what are you wheeling on about?"

"Sometimes you got to antagonize a classy broad like Jacqueline to get noticed is all I'm saying. You can work on the love part later."

"Are you serious? Are you pedaling?"

"I'm seriously pedaling," Stumpy shouted.

I thought about what Stumpy had said as we haphazardly pedaled and limped our way into Duras.

Stumpy and I parked the tandem and strolled down Duras's crowded streets. The sun-soaked village was lined with vendors for market day and it buzzed with festivity. The aromas of sausage, cheese, and roasted chicken drifted among the different stands. Area wineries had wine tastings and were selling last year's wine. We walked up and down the hilly, winding lanes, seeking refuge in shade when we could. We bought fresh baguettes, sausage, and cheese. We stopped at the St. Sebastian booth and offered to help, but the nuns shooed us away.

Someone whistled a high-pitched whistle. "Jason Barnes."

I looked around.

Stumpy pointed to the Duras Hotel. "Up there."

Jacqueline leaned out a second floor window. The hotel was made of light brown stone like most of the town's buildings. Vines grew up the side of the wall. Light blue shutters adorned the windows. Jacqueline had shouted over the hotel's café, but she looked like she didn't care.

I waved nonchalantly.

Jacqueline pointed at me. "Stay right there."

"She's cute," Stumpy said.

"She's at least five-foot-seven. Don't get any ideas."

Jacqueline hurried out of the hotel and around tables at the café to reach us. She wore khaki shorts, flats, and a white t-shirt. Her hair was pulled back behind her ears and fell down to her shoulders in back. She held a folded newspaper in one hand.

I did not smile. "Bonjour, Madame. Enjoying market day?"

"No."

I put my arm around Stumpy. "This is Stumpy, my good friend I was telling you about."

She shook hands with Stumpy and greeted him matter-of-factly. "Bonjour, Stumpy. Is that an American name?"

"Nickname," Stumpy said. "It's unique—synonymous with 'player.'"

"I don't understand."

I shook my head. "It doesn't matter."

The newspaper fluttered in Jacqueline's hand. "I thought you were going to convince the Morceau sisters to sell? 'Good at bullshitting old ladies' you said."

"Ha," Stumpy said.

Jacqueline fleetingly looked at Stumpy and then at me. A vendor shouted behind us, hawking his fois grois.

"I tried," I said disinterestedly, "but I don't think the sisters are going to come around."

"Come around?" Jacqueline unfolded the daily *Duras Journal* and held it in front of our faces. A photograph showed the Morceau sisters standing with their arms defiantly crossed in front of the abbey. "They are the opposite of coming around."

"I don't understand what it says," I said.

Jacqueline pointed to the headlines. "It says." Shoppers crowded around us as the market became busier. A couple holding hands bumped Jacqueline, forcing her closer to me. "It says—"

A family pressed by behind me, and I was pushed closer to Jacqueline. Her shoulders leaned against my chest as she read, "*The St. Sebastian Sisters Protest Government's Hydroelectric Project.*"

I kept taking deeper breaths, she smelled so good. "I heard about this project. I'm surprised someone didn't tell me about it sooner, though."

"I had my orders." Her lips quivered. She looked beautiful, and I stared at her face as she talked. "I can understand the nun's position, but I thought you and I were on the same side in this matter." She tapped the paper lightly and read, "*Monsieur Jason Barnes . . .*" Jacqueline pointed at me. "That's you, no?" She read on, "*Monsieur Jason Barnes, the new vintner, says, 'We will fight the government with every means available to us. This is not only our fight, but also Duras's fight. This is a fight for the people of France to save their land.'*" Jacqueline punched the paper. "And as you Americans like to say, 'blah, blah, blah.'"

I tried to touch Jacqueline's arm, but she pulled away. "That's not a small detail you failed to mention to me. Hydroelectric plant? A dam? You planned to flood the land? What did you expect our reaction would be?"

"I told you there were things I couldn't reveal." She pursed her lips and squinted her eyes. Someone's elbow bumped me in the back. "And like I thought you would really care with your cash-in-and-be-a-Paris-playboy talk."

"I, I,—"

"Ay, yi, yi," Stumpy said nervously, uncomfortable to be amidst the argument.

"I told you negotiations could be tough. I'm sorry, but I have no choice." Jacqueline pushed the paper toward me and made me take it. "It doesn't matter if you want to sell or not. The government can exercise their right of eminent domain and force you and the sisters to sell."

"Another item you conveniently forgot to mention."

"We were hoping it wouldn't have to come to that."

"If the government is going to try and take the vineyard then we are going to fight."

"I have a job to do. You are making this very difficult for me." She turned to walk away.

"Well I don't feel like singing either."

She waved her hands chaotically and made her way into the hotel.

"You did it," Stumpy said.

"I did it all right."

"No, it's good. She really notices you, now. You have her respect." Stumpy touched my shoulder. "She has strong emotions for you."

"She hates me."

"Hate is intense like love." Stumpy looked around. "And we are in France. It all turns to love in the end."

"You are an optimist, my friend."

We started walking. A wonderful spicy smell filled my nose. Stumpy and I followed the scent into a hot tent-covered booth. A Spanish woman held a long wooden ladle and stirred a four-foot wide pan full of paella. Fragrant steam rose as she stirred the yellow Spanish rice, pink finger-length prawns, quarter-round sausages, onions, and peppers.

"Oh, yes." Stumpy pointed to a large plastic container. The woman smiled at us and scooped in at least four pounds of paella. Stumpy paid, and we left for home. "We're going to feast tonight."

When we returned from town, Stumpy and I opened a bottle of wine and sat on the porch. We decided to save our paella for supper and instead ate fresh cheese, sausage, and baguettes. A breeze blew the recently formed clouds away and the sun warmed the patio. We clinked glasses and feasted on our simple fare. Stumpy's mood brightened, and the wine went down.

"I feel like Melanie is in prison. I want to break into the abbey and carry her off."

I swallowed a sausage-and-brie-topped baguette slice and took a sip of wine. "This is the life, huh?"

"Living the dream."

"Look, we can't blow this second chance. There's only fourteen days until the sixty grand is due. Can you please hold off on Sister Melanie until after the harvest this time? Once I sign those papers and inherit the land, you can do whatever you want."

Stumpy grimaced.

"If you can't control yourself . . ." I opened my palm to the vineyard. ". . . this is all gone as far as we're concerned."

"Okay, okay. I know."

The house phone rang. I walked into the kitchen and answered it. It was Jacqueline. She talked excitedly fast and it was difficult to understand her. "My bosses, you see. I feel horrible—not like me at all. You hate me for positive."

She sounded frantic. I had to interrupt. "Whoa. Ease back on the gas, girl."

"You don't understand the position I—"

"Jacqueline!"

Silence.

"Why don't you come over here? Stumpy's making paella. We can talk."

Silence.

"Paella? I love paella." She paused. "Okay, I suppose I could do that."

I walked around the house excitedly. "She's coming over. We're having dinner. It's going to be like a date, except, you'll be here."

"I'll leave."

"No, no—too obvious. She thinks you're making the paella."

Stumpy caught my excitement. He talked enthusiastically. "I'll serve you out on the patio. It'll be romantic."

Stumpy and I went to work creating an elegant patio dinner for two. We strung up lights, set out candles, and placed a small table in the patio corner that offered the best view.

Stumpy worked in the kitchen while I cleaned and straightened.

A kitchen towel hit me in the head. Stumpy laughed and put his hands on his hips. "Dawg, you really like this girl."

I looked to the ground, embarrassed. "Yeah, I suppose so."

Stumpy walked over and reached out his fist to me. I punched his knuckles.

"Well, damn, it's about time you stopped being so bitter and took a chance on love again."

I didn't know what to say. Laura had ripped my soul apart, and I hadn't thought love was possible again. I still had plenty of doubts, but the feelings I got when I was with Jacqueline were a pleasure impossible to ignore.

Stumpy slapped me on the shoulder. "You still got the old J-man charm?"

I smiled. "I still got it." I punched him in the shoulder. "You still got it?"

"I never had it."

I laughed. "You got it now. My God, you hit on a flight attendant and then a nun. That's some NASA kind of confidence."

Stumpy shuffled his feet and looked embarrassed. "Betsy didn't like me."

I punched him again. "Betsy, that's her name. I'm telling you she dug you. She didn't respond to that online form?"

"No. Forget about Betsy. Melanie is for me."

"And Jacqueline is for me. We are moving on, my friend."

"All right, then." Stumpy winked at me. "We're going to impress Jacqueline tonight." He walked back into the kitchen singing "Voulez-Vous."

I put on loafers, khakis, and a red polo shirt, but Stumpy said it was too business-casual-like and sent me back upstairs to change. We settled on sandals, jeans, and a button-down shirt with thin green stripes.

Jacqueline arrived wearing a pink A-line dress with a glossy black belt above the waist. Wow. "You look nice."

She smiled and blushed. "And you." She handed me a bottle of champagne.

"*Merci*." I inspected the bottle and led her into the kitchen where we greeted Stumpy. He stirred a large skillet of paella and added a dash of salt. He grabbed a spice jar and sprinkled it into the mix.

"It looks delicious," Jacqueline said. She looked intently into the yellow rice that contained shrimp, scallops, mussels, and sausage.

"It's an old family recipe," Stumpy said.

"Are you Spanish?"

Stumpy looked flustered for a moment, and then recovered. "Somewhere down the line, but I forget." He brushed his hands at us. "Now, out. I will bring some wine."

We walked onto the patio. Jacqueline gasped. "Oh my goodness, the view."

The fiery orange sun was just about to dip behind the far ridge. The vines waved goodbye, their leaves fluttering in the light breeze. As the sun set further, the ridge's shadow inched toward us.

Stumpy appeared in a white apron bordered with grapevines. He held an open bottle of St. Sebastian in one hand and two wine glasses in the other. He handed us the glasses and poured. "Sit, sit." He walked over and set the bottle on the square table. He pulled out a chair for Jacqueline. I sat down kitty-corner close to her.

"You're not joining us?" Jacqueline asked.

Stumpy shook his head and held up his hands. "You have things to discuss—and I love to serve." He bowed and returned to the kitchen.

I held up my glass. "*Santé.*"

We clinked glasses. "*Santé.*"

The sky turned purple like our rich St. Sebastian wine. Jacqueline looked out over the vineyard as dusk blurred the distant abbey and grapevines like an impressionist painting. "You'd have to be a fool not to fight for this land."

I looked out and felt the beauty, but also the history and my place in it. A part of me still wanted to cash in, but it would be a true shame to have the vineyard drowned.

The sky's final glow blackened, and the stars took over. A few outdoor lights dotted the distant hills, but otherwise it felt like we were on our own platform jutted into the heavens.

"Some people are actually very happy to get cash for their land," Jacqueline said.

"Greedy bastards."

She laughed.

We both laughed.

She lifted her glass. "To the greedy bastards. They make my life easier."

I clinked her glass, looked into her eyes, and smiled.

Stumpy walked in silently with steaming plates of paella. The rice, meat, and spices created a tantalizing fiesta of smells. Jacqueline's eyes opened wide with anticipation. He set the plates down and returned to the kitchen.

"This is so good." Jacqueline used her fork to arrange the paella on her plate before taking another bite. "Stumpy is a wonder."

I raised my glass. "To Stumpy." I yelled into the house, "Stumpy, you are a wonder."

Stumpy came to the door and bowed, taking full credit for the market lady's paella. He did a little hop and slapped his hands against his face. "I forgot the champagne. I should have served the champagne as an aperitif."

"For dessert," I said. "Champagne for dessert." I held up my wine glass to Jacqueline. "To your job and the vineyard. May it all work out." We clinked glasses in agreement. *And to us,* I thought. Could there be a future for Jacqueline and I amidst such tension?

Stumpy came outside with an ice bucket and the champagne Jacqueline had brought. He held the bottle for us to inspect and said with perfect pronunciation, "It's a Perrier-Jouët Brut Fleur de Champagne."

I looked at Stumpy in shock.

He went to work on the cork.

"I can't wait," Jacqueline said.

"Come on, Stumpy. Put some muscle into it. Do I have to call a nun over here to help you?"

Stumpy reached over to punch me in the arm. He leaned the bottle unintentionally with his other hand and the cork popped straight into Jacqueline's eye. She covered her face with her hands and bent over. The champagne spilled forth and dripped from the table onto her dress.

I jumped up quickly and hit my knee on the underside of the table. I hobbled over to Jacqueline. Stumpy ran into the kitchen.

The dogs appeared out of nowhere, barking and biting at my heels. I swatted at one and missed.

"Matthew! Mark!" Stumpy pointed and the dogs backed off.

I put my hand on Jacqueline's back. "Are you okay?"

Stumpy hurried out of the house looking worried and guilty. "I'm sorry. Sorry, sorry, sorry."

I held some ice from the champagne bucket by Jacqueline's face. "Here."

Stumpy pushed his paw toward her. He held a pill. "Take this."

"What's that?" I said.

"Zoloft. It makes you feel better."

"She can't take Zoloft for her eye."

"It's all we have."

I looked at Stumpy. "Why do you have Zoloft?"

He looked guilty and confused. "I don't know. Why do people have Zoloft?"

Stumpy was always so positive. Why would he need an antidepressant? I suppose his life wasn't so great either. It mirrored mine, more or less, except that I had failed to be as good a friend as he was.

Jacqueline started to cry.

I didn't know what to do. Stumpy looked at me equally perplexed.

Jacqueline stood up and leaned into me, sobbing. I wrapped my arms around her.

"I don't want to flood your land. You think I like flooding people's land?"

"It's just your job, like you said."

Her head rested against my chest. She put her arms around me and we stood content.

Stumpy gave me a thumbs up. He then walked off the cement patio, followed by the dogs, into the vines. They disappeared into the dark. I wanted to call out to him, but I had seen him do stranger things, and I didn't want to ruin my moment with Jacqueline.

"We should take you to a doctor."

Jacqueline stopped crying and looked at me. Her eye looked okay. It was at least open and functioning and didn't appear to be bruised.

"No, I can see. I'm fine." She looked around. "Where did Stumpy go?"

"Probably down to his shed to work on the backpacks."

I tried to kiss her. We were already wrapped up in an arm package, so a kiss seemed a natural next step, but she turned her cheek like a good Christian and pulled away.

What? Did she not like me?

Jacqueline put her hand on my face. "I'm sorry, Jason. Perhaps another time."

Jacqueline left, and I went out back in search for Stumpy, walking in the dark between the sleeping vines toward the shed. The stars enveloped me in the still night air and all was quiet in the vineyard.

A dim light shone in the shed. Through the window I saw Stumpy walking in a circle, adjusting a double-hauler strapped to his back. He stopped and sat down on a crate and buried his face in his hands. I felt miserable.

I walked in. "What's wrong, buddy?"

Stumpy looked up, surprised. "What are you doing here? You and Jacqueline were . . ." He shook his head. "You couldn't close?"

"It wasn't like that."

"But she likes you."

I smiled at the thought. "She might a little. Thanks to you, romance maker."

"I cork-eyed her. I can't do anything right."

"But your heart is good, Stumpy. That's what counts. You don't really need Zoloft, do you?"

Stumpy looked at me with an expression I don't think I've ever seen on him. His face wore a forlorn look that made me want to cry. "For a while I needed it. After you and Laura broke up. I was in the dumps, too."

"I'm sorry, man."

"It's okay. You had your own problems. I couldn't find a girl to like me, and seeing you and Laura—the perfect couple as far as I could tell—split up, was just demoralizing."

I felt like a drowned golf ball covered with pond scum. "Oh, man. I don't know what to say other than I'm sorry. I wish I would have known."

"I said it's okay. I haven't needed to take the pills in a while." Stumpy smiled and regained some of his usual cheerfulness. "And I definitely don't need them here. I just brought them along in case of an emergency."

"Like for an eye wound?"

We both laughed. "Yeah, I guess that didn't make too much sense."

He put his face back in his hands. "I wish I could see Melanie. We're so close, but it's like our relationship doesn't exist."

"Why don't you write her a letter?"

Stumpy looked at me like I was the area melon-head. "Like a letter from me is going to crack the Sister's wall."

"Write her a note." I shrugged. "I can make deliveries behind the wall."

Stumpy jumped up. "Like a double agent? You'd do that?"

"Sure. She might even write back and you two could be pen pals for a while until you figure out what to do next."

Stumpy shook my hand vigorously. "Thank you, Jason. You're the best."

CHAPTER 13

The next morning I awoke to a perfect day. It was still cool, and the new sun had yet to reach full strength. The fresh air had a crisp ozone smell from the recently departed night. I met Sister Claudette and we walked among the rows on our now ritual morning walk. She was reluctantly growing fond of me, I think, and I her. Oh sure, she was an old-fashioned stodge podge, but I admired her passion. She loved the grapes. And she loved this vineyard like a baby.

"I'm happy your friend has restrained himself from trying to see Sister Melanie."

"He may be a Baptist, but he respects the rules and the institution," I said, feeling guilty. I had delivered a note from Stumpy and then returned one from Sister Melanie. The love note express looked likely to flourish.

Sister Claudette appeared doubtful. "Yes, well, hopefully that little episode is behind us." She tasted a grape every ten yards or so and seemed particularly upbeat this morning. "What do you think?" Her stern face softened and she looked happy, a rare moment.

"The grapes?" I bit into another. Crisp, sweet, and juicy. "About the best yet."

"Yes." She smiled and put her hands together. "It's time."

"The harvest?"

"Yes, the harvest. It's time to begin."

I looked left and right. "I'll go round up the troops."

She put her hands on my shoulders. "Easy, Jason. How about a prayer first?"

We bowed our heads and Sister Claudette chattered on. "Lord bless these grapes as we are about to reap their goodness and turn them into wine."

"Like Jesus," I said. I opened one eye and saw Sister Claudette smile.

"Like Jesus," she said. "And bless the good nuns, and Jason, and his friend, as they come to know this land. May we all work diligently to harvest your fruit and to obey your commands. Amen."

"Amen."

She smiled. "Okay, go!"

I turned and ran toward the abbey yelling at the shed on my way. "Stumpmeister!"

Stumpy popped his noggin out of the door and shot his "what's up?" look my way.

"Rally ho, my friend, rally ho. Ready the crates. The grapes are coming home."

I ran into the abbey courtyard shouting at every nun I saw. *"Allez, allez, allez."*

Matthew and Mark joined me and ran by my side, barking like they were repeating me.

I found Sister Lucia in the office. She came around her desk and grabbed my hands. "Sister Claudette? She tasted the grapes? She approved?"

"Yes. The grapes are ready."

Sister Lucia's face beamed with anticipation. "I love the harvest."

"We have work to do. I have to find the crew leaders," I said.

"And I will go get the tanker truck, but let's say a harvest prayer first."

"Ah, Sister. I prayed too much for today. God might catch on to me." I ran out the door, Sister Lucia's shocked face frowning after me.

Out in the vineyard the tractors revved their engines and rumbled a throaty roar as they pulled trailers filled with nuns out into the fields. The nuns climbed off the trailers and spread into the rows and to the vines, silent and thoughtful. The picking began.

Stumpy worked feverishly from his shed, handing out backpacks and helping nuns adjust them to the proper fit.

I was appalled to see that hardly anyone was utilizing the double-haulers. I ran down and tried stacking second crates on some of the beefier nuns. A few reluctantly complied, but most flatly refused.

"Stumpy you have to start everyone off with two crates."

Stumpy ignored me. He was staring into Sister Melanie's eyes. All hands were on deck and Sister Melanie's kitchen confinement was lifted for picking duty. Stumpy slowly adjusted her backpack, taking an embarrassingly long time. The waiting nuns glared.

"Hurry up, there," I shouted as I felt it my duty as vintner. "The purple babies are waiting, ladies. Save them grapes!"

Stumpy and Sister Melanie shot me looks, but separated, and the work went on.

The nuns moved methodically down the rows, snipping grape clusters with their plier-like cutters. When their crates were full, the nuns walked to the end of the row where other nuns stacked them on a waiting trailer. They would then take a new crate and return to picking. When the empty crates were replaced with full crates, the tractor hauled the grapes off to the winery barn where the sorting and crushing would immediately take place. The juice was pumped into the waiting tanker truck, and once full, driven over to Chateaux Dubois.

I walked up and down the rows with my own crates, filling in when I found an open spot. I encouraged all the good nuns to work fast and to handle the grapes with care. "We make the wine," I would say. "Like Jesus," they would chant.

I had been walking among the rows soliciting the nuns to try the double-hauler. I found Sister Melanie, by herself, slowly picking grapes at a far end. I was confident Sister Melanie would help out; after all, I had been faithfully delivering Stumpy's love notes. I held out a red plastic crate toward her. "Carrying an extra crate is a small way to help out in a big way." I smiled, walked closer, and was about to say hello when I smelled the distinct aroma of marijuana. "Holy smokes." Sister Melanie had a small joint in her hand and was taking a defiant puff.

Sister Melanie jerked her head and when she recognized me, grimaced and flipped me the bird. "Go fuck yourself."

"Wait, what?" I was so shocked I felt like I was choking on a grape. She brushed me off. "Leave me alone. Go fuck yourself."

I walked away quickly, wondering on the order of the universe and life in general. I troubled over whether to sink Stumpy's infatuation barge with my new knowledge or to just let him swim on and discover the shipwreck on his own.

That evening, exhausted over the long workday, Stumpy and I watched some flashy French variety show on TV and laughed at the stupidity. We sat side-by-side on the beige couch. The two lamps on the end tables were dim. The moonless sky caused an all-encompassing blackness outside. The light from the TV caused shadows to flicker around the high ceiling and walls.

I couldn't contain the truth any longer. I felt it my duty to tell him. "Dude, I have to tell you something."

Stumpy looked at me with rapt, innocent attention. It was horrible to have to stomp on his naiveté. "I don't think Sister Melanie is praying the same prayers as the other nuns."

Stumpy gave me the old "I'm-trying-to-understand-you-but-it's-all-spilled-Legos-to-me-right-now" look. I didn't hold back and snapped it all together at once for the poor sod. "I saw Sister Melanie today and . . ." I took a deep breath. "And she's an obnoxious, foul-mouthed, dope-smoking nun."

Stumpy smiled all dizzy love-like. "Yeah, she's got some spunk, huh?"

Stumpy and I were slapping together different sets. "Spunk? I thought you were into her because of that virginal nun thing she has going on."

"That, too. She's so mysterious."

"Mysterious? Are you hiding some pieces? We're talking about a nun here."

Stumpy reared back his head and laughed condescendingly, like I didn't know the difference between a Bordeaux and a Riesling. Well neither of us did a few weeks ago, but that was beside the point—this nun was crazy.

"She's not a nun," Stumpy said.

"Not, what? Who not what nun?"

"Sister Melanie is not a nun and has no Sisters."

I stared stupefied.

Stumpy became animated. "She's not a nun. Never was. She's some novelist immersing herself in her work. She calls it method writing or something like that."

"What a load of crap."

"No clue about the writing. All I know is she's not a nun." Stumpy shook my shoulders. "She's going to stick it out until after the harvest and then we can date free and clear—no vows attached."

Stumpy and I were both close to finding love, but Jacqueline and Melanie's jobs were standing in our way. Jobs were always messing us up. "These women we've met sure are dedicated to their work."

"They need us, Jason." Stumpy held his hand up like he was clutching a strawberry. "They need us to bring romance into their lives; to show them how to really live."

I laughed, reached over, and gave Stumpy's noggin a push with the palm of my hand. "I sure hope they're thinking the same thing."

Stumpy laughed. "But seriously. Can you keep Melanie's secret? She spent a lot of time creating a fake identity and applying to work during the harvest. She'd kill me if I ruined her research."

"Secret! I've been delivering love notes and keeping quiet that you're courting a nun—that could cost me a vineyard worth ten million, and you're asking me if I can keep a secret?"

"Don't forget, I'm risking ten percent. That's a million."

I pointed at him. "Don't you forget."

Early the next morning, when the sun was still low, I walked out of the kitchen with a bowl of granola. I was aiming for the sofa when I stopped. There stood Stumpy in his flannel pajamas talking to Sister Melanie. I shouted out a garbled, "Hey," through my mouthful of toasted oats and other whole grains. Stumpy and Sister Melanie looked at me as I forcibly swallowed quicker than I had planned.

I shook my bowl at them. "What are you two doing?" Had she spent the night? Stumpy was risking everything.

"Melanie just arrived," Stumpy said.

I noticed she was not in her usual nun garb. "Don't think you can disguise yourself in civvies. I recognized you right off, Sister Melanie."

"Don't ever call me Sister again. It's Goddamn Melanie."

"Okay, Goddamn Melanie. You're probably the only one."

"I quit, boss man. Find another mule for your double hauler."

"You said mule, not me." She quit? Oh, man. The sisters would be all fired up.

"Melanie is leaving," Stumpy said.

"Oh." I should be nice. I didn't want Stumpy to lose Melanie.

"I want to see my family, and I'm sick of this prison of prayers. All these rules could squeeze the soul out of a person."

"Amen," I said.

"Sorry I was a little cranky with you yesterday, but I was at my limit."

I laughed. "I understand, now."

Melanie had a suitcase by the door. "Do you have to leave?" Stumpy said.

"Are you going to write about us?" I asked.

"I do have to leave." She looked at me. "I'm writing a novel."

My head was turning. Maybe Melanie could do us some good. "I was thinking more immediate, newsworthy writing, like our current David versus Goliath conflict."

Melanie considered. "I'll think about it."

She wrapped her arms around Stumpy and they kissed. "I'll come back after the sisters have cooled off."

We harvested three days straight, working as fast as we could to pull in the grapes. I estimated we had two more days to go. I had eleven days before the court payment was due, but I tried not to think about it. I could only labor on and hope.

Pristine, sunny weather kept us cheerful, and the grapes remained sweet. I followed Sister Claudette around, and we continued to taste the grapes—directing which sections of the vineyard should be picked next. The tractors trailered the filled crates in from the fields. We put the bunches in a vibrating conveyor belt and sorted them by hand to pick out the sticks and leaves so only the finest grapes remained. After sailing the berries into the crusher, we pumped the juice into the tanker truck. When full, Sister Lucia and Stumpy would drive the truck over to Chateaux Dubois.

The sisters were impressed with me. I could tell by their nods and lack of criticism. Stumpy had been goof-proof, too, for that matter, though he remained melancholy without Melanie.

It was the fourth harvest day. Jacqueline had gone back to Paris, and I hadn't seen her since the cork-popping incident. She was scheduled to visit with two of her big-fish bosses today to look over the land, and even though it was under adverse circumstances, I could not wait.

I worked the vineyard all morning, but I was distracted with the thought of Jacqueline visiting. I kept looking toward the convent, waiting for her to show up. As the morning wore on, I worked my way over so I could catch glimpses further down the road.

And then her car pulled into the parking area. She got out with two gruff older men. My heart leapt. I wanted to run to her, but I forced myself to remain calm.

I escorted Jacqueline and her bosses around the vineyard. The nuns watched and bristled, silently voicing their displeasure at the government invaders. I felt guilty as Judas.

I wanted to talk to Jacqueline, to touch her, hold her, but I was forced to remain professional. Jacqueline, though, was having fun. Her bosses couldn't speak English at all, and she translated all their questions for me, but she would keep adding things like, "He thinks you're cute," or "He heard you can sing. He wants you to fall to your knees and sing to him." It was funny, I admit, but I was trying to be a respectable vintner, a fierce adversary that these guys were going to have to deal with.

We entered the winery barn where the crushing was taking place. The barn was lit up, white and spotless. Our one giant stainless steel cask stood off in the corner. Stacked empty oak barrels stood along the far wall waiting for this year's wine. A stairwell led down to our natural cave cellar where wine bottles and oak barrels of St. Sebastian wine continued to age.

Sister Claudette and Sister Lucia came in with a tractor-load of grapes.

"These grapes are ours to keep, Jason," Sister Claudette said ignoring the visitors. The sisters supervised the other nuns as they sorted these, our best grapes, into the conveyor separator and then crusher, making sure everything was perfect.

"These grapes are from our finest vines in the vineyard," I explained. "These are the ones that we will make into St. Sebastian wine." I took the hose from the crusher and fitted the stainless steel coupling into our cask. Jacqueline watched me as I completed the job. I was showing off, I admit. Her eyes sparkled at me, and I had to file away in my book of schemes that a woman really digs a hard-working man—a simple fact that had escaped me over the years.

When I walked them to the car I snuck a quick word with Jacqueline. "Can I see you later?"

"No."

"Wait, what?"

"Tomorrow night." She squeezed my hand quickly and walked ahead.

CHAPTER 14

The next morning the story broke. It was on the last harvest day. I woke early, anxious to get to work. The sun was just lighting up the drive when I picked up our French national paper, *Le Monde*. The headlines surprised me. My French was limited, but I knew *Vignoble St. Sebastian*, and I recognized our picturesque abbey on the front page. We were in the news.

I went online to read a translation. Melanie had taken my suggestion. In a short investigative piece, she highlighted our poor godly vineyard's plight against the damn French machine. Panoramic pictures showed the rolling valley and the bountiful vines.

Melanie's prose could have brought tears to a prison warden's eyes. She really had done the nuns and the vineyard justice. Despite her hostility toward the sisters, I had to respect Melanie. She did the right thing when it counted. Of course Melanie had also thrown in a few banners showcasing her forthcoming book, some hogwash about a romantic comedy set in a vineyard that she hoped some hungry readers would turn the pages over.

Other news outlets quickly picked up the story. That afternoon the television trucks showed up. They filmed the vineyard and crowded around Sister Claudette to interview her. More news people arrived and then Jacqueline. I worried for her; she was about to be grilled. She smiled at me though, and looked unconcerned.

Once one newsman spotted Jacqueline, the rest surrounded her. She pulled out a piece of paper from her briefcase and read a prepared statement, which Sister Lucia translated for me: *"After much consideration, the Ministry of Energy has determined that a planned hydroelectric plant to be located outside the town of Duras would adversely affect individuals and the land greater than previously anticipated. Therefore, the current hydroelectric project at this location has been cancelled."*

The government had given up. There would be no dam. There would be no flood. Sister Claudette and Sister Lucia hugged. A group of watching nuns cheered. The reporters pestered Jacqueline with more questions, but she refused them.

Jacqueline walked over to me and put her hand on my shoulder. She wore a charcoal-colored business suit, and her hair and makeup were pristine. "You win."

The vineyard and my ancestors had been saved from the flood, but I must admit I was a little disappointed the government was no longer interested. I didn't want the land flooded, but it's comforting to have a buyer in the wings. "And you win as well, right?"

She nodded. "I failed my job, but yes, I feel good that this place will be saved."

The reporters packed up their trucks and drove away. Jacqueline had handled herself with a professionalism I could never have mustered. "You didn't fail," I said.

"Thank you. You're right. We've both won here today." She looked over the vineyard. "It's so beautiful. It's such a relief I won't have ruining this place on my conscience."

I watched Jacqueline admiring the vineyard. She smiled and breathed in the land's goodness. As I looked at her and the vineyard it felt like two puzzle pieces connected in my brain. I needed this place. I needed Jacqueline. I wanted Jacqueline and the vineyard, but as each hour went by I came closer to the day I could face jail and lose them both.

Jacqueline touched my arm. "Are you all right?"

"Yes, yes, of course. It's a relief." I laughed. "But I am out seven million Euros."

"And I might be out a job."

"They're going to fire you? The low-down dirty bastards."

She laughed. "Yes, but no. I'm going to quit. I can't consciously displace people anymore. I'll have to find something else."

"I can help you. I'm an expert at quitting and finding jobs."

"Thank you, Jason. I'd appreciate your insights. But right now the important thing is that the vineyard has been saved."

I raised my hands in the air. "Hallelujah."

Jacqueline clapped. "A celebration is in order."

"Champagne?"

She held up her hands. "No champagne."

We both laughed.

"A proper dinner," I said. "With professional waiters."

She became serious. "I leave in the morning." Her smile returned. "But tonight. Can we go out?"

"Hotel Duras cafe?"

She kissed my cheek and we planned to meet for dinner.

Only a few other people were eating at the café. Quiet whispers flickered the table candles in the cool night air. Jacqueline and I smiled at each other and I felt content. The tall lanky waiter uncorked a bottle of St. Sebastian. I covered my eyes and Jacqueline laughed. The waiter remained stone-faced and stuck to the task. He poured, and I immediately smelled the wine's richness, and the fruit I had come to know. I declined to taste when offered. "I'm biased."

Jacqueline took a sip. "Excellent."

"Thank the Lord."

"The sisters are getting to you."

"What? No, well yes, but not in that way." I liked the sisters, and we grew closer every day, but they could keep their rituals. Stumpy, the good Baptist, however, kind of liked the Catholic water and was slowly immersing himself into the bath.

"I wanted to be a nun once."

"A nun! Wait, what?"

She nodded. "I was only eight years old. I thought it would be so much fun to live in a convent; like a never-ending sleep over party."

"Then let me guess—you met a real nun and became terrified."

Jacqueline laughed and we each took a sip of wine. "Not exactly. Mother took me to a convent to visit her cousin who was a nun."

"And she was just horrifically ugly?" I said.

"No! But we ate at the convent and the food *was* horrific. It was so awful I decided right then and there I couldn't be a nun. I didn't want to be rude about the food, so I told my mom and her cousin that I had decided not to become a nun because I didn't want to turn into a virgin."

I started laughing and nearly spit out a piece of bread I was chewing on. "Obviously you didn't know what you were saying."

"Yes, obviously, Jason." Jacqueline rolled her eyes exasperatingly at me.

"So if the nuns made good food you'd probably be one?"

"Probably. What about you? What would it have taken for you to become a monk?"

"Ha!" The question was too absurd. "More than food." But then I started thinking about it and my mind wandered. "Maybe I could be a monk for a short while. Say like if I was a young prince secretly sent to a monastery for protection, but then, right before my evil stepbrother was about to claim the thrown, all my knights would come for me, and we'd march into, into . . . a big city, with me holding my glorious sword, Jazor, and I'd claim my kingdom."

Jacqueline was laughing and clapping. "Please sit down."

I looked around. I was standing, brandishing my butter knife as a sword.

The lanky waiter walked by me. "Will you be singing tonight, sir?"

"No. I'm sorry." I sat back down. "Tell me another story about you."

Jacqueline told another childhood memory, and then the food arrived. She had duck as thick as a T-bone. I had beef bourguignon, my favorite.

"Do you still want to sell the land and become a Paris playboy?"

I didn't want to admit that if the harvest didn't work out I would be in jail in nine days without any land to sell. "I don't know. I'm concentrating on the harvest right now, but you never know."

"You like being a vintner, no?"

"I like the work, but I worry if I'll be any good at it. I have a lot to learn. And I'm still trying it out—you know? The vineyard is a great gift, that's for sure, and it's growing on me. I've got some ideas to bring St. Sebastian into the big time. We could use some serious marketing, especially in the States, maybe even Japan and China. And we need more capacity; God knows we have the grapes. I'd like to build a bigger winery and turn all our grapes into wine. With some fancy packaging and increased demand and fine wine prices we could turn St. Sebastian into one of the grand vineyards."

Jacqueline touched my arm and exhaled. She looked lovingly into my eyes. "You are a dreamer."

"I'm a hard worker," I said defensively.

She laughed and then sighed. "Yes, and you are a hard worker as well. I envy you."

"You do?"

"Yes. You are carefree, but at the same time you have a purpose and a plan and seem to know what you want to do."

"Wait, what? I do?" No one had ever said anything like that about me.

Jacqueline laughed. "Yes, Jason." She looked at me thoughtfully and I wanted to kiss her. "Haven't you been listening to yourself?"

I thought back to what I had been saying, what I had been feeling about the vineyard. It all seemed so crazy. I had come to France to sell this place. What was happening to me? I shuddered. "What about you, Jacqueline? You're the career-oriented one." I loved saying her name, pronouncing her name in the French manner, *Jacqualeen*, such a beautiful sounding name. "What are your dreams?"

"I thought I wanted a career in the Ministry of Energy, but after this vineyard fiasco I don't know. I want something else. I want to prove to myself and everyone else that I can make it somewhere in the big world." She paused and thought. "I guess I want to make my parents proud."

"That's cool," I said. "You're lucky to have parents that care."

The waiter brought dessert. We shared a rich crème brulee infused with lavender that tasted so good I savored it in my mouth for as long as I could. "I just love the food here."

"Me, too." Her eyes lit up. "And the breakfast from room service is magnificent."

"Omelets?"

"Omelets, *oui*, and quiche and croissants." Her voice softened and her eyes narrowed seductively. "You should join me and try it."

"But I would have to—oh." Sometimes I'm not the quickest at key moments. Jacqueline laughed and looked at me coyly as if to say, "Well?"

"Yes, I agree," I said stupidly.

We walked around town, holding hands, looking at the shops and buildings. We walked underneath dim street lamps, across darkened alleys, and between building shadows. The night was quiet and lonely. A pigeon fluttered, startling us. Jacqueline pressed closer to me. I held her hand, and she smiled. We walked along the outer wall and past the town's castle.

We approached the Hotel, and our pace quickened. Our legs moved as one, propelling us toward our unstated mutual goal. We giggled our way through the lobby. The elevator doors opened, and we fell into the cab. Our eyes met, and when the doors closed our lips came together, slowly, as if on their own accord, touching softly. We pulled away and looked at each other in a magical moment, and then hungrily kissed each other.

I kissed her neck and shoulders. She grabbed the back of my head and I tried to French kiss her. Why not? I was in France and I didn't want to disappoint. She laughed and pulled away. "You silly American."

I felt stupid and my face warmed. Jacqueline smiled and pulled me toward her and then French kissed me, gently moving her tongue into my mouth. I kissed her back and lost myself. We twisted and pressed together. My hand ran up her waist to her chest. She brushed it away. "We're in the elevator!"

I looked around completely disoriented and surprised.

The doors opened. Jacqueline grabbed my hand and pulled me toward her room. We stumbled inside and she fell backward onto the bed. I tried to lie on top of her but she put a foot into my chest and kicked me away.

I didn't know what to do.

"Dance!" She giggled.

"What?"

"Dance like an American—like a cowboy."

"I can't dance."

Jacqueline sexed me with her eyes and unbuttoned her blouse. "Dance for me, cowboy." She pulled her skirt high above her knees.

I gulped. At that point I could have done the cancan with Moulin Rouge's best. I put my hands on my hips and kicked my pretend cowboy boots out left and then right. I shuffled like a square dancer to the end of the bed where I did two more mini cowboy kicks.

Jacqueline clapped her hands and laughed.

"Yeehaw!" I dove into the bed. Jacqueline wrapped me in her arms. We rolled and kissed, and I fell into a French dream.

Jacqueline was right. The breakfast from room service was amazing.

"Sixty-eight thousand big ones," I whispered to myself. I stood with Sister Claudette at Chateaux Dubois in the doorway of the warehouse with the vineyard's owner, Claude Dubois. Chateaux Dubois was thirty kilometers away from St. Sebastian, and using a tanker truck was more convenient and efficient for us.

"Monsieur Dubois prefers how we crush the grapes right away at St. Sebastian," Sister Claudette said. "In fact, he gives us a slightly better price."

"I'll drink to that."

A row of shiny steel fermenting casts loomed over us. Throughout the week, our stainless steel tanker truck had made three trips emptying our juice into his vats. We were waiting for our final tanker of juice to arrive.

Considering the bills and prepaid expenses, after we received payment from Chateaux Dubois my take would convert to sixty-eight thousand dollars. I would have enough to pay the court with eight grand left over. Hammersmith could retrieve my passport, express it over to me, and I would inherit the vineyard.

Monsieur Dubois stood in blue polyester shorts. A short sleeve plaid shirt barely covered his barrel-like belly. *"Je pense qu'il y a un problème."*

Monsieur Dubois had the check in his hand when we first saw the final tanker delivery come rolling in. The truck was slowing down to turn into Chateaux Dubois.

"Oh, no," Sister Claudette said. She walked quickly out of the warehouse. "That's juice."

I saw the problem. A steady stream of juice flowed from the bottom outflow valve. The tanker truck drove up the drive. "Stop!" Sister Claudette shouted. The outflow valve flew off and dangled by a short chain. Purple grape juice gushed out, spreading on the drive like a bloody river as the truck continued toward us.

"Oh la vache!" Monsieur Dubois cried.

Sister Lucia drove, and Stumpy rode shotgun. They looked like they were singing and swaying to music. Matthew and Mark were perched on Stumpy's lap, peering over the dash.

Sister Claudette walked rapidly toward the truck. She looked like she wanted to run.

She waved her hands. The juice stopped flowing from the valve. The truck stopped, and Sister Claudette replaced the valve cap, impossibly trying to save our juice. She walked around to the cab and opened the door. She machine-gunned some French words toward Sister Lucia and Stumpy. Sister Lucia stopped smiling.

I opened Stumpy's door.

"Did you tighten the discharge valve?" Sister Lucia asked Stumpy. "Righty-tighty, remember?"

Stumpy looked blank. He held his hand and mimicked tightening the valve. He turned his hand left, then right, and looked confused.

I climbed on top of the tanker with Monsieur Dubois, opened the top hatch and looked inside. Only a small amount of juice coated the bottom.

Monsieur Dubois climbed off the tanker. "This is no good. I'll have to rewrite the check."

"Wait, what? No, sir, we can get more juice. Don't change that check."

"That's our last juice," Sister Claudette said.

I wasn't about to give up. I needed that check. "We can sell him our private stock. There's enough in our vat for a tanker load."

Both the sisters looked crossly at me. "Then there would be no St. Sebastian wine this year," Sister Lucia said.

"And there has been St. Sebastian wine for three hundred and eighty-seven years now," Sister Claudette said.

I hung my head.

Monsieur Dubois walked toward his office.

I looked at Stumpy. "You really burned the beans this time."

The dogs stood next to Stumpy. One of them growled at me, Matthew or Mark—I couldn't tell the difference.

"Things happen," Sister Lucia said. "God's will moves in mysterious ways."

Monsieur Dubois reappeared and handed us a new check. Sister Claudette showed it to me and I quickly calculated. My profits would be twenty nine thousand five hundred Euros. I needed thirteen thousand one hundred more Euros by the end of the week to pay the court sixty thousand dollars and salvage my inheritance.

I walked toward the Citroen, feeling ambushed. I bumped into Stumpy and walked on. "If God's will moves through you, then I'm an atheist."

CHAPTER 15

I stood before Sister Lucia and Sister Claudette in their bright office. I had one week to come up with the money, and I was presenting them with a fundraising scheme, er, idea, I had thought of. An industrial-looking clock ticked the seconds by on the wall. Sister Lucia smiled at me. Sister Claudette looked skeptical. The smells of the vineyard and sounds of chirping sparrows floated through the open window. "The vineyard party should be a festival for the whole town," I said.

Sister Lucia clapped her hands. "I love the idea."

Sister Claudette tapped her fingers on her desk. "And we charge money?"

I walked across the office linoleum floor, accentuating my points like a professional pitchman. "Twenty Euros a pop. But we'll give free vineyard tours and wine tastings. And how about a tour of the abbey? Lots of folks are interested in what nun life is like. Of course we'll have to charge for some things, like games and rides."

"What games?"

"I don't know yet, but we'll come up with something."

"I could run a shell game," Sister Lucia said.

Sister Claudette and I looked at her with surprise.

Sister Lucia juggled her hands moving imaginary shells. "You remember, Claudette? I was quite good at it as a kid."

"You're hired." I winked at Sister Lucia. "We can sell wine and have the market vendors sell their goods. We'll charge them each a fee."

Sister Lucia practiced moving three paper clips around her desk in confusing patterns. "It will be fun, Claudette."

"We'll split the profits. It will be great community involvement for St. Sebastian. We can advertise that half the profits benefit charity." I paused and pointed at them to clarify. "That would be your profits."

Sister Claudette stood up and looked out the window as if searching for the right decision. "I don't like it."

"Oh, please, Claudette." Sister Lucia stood next to her sister. "There used to be festivals here all the time. We should bring back the tradition."

"But this is a profit-making scheme." Sister Claudette turned toward me. "Why do you need this money so badly again?"

I had never really told them the truth, and I didn't want to now. Why should they help a man in trouble with the law? "I owe my stepbrother some money. I don't like having a personal debt hanging over my head."

The sisters looked at each other long and hard, silently communicating. It made me nervous.

"Okay." Sister Claudette shook her head in exasperation. "It's against my intuition, but okay."

"Yes! Thank you, Sister." Today was Friday. The gig would go off Monday night. My payment was due next Friday. I looked at Sister Lucia. "Round up some more nuns who know carnival tricks. We'll have a 'Battle the Sisters for Prizes' area. Who could resist that?"

I left the office and searched out Stumpy. We printed flyers, *La Grande Fête du Vin,* and posted them throughout the town. I wanted to tell Jacqueline about the festival. I'm sure she would have liked to help out, but she had to go back to Paris to wrap things up with her job. I really didn't know when I'd see her again; all I knew is that I wanted to.

I placed some flyers on a table next to travel brochures at the Hotel Duras. The old lanky waiter walked by and looked over my shoulder. "*Très cher.*"

"Too expensive? You think?"

He stopped another waiter walking by and pointed at the flyer. The waiter shook his head. "Twenty Euros. Bah."

I felt a pang of worry. I needed people to come to the festival. "How much would be right?"

"Five Euros," The lanky waiter said. "Saint Mark's charges five Euros for their festival. People like the Saint Sebastian Sisters. For five Euros they will go."

"Okay. Five Euros." I borrowed his pen and began crossing out twenty Euros and writing "5" on the flyers. I stuck my head out the door and yelled at Stumpy tacking flyers across the street. "We gotta change all the flyers."

I handed the pen back to the lanky waiter.

He refused it. "Keep it."

"Thank you. Thanks for everything."

He smiled, gave me a wink, and went back to work. I liked that old guy.

Stumpy and I posted flyers in the town hall and talked to the man in charge of the weekly market. He made some phone calls and lined up the area cheese, sausage, and other market vendors to sell at the festival.

Stumpy and I drove home. "It was a good day."

Stumpy's head rocked to music known only to him. "The festival is going to be fun."

"The profits are going to be fun."

Monday night arrived. The sun dangled in the west, and there were three hours until it would drop for the night. The air was warm and smelled like market day from all the vendors. We had a good turnout, and the crowd grew. I collected the vendor fees and had two nuns sell tickets at the gate. I counted people coming in and I calculated that with a healthy game operation I might pull off the cash I needed from this convent carnival.

Nuns drove tractors and pulled wagonloads of people around the vineyard for tours. Wine tastings were going strong, but sales were slow.

The big hit, though, as I had predicted, was the 'Battle Against the Nuns.'

Sister Mary Margaret mowed them down at the Ping-Pong table with her long arms and power serve.

Sisters Helga and Olga, cousins from former East Germany and Olympic weightlifters, took turns arm wrestling area farmers into shame.

Sister Lucia flipped her shells around like a gypsy and won most of her games.

A popular booth, which surprised me, was 'Pick Your Penance.' People bought tickets to reveal 'hypothetical' sins to a panel of nuns who would then come up with three possible penances. People could pick a penance they thought best. There were no winners other than that people received hypothetical penances to hypothetical sins. Sister Claudette worried we were breaking some church rules, but even she couldn't resist the fun.

Sister Claudette stood to the side of the booth and just had to pronounce her own, much sterner, penance to each sin. The lanky waiter was there smiling at Sister Claudette and he translated for me.

She shook her finger at a supposed sinner. "Count your blessings, Robert, I'd have you tilling our weeds for a month."

"I do count my blessings, Sister."

Sister Claudette actually laughed. To another sinner she said, "Oh, you got off easy, Stephen Randles. You'd be on your knees saying Hail Mary's until I died for that one."

"You'll never die, Sister." Stephen Randles said.

Sister Claudette shook her finger at him. "And don't you forget it."

Everyone laughed.

Stumpy and I hustled around and made sure all ran smooth. Every half hour we emptied the ticket cash box and brought the money inside to the office safe. Vendor sales seemed slow, which worried me because I had sort of guaranteed the vendors a minimum return.

After the third cash deposit, Stumpy and I felt like happy circus barons. I looked out the office window. The carnival still hopped, and the gaming nuns were still proving the good Lord was on their side.

A police car and a taxi pulled close to the front gate. Two local *gendarmes* stepped out of the police car. "Oh, crap. The cops."

Stumpy pointed with a shocked look. "And Eustace!"

"Eustace?"

Sure enough. My former stepbrother stepped out of the taxi. He was wearing a blue blazer, white khakis, and loafers. He looked like a yacht club member wannabe.

My heart revved up the RPMs to Autobahn speed. "They're going to arrest us."

"You think?"

I frantically grabbed at the Euros in the safe and put them back into the cash bag. "Yes, I think, and all because of your big mouth. Why'd you have to tell Laura we were going to France?" I pulled the strings taut on the bag. "Come on; we gotta hide."

Stumpy just stood there, maddeningly not alarmed. "Why would they arrest me?"

"For aiding and abetting my escape from the United States. You even paid for it."

"Oh."

I grabbed his shirt at his chest and pulled. "Now come on."

We hurried out of the office and ran down the hall. I sprinted with the cash in hand. Stumpy tried to keep up behind me. I darted out a side door and raced across the courtyard. Luckily all the nuns were at the party and the abbey was empty. Ugh. Matthew and Mark were there. They saw us and chased. I ran into the church and held the door waiting for Stumpy to lumber in. He finally made it with the dogs close at his heels. "Follow me." I ran to the back and then up the stairs to the choir loft. I set the cash on a pew and opened a bottom stained glass window air vent and peered outside.

Matthew and Mark barked.

"Sh!" Stumpy said and they quieted. "What are we doing?"

"We're hiding. I don't think you can arrest someone inside a church."

Outside Sister Claudette faced off with the gendarmes and Eustace. When they were done talking, Eustace looked around with a proprietorial grin. He got back in the taxi and rode away.

"I think that church asylum stuff is from olden times."

"Sh." Sister Claudette walked into the abbey with the two gendarmes. "We've got no other choice. Here they come." I lay down under a pew. "Keep quiet and think invisible."

It smelled dusty, and I kept rubbing my nose so as not to sneeze. We lay silent for several minutes. Nothing happened.

"I got to pee," Stumpy said.

"Christ." I crawled over aging wooden planks to the window and looked out. The nuns were cleaning up the carnival and the vendors were packing up. The gendarmes got back into their police car and drove off.

"They shut us down. Come on." I hurried and scampered down the stairs. I heard a thud and an "ow" come from Stumpy. I walked outside. The dogs pranced on each side of me, like I was their prisoner.

"What's going on?" The town's people walked toward their cars. "The party is just getting started."

Everyone ignored me and the *La Grande Fête du Vin* fizzled. Stumpy walked out of the church rubbing his head.

"There you two are." Sister Claudette stomped toward us.

"We can't shut down, Sister. I need a couple more hours."

"You can thank yourself that we're shutting down."

Eustace and the authorities had finally caught up to me. My shoulders dropped. "Can the church grant us asylum, Sister? Will you protect us?"

Her eyes saw me all at once, inside and out, and I felt ever the rascal that I was. "You failed to obtain a permit."

"The court in Kankakee wants a permit?"

Sister Claudette stared me down and I found it difficult to breathe. "One problem at a time." She had an angry patience about her that looked to find the whole truth. "The Duras Gendarmes wanted to see a permit for the festival. That's why we had to shut down."

"I paid for a permit." I reached into my pocket and pulled out a lopsidedly folded pink paper. "It's right here."

"Posted properly in your trousers," Sister Claudette said with a sarcasm I didn't know she was capable. "If you were here we wouldn't have had to shut down."

"That other man," I said.

"Your former stepbrother, Eustace."

"Eustace." I gritted my teeth. "We were hiding from him in the choir loft."

Sister Claudette looked at the bag of cash I held in my hand.

I felt guilty. I handed her the bag. "Just keeping it safe."

The round sausage vendor rolled over and spoke English for my benefit through a thick mustache. "Excuse me, Sister."

Sister Claudette's gaze fell on the sausage man and I felt temporary relief.

He stammered under her stare. "The vendors were guaranteed minimum sales." He looked around. "Sales were slow and with shutting down early we are nowhere near what we were promised."

Her gaze returned to me. "Promised?"

I merely shrugged. A jumble of accusations and problems had descended on me at once, not an unusual occurrence for one skateboarding on the curvy side of life. My standard M.O. was to plead innocence and talk circles. But I had come to like Sister Claudette, which presented a dilemma. I had never come to know and respect such an authoritarian figure and I couldn't muster up my usual B.S. tales. With Aunt Clara, it had been different. Aunt Clara was, well, not exactly mean, she was angry. She would be angry with me no matter what I did, and I found it easy to lie to her.

"We don't need minimum sales, but we would like our entrance fees refunded," Monsieur Sausage said.

Sister Claudette handed him the cash bag. "Take what you're due and distribute the refund to the others if you don't mind."

He took off his hat. "Thank you, Sister. We will make a donation of course."

I watched my profits waddle off with the sausage man. "So, the gendarmes didn't want to see me and Stumpy?"

"No."

"And Eustace. Was he looking for me?"

Sister Claudette glared at me accusingly. "No. I believe he thinks you're in the United States. He did mention, though, that you had some legal troubles."

If Eustace truly believed I was still moping off the main paths in the U.S. then I still had a squirrel's chance of bringing home the big nut. "You must believe me, Sister. Eustace is the cause of all my legal troubles."

Sister Claudette's face had no hint of softening. "You will have to explain these troubles to me."

"I will. The whole truth."

"If you remember, when I agreed to distribute to you the harvest profits you told me there was no good reason why you couldn't inherit the estate."

"Well, I, er."

She looked at Stumpy. "And I suppose you've been privy to all this?"

Stumpy reverted back to his idiot mode that had incensed Sister Claudette earlier. "I don't mess with privies."

"I don't—" Sister Claudette paused and decided not to pursue Stumpy's comment. She pointed at me. "Eustace claims the vineyard will be his on Friday. I knew about the Good Character Clause in the will, but I didn't ever think it germane."

"Probably because it's in English, not German," Stumpy said.

Sister Claudette and I looked at Stumpy and then forgave him because he was serious and smiling.

"Eustace owns the golf range I worked on. I stole a golf cart."

"Eustace fired him first," Stumpy said.

"I damaged some of his property."

"After Eustace shot him with a hose." Stumpy said. "And he tried to kill Jason with a flag pole."

Sister Claudette held up her hands. "Slow down. Explain it to me." She looked at Stumpy. "Without interruptions."

I told Sister Claudette and Sister Lucia the story, exactly how it happened. I told them about the agreement we had made with Aunt Clara the night before she died. The agreement Eustace had conveniently backed out of. We talked about the Good Character Clause, and they understood that if I were sentenced to jail in any country the vineyard would automatically pass to Eustace. "That's why I've been trying to make some money. If I don't pay the damages by Friday, I'll be automatically convicted, and Eustace will inherit the vineyard."

King Sausage returned and handed Aunt Clara the cash bag. She took out a fistful of Euros and handed them to Stumpy. "Pass out refunds to the townsfolk."

Sister Lucia looked concerned, like she wanted to help. "Can we not help him, Claudette? How much do you need, Jason?"

"Eighteen thousand five hundred dollars. Thirteen thousand one hundred Euros." Good God, were the sisters going to save me?

Sister Claudette huffed irritably at Sister Lucia. "How much money do you have, Sister?"

"I meant—"

"I know what you meant and the convent's mission does not include loaning money to pay the debts of a criminal. Imagine Rome's reaction during the next audit?"

My hopes bubbled out. "You could put it under Investments—other."

"No," Sister Claudette said sharply. "No hocus pocus. I never liked how Eustace's father treated Clara. I don't know why Clara created the possibility the vineyard could pass outside her own family, but she did. My guess is that your character flaws wore her down over the years and this clause was an attempt to keep you focused or to teach you a big lesson."

"That's Aunt Clara," Stumpy said. "She loved spooning out the lessons to Jason and me."

"I don't know if I like this Eustace either after meeting him. He's awfully smug about checking out his future property. But who knows? He might be a good partner."

Sister Lucia touched Sister Claudette's arm. "Oh, no, you don't mean that, Sister."

Sister Claudette shook her sister's hand free. She was irritated with us all. "Let God's will be done." She walked toward the abbey. Sister Lucia quick-stepped behind her. "Can we talk some more, Claudette?"

Sister Claudette continued on in silence. Sister Lucia spoke softly, pleading with her as they walked.

"Excuse me," I called. "Can you and all the other nuns keep our presence here a secret?"

"The nuns don't talk," Stumpy said.

"We will not lie," Sister Claudette said. "But we will not say more than we have to."

It's the best we could hope for. I looked at Stumpy. We shrugged our shoulders at the same time. "We need a plan," he said.

I laughed. "We do need a plan."

CHAPTER 16

"What did Hammersmith say?" Stumpy asked.

Stumpy and I sat on the patio Tuesday afternoon. The bees worked feverishly in the purple lilacs. We had three days left. We drank beer for the first time in France because it was hot out, and drinking beer is how we typically brainstormed during a crisis.

"No one answered. They must have cut out early today. I'll email him."

A small hummingbird floated by, unconcerned with our problems or us. Stumpy emptied his Kronenbourg in one gulp. He went into the kitchen and came back with two more. He set one down next to me even though I had only taken a sip of my first. He paced and started sucking on his second bottle.

"Easy there, Blotto."

"Why are you so calm? We have to figure something out."

Usually I was the panicked one. "Why are you so not calm? I thought you didn't care about the money, Mister Love Panda. You can see Melanie regardless."

Stumpy stopped pacing. He looked at me wild-eyed and then breathed. "Not if I'm arrested for aiding and abetting."

"I escaped on my own. Don't worry; I won't sell you out."

"I don't care about that. And I don't care about the money. It's just that . . . I feel like I belong here. I love this place. My work is important. The nuns are so nice and they don't yell at me—ever."

"They can't talk most of the time."

"Yes, well." He paused. "But they smile and don't frown like everyone back home. The past weeks have been the best thing that has ever happened to me. I could live here and never have to take another pill." Stumpy fell to his knees, clasped his hands prayer-like and shook them pleadingly. "I want to stay here. We gotta figure something out."

Stumpy's heartfelt speech got to me. The past weeks had been pretty good. Maybe the best ever. I had met Jacqueline. Man, I wish she were here now—well maybe not—I wasn't expecting to see her until after the final due date, so better that I straighten this mess out and that she never learn of my potential status as a felon. I felt empowered. I stood up with determination. "Okay, this is what we're going to do."

Stumpy nodded and smiled and looked hopeful.

"You got any ideas?"

His face fell. "Come on, Jason. You're the idea man."

"Okay, okay." I grabbed my beer and drank and paced. "You got any money?"

"No."

"Stocks, bonds, IRAs, or 401k?"

Stumpy put his hands on his head and pulled at his hair. "Stop confusing me."

"Okay, okay." I drank some more. "I'll work on the money part. But our first problem is to make sure Eustace doesn't figure out we're here."

"Can't we just stay hidden here? I know a couple of nuns who've got an Xbox hidden in their room. I'm sure they'd let us use it."

I grabbed two more beers out of the fridge. "There's too much we have to do. And I've got to be out searching on some cash."

"I hope the townspeople don't give us away."

"Eustace isn't going to talk to any townspeople." I slapped my forehead. "Oh, shit. He'll probably try to see Aceau."

"What asshole?"

"Not *asshole. Aceau*—the lawyer. If Eustace is going to claim the estate, he's got to deal with Aceau."

"And that asshole knows you're here."

I had an idea. "Let's go." I went to the side of the house and hopped on the tandem. I motioned for Stumpy to do the same.

"Where are we going?"

We pedaled and I steered us down the drive. "We have to get rid of Aceau," I said.

"Whoa. I think we should talk about it more," Stumpy said. "We can't just get rid of people."

I turned the bike and stopped at the abbey. "Not like that."

Stumpy relaxed, but I still think he was nervous.

We walked through the cool cavernous church. Candles flickered in the side vestibules. The warm smell of incense permeated the air. Our footsteps echoed and our whispers sounded like shouts. Rows of rigid wooden pews sat empty and looked serene in their own constant worship. Stumpy sat in a pew. "We should pray on the plan." He bowed his head.

I slapped him and pulled his shirt. "Come on. I've already received my inspiration. There's no time for prayer."

Stumpy whispered something, did a bow to the altar, and followed me to the back of the church. I opened a door to a storage room and we walked inside. I flipped on a light to a dusty room with wooden cabinets and closets.

"What's this?" Stumpy asked.

"The nuns put on a play last year with some local actors. Sister Claudette was telling me about it. Some drivel called *The Modern Man in Jesus's Time*."

"You want us to put on a play?"

"A reality play." I walked to a large cabinet and opened the wood doors. An array of colorful, but musty smelling costumes filled the closet. "We're going to disguise ourselves."

Stumpy fingered through the costume rack. "As what—shepherds?"

I picked out a black three-piece suit that looked to be from the nineteenth century. I held it up to Stumpy. "This should work. You're going to play Aceau."

"But what's the play about?"

"It's about saving our vineyard. When is the last time you saw Eustace?"

"Remember when I was a kid and got that job passing out coupons at the driving range for the cheaper driving range that had opened up."

"Yeah, I remember. Eustace's dad banned you for life."

"That was after I had tried to save the gophers he was trying to kill."

I laughed.

"I've only seen Eustace once since then. I said hello to him, but I don't think he recognized me."

"Perfect." I found a shepherd's-size black beard. "Better wear this to make sure."

"What are you going to be?"

"I plan on staying out of the way, but just to be safe . . ." I rummaged through the costumes. I pulled out a heavy brown wool robe. "I can be a monk. I'll pretend I'm visiting the abbey on a pilgrimage."

"You have to shave your head."

I touched my head. I worked hard on sculpting my simple style. "No way."

"Shave your head, wear little round sunglasses, and paste a small goatee beard on your chin." Stumpy laughed. "You do that, and then I'll wear that beard."

"I don't know. What would Jacqueline say?"

"Good way to find out if she really likes you."

True, but did I want to take that risk?

"Remember—Six Flags try," Stumpy said.

I looked around for another costume but they were all biblical. Being a monk was my best option.

"That's the only way you'll look authentic. Eustace will never recognize you."

"Okay. I'll do it."

Stumpy insisted on shaving my head. That night he hacked the rooftop down with scissors and smoothed it all out with a disposable Gillette. We went to our rooms and tried on our costumes. I pulled the prickly robe over my T-shirt and shorts. I put on the sunglasses, sandals, and goatee beard and looked into the mirror. I had to laugh. I looked like a beatnik monk.

The doorbell chimes rang. I took a peek out my window and saw Melanie smoking a cigarette impatiently. I ran out of the room and collided into Stumpy. He had seen her, too. "It's Melanie."

His shirt was unbuttoned and his beard was on sideways. "I'll get the door. Put yourself together. We can test our disguises on her."

I walked to the door and slowly opened it. Melanie wore a red linen dress, her brown hair skimming her shoulders. It was the first time I had seen it down. She ground out her cigarette with her high heels.

"*Bonsoir.*"

She looked up surprised. *"Bonsoir, Monsieur. Ou est Stumpy et Jason?"*

"You are looking much happier, Melanie."

Her eyes opened wide and she stared at me. After a moment she put her hand to her mouth. "Jason?" She laughed. "Oh my god. What have you done?" She marched into the house past me. "What the fuck are you guys up to? Where's my Stumpy?"

I walked slowly and calmly like a monk into the room. "If you are referring to Monsieur Aceau, he will be down shortly."

"Have you guys been drinking?"

The beer bottles sat lined up on the sink counter. "Yes, but our new personas, though possibly conceived under the influence of alcohol, have a much grander purpose."

Stumpy appeared at the top of the steps. He had a full beard, square reading glasses, and a black fedora. His rounded midsection beautifully filled out his three-piece suit.

"Stumpy?"

"Madame."

He walked down the stairs and embraced Melanie, kissing her long on the lips. His glasses steamed up.

Melanie pulled away and laughed hysterically. She bent over and gasped for breath. "You guys should not be left alone."

"Heard that one before."

"What in God's name are you doing?"

I laughed at Stumpy, too. "You look like Mr. French."

Stumpy remained in character; dignified. "You date yourself, Grasshopper."

"Too many reruns. For you too, obviously, good sir."

Melanie threw her hands into the air. "What is going on?"

Stumpy pulled off his beard and smiled his childlike smile. He and Melanie kissed again.

She ran her hands over his suit jacket. "I couldn't take it anymore. I had to see you."

"Thank you for the story you wrote," Stumpy said. "It was a great article. You really saved us."

Melanie smiled, clearly pleased.

"Yes, thank you," I said. "It was awesome!"

Melanie waved her hands. "Yeah, well, whatever. Now what the hell are you guys up to?"

We gave Melanie the whole vineyard story: inheritance, Eustace, court, Aceau.

Melanie looked sympathetic. I think she liked underdog challenges. "What can I do?"

"Do you want a disguise, too?"

"Did you save your nun outfit, Sister?"

Melanie shot me a look. "I'm never dressing up as a nun again."

"But you could help us," I said. "Here's what I'm thinking."

Aceau's office was closed on Tuesdays so Eustace would probably try to see Aceau first thing Wednesday morning.

Stumpy and I sat in the front seat of our yellow Toyota rental in full costume. Aceau still lived with his mother in a two-story stone cottage off the main road into town. We parked our car across the street and sat low in our seats waiting for him to emerge. Melanie sat in back as herself, ready to act. Stumpy and I drank strong coffee out of miniature paper cups. Its steam and smell filled the car. The sun peaked its head over the horizon and the early morning dark left us. We were nervous and alert.

"But I don't speak French," Stumpy said.

"Neither does Eustace. Make up some words and speak with an accent."

"Can we go over the plan again? Won't the insurance company be mad? It doesn't feel honest. What if someone gets hurt?"

"Shut up, Stumpy. There's Aceau."

Aceau walked toward his car. I started our car, pulled back, and drove fast down the main road into town. Aceau would have to drive through the town square to reach his office. I dropped Melanie and Stumpy off and parked on a side street near the square and waited.

Aceau's car appeared. He drove down one side of the square and turned at the corner. I slowly accelerated. I saw Melanie walking quickly in my peripheral vision. Aceau's car approached my street. I pulled into the intersection and turned into him, colliding head on. Both cars had been going slow, but still the airbags exploded. At the same instant Melanie flung herself on top of our Toyota. She had a rock in her hand and brought it down hard on the windshield, creating a head-like circle shatter. She rolled toward Aceau's side and landed in the street, blood from a self-inflicted cut oozed over the side of her face.

Aceau recovered from the airbag, jumped out and ran to Melanie. A bit dazed, I pushed the airbag down and ran around the backside of Aceau's car. I reached inside his car and grabbed a thick set of keys out of the ignition.

I leaned over Melanie. Stumpy appeared and leaned over too. I handed him Aceau's keys as bystanders crowded around. Stumpy left the scene to unlock Aceau's office. Melanie looked delirious, and she spoke slowly with Aceau. He talked excitedly in French and then looked at me.

I turned and ran and ducked down an alley behind the Hotel Duras.

"*Arrêttez! Arrêttez!*" Aceau shouted.

I later learned their next conversation went something like this:

Melanie: It was that Monk's fault. He ran away.

Aceau: Yes, you are correct.

Melanie: Can you take me to the hospital? I can't move my neck.

Aceau: I will accompany you as long as you need.

I peeked into the hotel's café. Eustace exited by the maître d' stand holding a briefcase. He walked on the sidewalk toward Aceau's office. We had guessed right. Eustace was going to try and visit Aceau first thing.

I sprinted down the alley. My robe weighed me down and shifted uncomfortably. The pavement stung my bare feet. The wooden cross around my neck kept flying up, hitting me in the face.

I reached Aceau's office building and calmly opened the door. His office was at the end of a short corridor on the ground floor. He did not have a secretary. I walked by other professional-looking offices. My leather sandals clacked against the marble.

I opened Aceau's door slowly. Stumpy paced in front of a large wooden desk.

I stepped in and closed the door. "Eustace is coming."

Stumpy looked like he had a golf ball stuck in his throat. "Is everyone okay?"

I slapped him on the back. "Yes, yes." I grabbed a pen and notebook and pretzelled myself yogi-like underneath the desk.

A knock sounded at the door.

Stumpy whispered down at me. His forehead glistened with sweat. "I don't think I can do this. I'm not good at dishonesty."

"It's not dishonesty," I hissed. "It's a play, remember? Six Flags try! Now be professional—like Sebastian Cabot."

Stumpy recovered somewhat, and he breathed in and swelled up into Mr. French. "*Entre vous.*"

I heard Eustace's whine. "Bonjour. Parlez vous English?"

"*Oui.* I speak very good English, but I'm just in the process of leaving. Could you come back next week?"

"I've come all the way from the United States on a very important matter. I want to claim St. Sebastian winery as my inheritance." Eustace rambled on explaining all the details about my legal transgressions and his claim.

"I will need to see proof of these allegations against Monsieur Barnes," Stumpy said. "But I'm afraid you have caught me at a bad time. I'm leaving for a holiday at this moment."

"Where are you going?"

"Bordeaux."

I kicked Stumpy in the legs and wrote on the notepad, "No. Far Away. Like Nice."

Unfortunately, Stumpy thought I meant Bordeaux was too far away, and that he should go somewhere nice.

"Or someplace nice, like my mother's right here in town."

"Perfect. I don't want to ruin your time off, but it's vitally important. Could we meet on Friday afternoon? I will provide you proof of everything you need, and we can notarize the inheritance."

I wrote "no!" but showed it to Stumpy not knowing I held the letters upside down. They looked like "iou," but with Stumpy's occasional dyslexia he read "oui."

"*Oui*. We can meet Friday afternoon."

"You're a dumbass!" I wrote.

Stumpy's face turned red and he looked angrily at me.

"Something wrong?"

"No." Stumpy paused. "I'm just pleased that a fine gentleman as yourself is inheriting St. Sebastian and not some selfish criminal."

"I hope to do my part and be an active member of the business community."

"That is admirable, sir. I've not heard good things about this Monsieur Barnes, and these new revelations you speak of are quite alarming."

"He's a lazy scoundrel."

"A disgrace to his family, no doubt."

"Yes, he is a shame to his family name. Even his own lawyer has forsaken him."

Hammersmith has turned against me? Wait, what?

Stumpy stretched out his legs and ground his wingtip into the side of my head. "An embarrassment to his friends, too, I'm sure."

"He has no decent friends to call his own. I hear only some moronic childhood buddy will put up with him."

Stumpy stood up, kicking me in the shin. "You speak a tough truth. And at that I must wish you good day, sir."

"Friday afternoon, then."

I heard the door shut, and I crawled out from under the desk.

Stumpy and I stared at each other and decided not to get into it.

"There's still time to return to the accident. Text Melanie that we're good. Now let's switch costumes."

Stumpy stared at me blankly.

"Come on. You're the registered driver and I don't have a passport. You're going to have to take the heat."

"Can't we just leave?"

"No. They'll come looking for you at the vineyard and we don't want the sisters involved."

"I don't look like you."

"All monks look the same to people."

Stumpy gave in and we swapped costumes.

"But I have hair."

Two gendarmes worked the accident scene. Stumpy introduced himself and presented his license. "I ran to get help and got lost."

"You're an American monk?"

"Yes. I'm on a pilgrimage to Lourdes."

"*Un clé*," I shouted. I held up Aceau's keys and the oversized suit jacket fell down my forearm. I motioned where I had found the keys on the street and handed them to the gendarme. I stood off to the side as they took down Stumpy's information.

A taxi pulled up and Aceau got out. "The woman is fine. The woman is crazy." He walked up to Stumpy and the gendarme. I patted my beard down to make sure it was sticking. "The ambulance stopped and she jumped out and ran away." Aceau looked at Stumpy. "You're not the same monk."

Stumpy leaned into Aceau and whispered. "I rented this car. If you want the insurance to pay for your car's damage, then I am the same monk."

"This is the monk," Aceau said. "God help me today."

Both cars still functioned, and we were able to drive. We circled around and down a side hill to a small park. Melanie sat at a picnic table smoking a cigarette. She ran to our car. "Now, that was more fun than being a nun."

CHAPTER 17

When we were almost back to St. Sebastian we passed a stopped car where two unmarked country roads intersected. A woman stood outside the car holding her cell phone to the sky like she was searching for a signal.

"That was Laura!" Stumpy said.

I slammed on the brakes. "You're messing with me."

I looked in the rear view mirror. "That *is* Laura."

"Who is Laura?" Melanie asked.

I backed the car slowly toward Laura. "Laura is my ex-wife."

I stepped out of the car and waved. "Hey." My mind swirled. Laura was supposed to be an ocean away. I had hardly thought about her since arriving in France. But now here she was. I immediately began to worry about the possibility of Laura and Jacqueline meeting. Oh, jeez, oh my. I felt slightly nauseous.

Laura looked at me, concerned, possibly even frightened. Then I remembered I was disguised. I pulled my beard down and lifted my hat. "*Bonjour!*"

Laura waved wildly and ran to me. She looked happy. We hugged.

"My God, you're bald. And why are you wearing a beard?"

"It's a long story."

Laura looked around. Grape vines lined the roads and spread out as far as we could see. The sun beat down and the dry air was pure. "I feel like I'm in heaven."

A tractor pulling a wide wagon full of hay approached.

"We better move. Follow me to St. Sebastian."

I got back in the car, and we drove home.

"What's your ex-wife doing here?" Melanie asked.

"I'm wondering the same thing," I said.

Stumpy shifted in his seat and looked guilty.

"Stumpy?"

Silence.

"Wait, what! You invited her here?"

"I didn't invite her; she just came."

"And why would she do that?"

Silence.

"Stumpy?"

"She emailed me."

"And?"

"I couldn't help it. She hurt you so bad."

"So?"

"I told her you were in love, okay? I wanted to brag about you ... to show her—you know—that you could do it."

I ran my hand over my bald head, a new experience for me that was becoming addictive. "Oh, Stumpy."

"Laura said she 'had to see this for herself,' but I didn't think she meant right away. I never believed she'd actually come over here."

"Well, believe it." I ran my hand over my head again. That couldn't be the whole story. Laura had to be up to something.

We arrived at the house and stood in the driveway. Stumpy introduced Laura to Melanie. Laura had a suitcase and a travelling bag. My stomach did a panic clench. "Where are you staying?"

Laura looked taken aback. "Don't you have room?"

I should have known better, but it was a hassle to argue with Laura. "Okay, sure, fine."

Laura nodded, satisfied. She was in control. She blurted out, "Now why are you two dressed up like idiots?"

"Actually," Stumpy said. "We're wearing each other's costumes. They look more natural reversed."

Laura put her hands on her hips. "Really?"

"They're disguises," I said. "Eustace is here and we're hiding from him."

"That explains everything." Laura held up her hands like she was trying to stop a bus from running her over. "But with you two, nothing surprises me, and I don't even want to know. Are you going to show me this place or not?" She nodded her head toward the abbey. "Nice neighbors you've got there by the way."

We walked into the house. Laura gave herself a tour without asking.

"She makes him not a man," I heard Melanie whisper to Stumpy.

My face burned. *That's not true,* I wanted to say, but I kept quiet. Did people really think Laura controlled me?

Stumpy and I changed out of our disguises.

Actually, maybe Laura's arrival was an unintentional blessing. I had planned on calling her in an attempt to smooth talk her into lending me the eighteen grand I needed, but now, in person, I'd be able to give her the whole presentation. She'd find it much more difficult to reject me face to face, or so I hoped.

I poured Laura some wine. "I'll show you the vineyard." I grabbed a glass of the good juice for myself and walked with Laura out to the patio and into the vines. "So what are you doing here?"

She pulled at a vine leaf. "Tom and I haven't been getting along so well."

"Oh."

"His bond trading hasn't worked out this year."

"Derivatives in the dumps?"

She didn't say anything.

"Losing-money-Tom not as appealing as making-money-Tom?"

"Fuck you, Jason. You have no idea what I've been going through. We haven't made a mortgage payment in six months. I used all my miles just to get here."

My hopes deflated. Laura wasn't going to lend me a dime. "Fuck you, Laura. Like I'm supposed to feel bad about you and Tom."

Laura stopped and looked at me. Her face softened. I thought she might cry. "I'm sorry. You're right. I just needed to get away."

"Here. Have some more wine."

"Thank you." She laughed nervously, which was not like Laura at all.

"What's wrong, Laura. Why did you really come here?"

"Well." She paused. "I'm divorcing Tom. I was wondering if you could lend me some money?"

Man, I didn't want to get messed up with Laura and her problems. "Bad idea, Laura. Go home and reconsider."

"No need. I've decided."

"You'll look bad. Love 'em and leave 'em Laura, that's what they'll say."

"Fuck you, again, Jason."

"Fuck you, again, Laura. I'm in need of the hard stuff myself."

"Oh," She said, her hopes deflated. "I should have figured, but with this vineyard and all . . ."

"Yeah, well."

Laura and I walked back to the house and I filled her in on all my troubles.

"Did you know your aunt's lawyer went out of business?"

"Out of business? Hammerhead? He's my lawyer too. No wonder he hasn't returned my calls."

"He just up and left town. You know Sheila worked for him. Now she's stuck without a job."

Damn. I was going to need Hammerschmuck to deal with the court one way or the other. I tried to put on a man-with-no-troubles face. "Oh, well. *C'est la vie.*" But then I got scared. "You didn't tell Eustace we were here, did you?"

"I don't ever see Eustace." She gave me a look that said she was not a gossip. "And no, I didn't tell anyone. Stumpy told me not to."

We sat in the main room. Stumpy and Melanie sat on the couch. Laura and I sat in opposite-facing end chairs. Two bottles of wine and four glasses sat on the coffee table in front of us.

Melanie drank more than her share. Stumpy opened up another bottle. Melanie continued her course and was the first overboard at the makeshift party. Stumpy had never seen her drunk, and I think it unnerved him.

The doorbell chimed.

Laura opened the door and there stood Betsy in her American Airlines uniform and rollaway suitcase. One look at her height told everyone in the room she was Stumpy's guest.

Betsy held out her hands toward Stumpy like she wanted him to run to her and give her a hug. "Online form! You scored a ninety-six percent—the highest ever—we are basically a perfect match."

Melanie put her arm around Stumpy's neck and called out to Betsy. "Back of the cabin, missy. First class is full."

Betsy looked Stumpy and Melanie over and was not deterred. "Ah, you have a date I see, Neil."

"Neil? Who the fuck is Neil?" Melanie said.

Stumpy seemed distressed. "Uh, Neil's my real name."

Betsy walked primly across the room, unconcerned with the other passengers. She stood in front of Stumpy. "Sorry to barge in, but I just had to tell you. Continue your date; I'm not the jealous type. I know we are destined to be."

Melanie looked hurt and worried. "Why didn't you tell me your name was Neil?"

"Because, because, Neil's my name for like official stuff and when I'm in trouble. You didn't have an online form."

Melanie stood up. "Because I'm not running an escort service!"

Betsy ignored the jab and talked to the rest of us in the room. "The fact that Neil wants to be a pilot sealed the deal for us."

"Pilot?" I slapped Stumpy on the shoulder and whispered into his ear. "Two women who like you at the same party." I laughed at Stumpy's uncomfortable good fortune. "You're going to be a jet-fighter ace."

Melanie smacked her wine glass down. "Another pour, Sommelier Stump."

Laura pushed her iPhone into the Bose player and turned on some Euro-hop music. "Let's dance." She twirled and danced alone.

I poured Betsy a glass of wine and brought her a chair.

Stumpy looked confused.

"Someone dance with me," Laura pleaded.

"Neil can break-dance," Betsy said.

Melanie held up a bottle of wine. "He's a freaking American superhero." She poured herself some more wine.

God forbid that Stumpy ever fly a plane, but he could break dance.

Betsy started to dance. She and Laura swayed together and made up their own routine. They held their arms out and motioned me forward. "Dance, Jason!"

I stood and backed up. "No way."

Melanie jumped up, grabbed Stumpy by the arm and pulled him toward her. "He's my date. Show us what you got, Neil." The three women danced around Stumpy. He looked bewildered and confused. I thought it hilarious.

"Dance!" Betsy and Laura said.

"Dance!" Melanie said.

Stumpy looked at me for help. It was too much fun. I threw a pillow at him and hit him in the gut. I jumped up on the coffee table and started dancing, flailing my arms around. "Come on, Stumpy. Dance. Six Flags try!"

Stumpy was confused, angry, and happy. He began to dance. He danced like a madman—as if dancing would solve his dilemma.

The ladies clapped and urged Stumpy on.

He jerked and twisted and then broke it down, spinning around on the floor like a chubby top.

"Wooh!" I yelled and kicked my legs. I couldn't stop laughing. I spun around and started throwing couch cushions. It felt exhilarating. A wine bottle crashed off the coffee table and shattered. A pillow hit me in the side of the head. I spun around and did a pro-wrestler jump onto the couch.

The music stopped. I looked up. Before me stood three angels looking fierce as devils: Sister Claudette, Sister Lucia, and Jacqueline.

They stood staring in shock. Only after a pause did Sister Lucia relax and smile. Stumpy stood up between the three women, his shirt soaked in sweat.

"This house has gone through many changes," Sister Claudette said. "But never did I expect it to turn into a brothel."

"Matthew! Mark! No!" I had never seen Sister Lucia so upset. The dogs were greedily licking up the spilled wine.

"Just some communion for the little saints," I said as I walked around the room. "Sisters you're overreacting. We're only having a little party. These are our friends, Betsy and Laura."

Jacqueline would not take her eyes off me, and she looked hurt. She raised an eyebrow. "That explains everything then?"

"Is this Laura, your ex-wife Laura?" Sister Claudette said.

Jacqueline's face elongated. "Wife?" She let out a gasp.

"A long time ago—a big mistake for both of us," I said. "Right, Laura?"

"Yes, a big mistake," Laura said.

"She's happily remarried and everything," I said.

Laura coughed. "Yes, happily."

"Then what is she doing here?" Sister Claudette said.

"Good question," Jacqueline huffed.

"I don't like it," Sister Claudette said.

"I don't either," Jacqueline said. "What did you do with your hair?"

I ran my hand over my head. "It feels more spiritual."

"I don't like your hair, or what is happening in this house," Sister Claudette said. "This kind of debauchery cannot go on here."

"Debauchery? Sister this is almost my own house."

She motioned to Melanie and Betsy. "Winos and prostitutes!"

Betsy put her hands on her hips. "I beg your pardon?"

Sister Claudette looked up and down condescendingly at Betsy. "Is that a real uniform or did they make you dress up?"

Betsy put her hands on her hips. "I should ask you the same."

Sister Claudette looked like she might explode. I jumped between her and Betsy.

"Come on, Sister. It's just a little party."

Sister Lucia tried to help. "Remember the time we had after your high school graduation, Claudette?"

Sister Claudette stared Sister Lucia down and won. "I have the interests of eighty-two nuns to look after. We cannot have this type of sinful activity going on in our vicinity. Jason, if we are to be partners in producing wine, that includes being partners in behavior as far as I'm concerned."

"Well join the party then, Sister," Melanie shouted.

I was in no position to argue. I lowered my head. "Of course, Sister."

"It's late," Sister Claudette said. "You women should leave."

"But I was going to stay here," Laura said.

Jacqueline glared at me. "I bet."

"I was staying, too," Betsy said.

Sister Claudette looked at Betsy and took a moment to reign in her anger. "There's room in the abbey. You are all welcome to stay."

"Christ almighty," Melanie said. "I'm going back to the penguin pen."

"Pack your bags, ladies, and follow me," Sister Claudette said.

I hopped around like a porter and helped the women with their bags. All the while, I felt Sister Claudette's soul-searching gaze. I finally stopped and looked at her. "What?"

"Eustace is looking more attractive by the day." She turned and walked out the door with Sister Lucia, followed by Laura, Betsy, and Melanie.

I ran outside and called to Jacqueline. She had just entered her car. I leaned down by her window, which she had lowered halfway.

"What do you want?"

"Room service breakfast?"

"You've got to be kidding."

"Yes, I'm joking."

"Of course you are! Everything with you is a joke! You do what you want. Sleep with a gullible French girl one night and back with your wife the next."

"She's not my wife."

I thought Jacqueline was pretty angry, but she got even angrier. "You are a bullshitter. I know what it means now. You bullshit old ladies. You bullshit your friends. You bullshit me! I want no more part of your games and jokes."

"Jacqueline, please. Let me talk."

"Leave me alone you Paris playboy asshole. I never want to see you again." She slammed on the gas, the car lurched, and she sped off.

I walked back into the house.

Stumpy was cleaning up the broken bottle and spilled wine.

"Just our party now," I said.

"Like old times."

Empty wine bottles and partially filled glasses littered the room. Pillows and cushions were scattered everywhere.

"Dude, you had two women eyeing you up for keeps," I said. "Damn, you're the man."

"I was scared."

"You should be." I uncorked a new bottle. "Women are nothing but misery, and now you've got double."

I poured us each more wine. "Jacqueline and I are done." As I said it, I felt it. She was gone. I ruined it by being me. She was right. I am a bullshitter. I'm a no-good scoundrel who thinks only of himself.

"You'll make it right."

"I don't think so. Not this time."

Jacqueline hated me. Sister Claudette was leaning in the same direction, even hinting she'd rather Eustace inherit the vineyard—just like Aunt Clara. Well fuck them all! If they really thought I was a no-good selfish bastard then I'd be a no-good selfish bastard. I grabbed a bottle of wine. "I'm going for a walk."

CHAPTER 18

I took the wine bottle onto the patio. A bat swooped and circled, devouring bugs swarming in the dim light. I stepped off the concrete and walked down the hill into the vines and grass and dirt. Clouds descended ominously toward me, screening the stars and darkening the sky. I drank from the bottle, letting the wine flow fast down the back of my throat. Acid burned in my stomach. The heavy clouds lowered into fog, and when I breathed I inhaled a damp mist that tasted like cold copper. I drank more and felt a euphoric madness, an overpowering feeling that I had been terribly wronged. I deserved this land.

I rounded the ridge. The vine leaves sagged, heavy and wet, as I passed. The fog grew thick and the final hill seemed formidable, but still I climbed. I climbed and stumbled over rocks, holding myself up with my free hand while protecting the wine with the other. I stopped and drank deep. The fermented grapes' history swirled in my mind. I stopped at the cemetery and sat on the family vault and drank again. I became one with the wine and I felt its power, the power its ancestors must have held over my own. I drank the bottle, holding it upright until the last drop fell on my eager tongue. I stood up and threw the bottle high into the air down the hill.

I knew what I had to do; knew the evil mission that would save me. I climbed to the top of the hill and stumbled through the chapel door. I sat in a pew and faked a prayer. I opened my eyes slightly and looked at the relic case. The relics were the answer. Jacqueline, Sister Claudette, Aunt Clara, they had driven me to them. I looked at the cups and then back at the altar. I lay down on the pew and looked up to the arched ceiling. I rolled over and fell to the ground and crawled. I crawled to the cabinet, thirsty for one of the cups.

The glass case door had a small rusty lock. I pulled on it and it easily opened. I reached down to the bottom row and grabbed a gold chalice that was at one end. I pulled it out quickly, and then carefully shut the door. The deed was done.

I held the cup tight against my chest and stood up. I stared at the ground, my eyes averting the altar and the cross. I muscled through the door and fell outside into a puddle of mud. I pushed myself up and ran. I ran recklessly down the hill and through the vineyard, clutching the cup, feeling its coolness against my fingers. I thought I heard a dog bark. The fog covered my skin in a heavy film and coalesced into water droplets that fell from my brow and nose and chin. I ran on, fueled by the wine and the cup and the imagined mad bats diving at me in the dark.

I reached the house, entered the back door, and turned on the kitchen light—basking in its safety. Stumpy must have gone to sleep already. I grabbed an old towel from the cupboard and dried myself off. I rubbed down the cup, and it shined a golden hue. Four red ruby-like gems were situated around the perimeter, dividing the cup into quarters. Underneath each jewel a crusade-like battle scene was etched. I was certain it would fetch my price. I wrapped the cup with the towel, stealthily snuck into my room, and hid it in the closet. I breathed a guilty sigh of relief.

CHAPTER 19

The next day, the hot morning sun assuaged my anger. I thought of Jacqueline and missed her. I thought of Sister Claudette—and what I had done—and felt a little guilt, but not enough to turn back.

Stumpy and I breakfasted in the abbey dining hall with eighty-two nuns and our guests. We sat in different-colored plastic chairs at long, white folding tables. I had a bowl of oatmeal and some yogurt. Stumpy had a plastic tray stacked with scrambled eggs and bacon. Laura and Betsy were in high spirits, clearly enjoying their convent stay. The nuns ate in silence, but for our friends, it was impossible.

"I feel like I'm at camp," Laura said.

"I so love not having to decide what to do," Betsy said.

Sister Claudette had given them jobs, and, unbelievably, they looked forward to working in the vineyard.

Sister Claudette wasn't speaking to me, and it made me uneasy. "You know, Sister Claudette, this might be a good gig," I said.

Silence.

"What *gig*?" She finally said.

"You could rent rooms like a hotel and charge to work the vineyard. People love stuff like that. We could cut down on the number of visiting nuns and make some money as well."

Sister Claudette smiled a begrudging smile.

"Thanks for making—I mean letting—our friends stay here. Probably better that way."

She nodded.

"I understand your thought wagon. This place has a reputation—the abbey, the vineyard. It's all intertwined. If anything scandalous happens it could hurt business."

Sister Claudette nodded again, longer this time. "A small hotel inside the abbey isn't a bad idea."

I smiled. I could do this. I could work with Sister Claudette. I could be an honest businessman. I just had to make one underhanded little transaction to make it all happen. That's the way the world works. I'd make it up to the Sisters, anyway, I promised.

Since I wasn't *officially* in France, Stumpy opened a French bank account to deposit the harvest profits.

We had twenty-nine thousand five hundred Euros in the account. I needed thirteen thousand one hundred more. I had to pay the court by tomorrow. Every second counted.

I had to sell the golden cup. "Stumpy, let me use your eBay account."

"Why?"

"Just trust me."

"Definitely no, then."

"I'm going to sell some assets and I need an eBay account."

"Like what assets?"

"Like, I don't know, maybe some double-haulers. What's it matter?"

"Double-haulers are going to save the vineyard?"

"No, you're right, they're not. Just let me use your account."

"No way."

I marched up to my room and brought the cup out from its hiding place. I carried it to the balcony and held it over my head like in a victory celebration. "This is what I'm going to sell."

Stumpy's eyes went wide. "The Holy Grail."

"Do you think it'll fetch thirteen thousand one hundred Euros?" I came downstairs. Stumpy tried to touch the cup, but I kept pulling it away from him.

"You want to use my account or not?"

I handed him the cup and he ran his fingers over it greedily. "It's beautiful."

"What do you think?"

"Ten grand tops."

I had almost won him over. "Okay, cool. Let's put it on eBay and find out."

"Where'd you get it?"

"Oh my God," I said. "You're nothing but a henpecker."

"It's my account. I want to know."

I figured if Stumpy was in on the truth then maybe my sin would be cut in half. "I borrowed it, okay. After I inherit the vineyard and the grapes are popping, I'll buy it back or replace it with a better one."

"Where'd you borrow it?"

"Jesus, Joseph, and Mary. You could be Aunt Clara."

He just looked at me as if to say, "Well?"

"The chapel on the hill. Okay? I took it out of the relics cabinet."

"My God. You stole from a church."

"I told you I'd replace it."

"I don't know, Jason."

"Are you going to give me your eBay account info?"

"I don't want to be a part of this." We looked at each other and assessed our positions. Stumpy became nervous. "Don't talk to me anymore."

"Not a chance." I breathed in deep. "Look. This land is my land." I put my hand on his shoulder. "This land is your land."

Stumpy waved his hands like a choir conductor. He bounced and then sang. *"From California to the New York island."*

I laughed politely. "Come on. Serious. The chapel sits on our land. We're not stealing. We're using what's ours to save what is rightfully ours. What could be wrong with that?"

"I don't know. It sort of makes sense when you explain it like that, but it still—it just feels wrong."

"Feels wrong?" I handed him the cup. "That feels real. Feels wrong? People do things that feel wrong all the time. That's how people survive. They cut corners sometimes. How about that English paper I let you use at the end of senior year. Did that feel wrong? I bet it did, but you graduated didn't you? And it all worked out for the best."

"I haven't been so happy after high school."

I'd forgotten about the Zoloft. "But you're happy here, right? You said yourself you felt like you belonged here." Stumpy gave a slight nod in agreement. "Well if we don't sell the cup we're out of here on Saturday and you're going to be delivering pizzas and crying over beers at Lucky Mike's alone, because I'll be in the clink. And, trust me, I'm not going to let you forget what could have been."

He started biting his nails. "I don't want to leave here."

"That's smart. What's your log-in?"

"Stumpmaster."

"Password?"

"Jasonbud."

"Jasonbud!"

I reacted too strongly. Stumpy couldn't handle the stress. He started to cry. "Jesus, Jason. I'm sorry. You're my only friend."

I felt hollow. When you got right down to it, Stumpy's friendship was all I had in the world. I relaxed and quieted my tone. "You're my best and only friend, Stumpy. You know that."

He nodded, wiped a tear, and smiled.

"We've done some crazy shit together."

He laughed.

"And this trip has been the craziest."

We both laughed. "That is for sure," he said.

"So are we going to save this place?"

"Yeah. Let's do it."

After weighing the cup, I figured it was worth at least twenty thousand Euros in gold, but we needed to cash in quick. We put it on eBay for a "Buy it Now" price of thirteen thousand one hundred Euros. All I could do now was hope.

"I'm going to town to see if I can bring Jacqueline back over to the good side."

"Not like that, you aren't."

"Not like what?"

"Eustace is probably staying at the hotel, too. You need your disguise."

I put my monk costume on: robe, sandals, sunglasses, and goatee. "You coming?"

"Naw. I want to watch this auction."

I walked into the hotel lobby, sat down, and sank deep into the burgundy sofa's old cushions. I picked up a paper to read. A wooden display stand stood next to the wall. It held glossy flyers for Dordogne river canoe trips and cave tours. An older couple speaking German walked out of the lobby holding hands.

A waiter wheeled a room service cart into the elevator. A crème colored cloth with gold fringe brushing the floor was draped over the cart. The waiter propped open the elevator door and returned for a second cart. The second cart looked the same as the first. It had a glass of orange juice, coffee, and a stainless steel room service plate cover on top. A slip of paper hung loosely over the end. "23" it said. Jacqueline's room!

The elevator doors closed. I walked calmly to the stairs and quickly climbed. I stopped at the second floor and reconnoitered the scene through the square window in the stairwell door. The waiter had both carts in the hall. Green carpeting covered the floor. The waiter knocked on a door, "*Bonjour,*" he said and wheeled a cart into the room directly across from Jacqueline's. When the door shut behind him I tip-toed to Jacqueline's cart, pulled the long tablecloth up, and climbed in underneath—compacting myself on the stainless steel bottom. I pulled the tablecloth down and remained motionless.

I hadn't really thought about what I was doing. The opportunity laid itself open, and I jumped. I guess I thought my popping out of the breakfast cart like white bread out of a toaster would bring such a laugh out of Jacqueline that she would be ready to forgive me.

A door shut, and the cart began to move. The waiter exclaimed something in French. It must have been about the added weight, but he kept going until stopping at Jacqueline's door. I heard him knock. I started to panic. What if it wasn't Jacqueline's room? She always reserved room 23. But what if last night was different? What if she decided to return home? What if 23 were already booked?

"*Bonjour, Madame.*"

"*Bonjour.*" I couldn't tell if the voice was Jacqueline's or not.

The cart moved and bumped over the threshold. Sweat dripped down my nervous face. What was I doing? I was going to freak her out. "*Bonne journée.*" I heard the waiter's footsteps leave and the door close behind him.

I rolled out from underneath the cloth and jumped up. "*Bon appetit!*"

A woman with short gray hair, a flower patterned blouse, and tan dress slacks stood by the window. She screamed in terror. Her hands shook uncontrollably in front of her face.

I had the wrong room. I was going to be arrested. After all we had been through, Stumpy was going to kill me.

Jacqueline came running out of the bathroom. "Ahh!"

"Wait, Jacqueline, it's me!"

She stopped and looked closely. She put her hand to her temple and dropped her head.

"*Tu connaites ce . . . ce . . ., moine?*" "You know this, this, monk?"

Jacqueline stood up straight. "Yes. I know this, this, idiot. What the hell are you doing? What the hell are you supposed to be?"

A knock sounded from the door. "Are you all right? Hello? Is everything okay in there?"

It was Eustace.

Jacqueline walked toward the door.

"Don't open that door," I begged.

I jumped behind the older woman and held her in front of me to hide.

"*Oh mon dieu!*"

Jacqueline looked at me hard, like she was seeing me for the first time.

"Please, Jacqueline! I can explain."

She began to open the door. I dove behind the bed. She opened the door a crack. "Everything is fine. Thank you, sir. My mother sometimes behaves hysterically."

Mother?

"Are you sure?"

"Quite."

"Strange," Eustace said. "I thought I heard a voice I recognized."

"Thank you, sir." She closed the door.

I stood up and straightened my robe. "Thank you."

Jacqueline pointed at the door. "Out."

"Just listen for a moment. I—"

"Out! I don't want an explanation, Jason. I want you out of this room and out of my life."

"This person is Jason? The love of your life, Jason?"

"Love of your life! Is that true? Did she say that?"

Jacqueline buried her face in her hands. "*Oh ma mère.*"

I looked at Jacqueline's mother. "*Je m'appelle Jason Barnes.*" We shook hands.

"Marjette."

"*Enchanté.*"

"Don't believe him." Jacqueline sat on the edge of the bed. "You have a wife! You never said anything about a wife."

"I don't have a wife. We're divorced. She's my ex-wife."

"Once a wife, always a wife."

"That's not true. Who says that?"

"I do. Because that's what it feels like to me."

"Look. I don't know anything about your past either."

Her eyes looked to the ceiling for a brief second. I had scored a point. "Okay, Jason. I will tell you about my past. I was in love with a man for three years—"

Marjette waved her hand in front of her face disapprovingly. "Psh."

"That's okay," I said. "I don't need to know."

Jacqueline looked at me cross. "Yes you do. I was in love with a man whom I thought was in love with me. After two years of dating I thought we were getting serious, but then I found out he had a wife, and in the end the wife won. I'm not going through that again."

"It's not like that," I said. "I've been divorced for five years. And Laura just showed up unannounced."

"Why is life so crazy with you? How do you have an answer for everything? Why are you hiding from that man in the hall?"

I pointed at the door. "That man is a bad man. That man is after me. He is trying to steal the vineyard." I motioned for Jacqueline's mother to sit at the table by the window. "Please, Madame. It's a long story. Let me explain." I served a plate of the food to Jacqueline and set the bulk of the goodies on the table in front of her mother. I sat down across from her and looked straight into her eyes. "Marjette. About a month ago my dear aunt who raised me passed away."

She put her hand to her heart. "*Je suis désolée.*"

"You are unstoppable," Jacqueline shook her head.

I proceeded to tell my story to Jacqueline's mother, knowing full well I had to convince her in any case. I put my version all out on the room service table except for some bad tasting morsels like possible jail time, illegally entering the country, and hawking some nuns' religious artifacts. But otherwise, it was all good quiche, and by the end of my spiel Marjette was full-up on breakfast and ready to call me a stand-up guy.

Jacqueline was putting on an earring. "So you say a few nice words to Mother and everything is okay? You think I'm supposed to fall into your arms now?"

I jumped up and grabbed her hand. "No. Of course not. Jacqueline, I think, I hope, that we have something special. Please, let me prove my words."

She stared at me a moment, and then squeezed my hand and nodded. I felt immediate relief. I think Jacqueline was still hurt, but at least I had a chance.

Jacqueline's mother wanted a vineyard tour, and we agreed to meet up later. I said goodbye and kept an eye out for Eustace as I left.

CHAPTER 20

I raced back to St. Sebastian. I could see Stumpy pacing on the patio from a quarter mile down the road. He ran into the drive to greet me. I blared the horn at him and yelled out the window. "I could have hit you."

His hands fluttered excitedly around my face and shoulders as I got out of the car. "It sold. It sold!"

"The cup?"

"Thirteen thousand one hundred Euros. Someone 'bought it now.'"

I grabbed his shirt at the chest and shook him. "We did it."

He pushed me, and we punched and jabbed each other and laughed with joy.

"Are they going to send us the cash through PayPal?"

"Someone in France bought it. They want to meet in person to make sure of everything."

I did a hop, spread my hands out, and looked at Stumpy questioningly.

"This afternoon in Bordeaux," he said.

"Let's do it."

"Let's go."

We ran into the house to get ready. I took off the monk disguise and put on my regular jeans and shirt and turned back into Jason Barnes. I went downstairs and pulled out a map of Bordeaux from the old bookshelf. I examined the spot we were supposed to meet the buyer. All we had to do was exchange the cup for cash, return to the bank, and wire the money to the court in Kankakee. If all went well it could be done this afternoon, but we needed to leave right away.

Stumpy put the cup into a backpack and we walked out the door. There stood Laura, Melanie, and Betsy.

"We're ready for our vineyard tour," Betsy said, chipper. "Will you be our pilot, Neil?"

Melanie scowled. I don't think she thought Stumpy could seriously like Betsy, but still, she wasn't going to let Betsy out of her sight.

Stumpy started fidgeting, and I thought he might say something he would regret. "Sorry, but we have to go," I said.

"Big business," Stumpy said.

"Can we see you later?" Betsy asked, hopeful.

"Yes. We'll be back in a couple of hours." Stumpy smiled.

Betsy smiled.

Melanie looked pleadingly at Stumpy.

"But we wanted a tour," Laura said

"Sister Claudette will give you a tour," I said.

Laura groaned. "She'll give us jobs."

"Ask Sister Lucia for a tour." I slapped Stumpy on the shoulder and pushed him toward the car. "Or give yourselves a tour. Just ask the nuns questions as you go."

I remembered Jacqueline and her mom. "Laura, could I have a word?"

Laura and I walked down the drive. "That woman with the sisters last night, Jacqueline . . ."

"You love her."

"Well, I, er, maybe. But listen. I sort of patched things up with her this morning, but she's obviously not thrilled that you're here."

"Is she going to be around?"

"Well, yes. I hope. That's the thing. She and her mother are coming out for a vineyard tour, too. I was wondering if—"

"I'll be nice."

"And—"

"And I'll talk you up without seeming like I want you back." She smiled at me flirtingly. "Like I'd want that."

I ignored her nonsense. "And don't mention anything about you divorcing Tom."

She raised her head defiantly. "I love my Tom."

"Okay, good, good. Thank you, Laura. I really like this girl. It's been a long time, you know?"

She looked sad. "I know."

I smiled. "We had some good times, huh?"

She laughed. "Oh, yes. And now you've got a sophisticated French woman." She waved her fingers in the air. "Oh la la, très chic! I should have never doubted you."

A taxi came up the road. "This must be Jacqueline and her mom now."

Laura and I were about three hundred yards from the house. The taxi slowly passed. I locked eyes for a second with the lone passenger. It was Eustace.

Eustace turned forward like nothing was amiss, and I hoped he didn't recognize me, but then his brain figured my face out despite my new baldness. The taxi stopped and the back door flew open. Eustace stepped out. "Jason!"

I bolted past him and gave him a quick shove in the process. I sprinted up the driveway. "Stumpy! Start the car. Stumpy!"

Eustace jumped back in the taxi and it followed, sniffing at my heels.

Stumpy had the car started and I jumped in the passenger seat. "It's Eustace. Go!"

The taxi stopped and Eustace walked toward our car.

Stumpy lurched the Toyota forward. Eustace waved his arms in panic and dodged the front bumper.

"Jason!"

Stumpy turned sharply to avoid Eustace and headed straight for the ladies. The car was in first gear and Stumpy pressed the gas, clutch, and brake repeatedly in no particular order. The ladies screamed and ran for cover. I grabbed the wheel and pointed us down the drive. Stumpy hit the gas hard, and we lurched our way to the main road. We stopped.

My mouth was dry, and I felt like vomiting. "Switch."

We each got out and ran around the car and met at the front. We tried to dodge each other left then right, but we were synchronized and collided. We pushed each other aside and got back in the car. I smoothly popped in the clutch and we raced down the road—destination Bordeaux.

"Do you think Eustace will tell on us?"

"Yeah, I would think so." I shook my head in frustration. "Hopefully the police will have better things to do than research an American complaining about another American entering France illegally."

"What if he tries to see Aceau again?"

"What of it now? He already knows I'm here."

"Eustace might go to Aceau for advice before he tells the police or anyone else."

Stumpy was rockin' the noggin for a change. "You're right, there."

"Coming into France the wrong way might cancel you from the will, too."

"Damn. You're probably right again, Stumpy. Since when did your genius Big Bang, Stephen Hawking?"

Stumpy slapped the front dash. "I think well under pressure. And my real name is Neil Hammond, Jason. Don't you know that?"

I sighed. "Look. All I know right now is we gotta sell this cup and deposit the cash and wire it to the court by tomorrow before Eustace or anybody else tries to arrest us."

"Us?"

"You aided and abetted, remember?"

Bordeaux was ninety kilometers away. We passed vineyards and farms, rolls of hay and grazing cows. The road curved through small towns until we caught expressway A62 in Langon. I sped up. Trucks and dodging cars roared by, immersing us into a more frenetic pace than we had been experiencing in vineyard life. It took us a good hour before we reached Bordeaux.

We parked on the street in the heart of Bordeaux's city government buildings. Giant columns rose from the street's edge, forming a sidewalk arcade that shaded our walk. We made our way to the water. A swift breeze came from the Atlantic, creating scattered ripples on the Gironde Estuary's surface. The air was cool and smelled faintly of fish. Industrial barges passed each other along the wide waterway.

We stood and looked at each other. We paced and looked at each other again. Stumpy shrugged. I shrugged. We did this for a few minutes and then a short, skinny man approached us. He was young. He wore a low V-neck shirt that exposed a hairy chest, and his hair was slicked back into a ponytail. "*Bonjour.*"

"*Bonjour.*"

He spoke French and talked on and on but it meant nothing to us. Finally he made some hand gestures that resembled a box and stopped talking. He looked at us expectantly.

"He wants to see the cup, I think."

Stumpy unzipped the backpack.

"Careful."

He set the backpack down and slowly unwrapped the cup.

The man's eyes lit up. "*Oui.*"

He reached out and touched the cup. Stumpy held on and wouldn't let him take it.

"Euros." I rubbed my thumb and fingers to signal money.

A car's horn honked. I didn't think anything of it at first, but then it sounded again, repeatedly. A black Mercedes limousine was parked twenty yards from us.

I put my hands on the cup. Stumpy, me, and the unknown man, all had a hold of it. "This isn't the guy."

We pushed and pulled until the man let go. Stumpy and I fell to the ground both holding onto the cup. The man ran away.

We stood up and brushed ourselves off. Stumpy held the cup like a football. I nodded to the Mercedes limo. "That must be our real buyer."

The limousine's windows were tinted. The back window opened slightly and a hand reached out. Stumpy and I approached carefully.

I held out my hand and motioned for money. "Euros."

A small cardboard box was handed out to us.

I opened the box and counted thirteen bound stacks of one hundred Euros, plus one hundred Euros more. Perfect. "*Ça va.*" I nudged Stumpy and he handed over the cup.

The back window rolled up, and the limousine sped off.

"Just like that."

"Easy as stomping grapes."

I shook Stumpy by the shoulders. "We did it." I almost dropped the box.

"Careful, the money."

We stuffed the box of cash into Stumpy's backpack, saddled him up, looked around for threats, and walked back the way we had come.

"Only two hours until the bank closes." I picked up the pace. Our footsteps clicked on the cement sidewalk. We turned the corner to the street our car was parked and ran smack into a swarm of kids. They came from nowhere and surrounded us. They begged for money as a pretense, but patted and pulled, searching for the good stuff.

Across the street I saw the man from our previous encounter. He leaned against a building and smiled as he watched us. The kids were after the cup, or possibly the cash. The man had probably watched the whole transaction take place.

Stumpy smiled at the kids and thought it all funny. "No, no."

"Stumpy. They're after the cash."

I grabbed Stumpy's backpack and pushed it up high on his back. Ruddy fingers pawed it, but they could only manage to open a couple zipper pockets. Stumpy and I swung around as I pulled the backpack over his head. The kids jumped at us and their combined weight began to pull us down. I wrapped both hands around the backpack and held it into my stomach. Stumpy bent over. I pushed him in the butt. "Go! Stumpy! Go! Like pee wee football."

Stumpy bulldogged forward, sending kids flying. I stayed close behind my blocker and broke free. We ran fast, and the kids chased us. Out of the corner of my eye I saw the mystery man running across the street to join the chase. I don't know if it was my imagination or not, but I thought I saw some other men appear around corners and run at us, too, but it was all a blur and I tried to focus straight ahead and just run.

Stumpy slowed down by our car.

They'd be on us before we could jump into the car. "Keep going," I shouted. We rounded the corner and headed for a busy street.

I saw the Mercedes limousine parked at a stoplight.

"Come on." I ran for the limousine, figuring the recent transaction had made us friends. I pulled on the back door and it opened. I dove in. Stumpy jumped in behind me and closed the door. The light turned green. "Go! Those kids are chasing us." The kids pounded on the side windows, but the limousine moved through the intersection and down the road.

We were safe from the kids, but I then wondered if it was all a sinister plan. Maybe the buyer in the limousine, the kids, and the mystery man were all working together.

"A deal's a deal," a man said in accented English. "No trade-backs. What are you fools doing?"

I recognized that voice, and since I was now more familiar with the language and accents, his English had become easier to understand. I pushed myself up into a seat and saw Aceau sitting primly with the cup in his lap.

"Aceau!"

Stumpy bumped his head on the limo's ceiling, spun his behind around and sat in a seat. "This is the asshole?"

"You bought the cup?"

Aceau wore his same suit. "Not me. I have an important client in Bordeaux who purchased the chalice. God knows why the transaction included you, but the deal is done. Now you must get out, my client will not like this at all."

"The deal is still good. Those kids were trying to rob us."

"You are bald." Aceau looked at me intently, like he knew me from somewhere else. But I don't think he put the synopsis together to place me as the monk.

I rubbed my head. "My girlfriend likes it this way."

Aceau did not respond, but nodded to the driver. After a few turns the limousine came to a stop.

Stumpy snickered. "See you later, asshole."

"Not a word of this to anyone," Aceau said.

"Not a word," I said.

CHAPTER 21

An hour later, we drove around Duras's town square, turned down Rue Chavassier, and parked in front of BNP Paribas bank. I had to stop myself from running in.

We walked into the deserted lobby. *"Bonjour."* A sullen teller glanced at us, wary at our eagerness. Stumpy still held on to the backpack like a football. We approached the teller. Stumpy slid the box of Euros across the counter to deposit. We received a balance slip that indicated we had forty-two thousand six hundred Euros. It was done.

We asked to wire some money and waited outside the office of a personal banker. After a few moments a young woman came out and introduced herself. *"Bonjour. Je m'appelle Isabelle."*

"Jason Barnes."

"Neil Hammond."

Isabelle had a black business skirt and an ivory blouse. She had red hair and wore black high heel shoes. Without the shoes I think she would have ignited Stumpy's love-fire, but as it was now, she had an inch on him. Stumpy remained unaware and unimpressed and I was silently thankful.

"The wire room is closed," Isabelle explained. "You may return between ten and three tomorrow."

Tomorrow was Friday, the due date. That would be cutting it way too close. I hadn't heard from the runaway Hammersmith, and I didn't know if wiring cash to the Kankakee County Court was even possible. "The transfer has to take place today. We're here now. We have the money. You don't understand the calamities that may befall us between today and tomorrow."

Isabelle looked at me strangely, like she hadn't comprehended.

"Bad things happen to us sometimes," Stumpy explained.

I felt desperate. "Please fire up the old wire and zap over the cash for us." I took a step closer to Isabelle and pleaded with my hands clutched together. "The future of St. Sebastian wine may be at stake."

Isabelle took a step backward, I think feeling a bit threatened.

"Do you like St. Sebastian wine?" Stumpy asked.

"I do," she said pertly. "But that is not the issue. I cannot 'zap' the wire. Nobody can now. The main office in Paris controls all the wire transfer times."

I felt defeated.

"First thing in the morning is the best we can do. I suggest you arrive at ten."

"But that will be three in the morning in the states. Everyone will be asleep."

"Have all the pertinent information available." Isabelle's eyes blinked rapidly. "If you have the correct numbers and wire instructions it will not matter if your institution is open or not."

"I, er, I don't know anything about our numbers." Damn, Hammersmith. "Could I make some calls to the United States and corral these financial doo-daddies?"

"Pardon?"

I explained the request in my best English. Word had meandered around Duras that Stumpy and I were the new St. Sebastian owners.

Isabelle brightened. She wanted to show us good service, and a telephone call was something she could help us with. Stumpy and I followed her into a glass-walled office. She sat behind her pristine desk. We sat in chairs before her. Isabelle turned her desk phone around and placed it in front of me. "Do you need privacy?"

"No. Just show me how to call the US."

I knuckle-punched the number and made a dozen calls, spending five minutes in computer voice hell until finally reaching the Kankakee County Court's collection department. An efficient-sounding man gave me the instructions to wire money. He also promised to notify Judge Crawford when the payment was received. All seemed in order, but then he asked me to name the bank and account owner on the bank account I would be wiring money from.

Questions were not good. "Um. It's a BNP Paribas bank in France. It's not my bank account. Is that a problem?"

"No. It should not be. As long as the damages are paid we are happy. Are you in France now?"

Was this guy chitchatting or was he trying to bust me? I couldn't admit I was in France. "I don't know where I am?"

"You don't know where you are?"

I looked around the office at Isabelle's plaques and family photographs searching for help. "No. Not at the moment. I could be anywhere."

"You're calling from an international number."

"I must be somewhere, then."

There was silence.

"Goodbye, then." There was no need to continue. I could only endanger myself more. "I'll call tomorrow to check the transfer."

"Goodbye."

I looked at Stumpy, worried about the man's questions. Eustace knew I was here and now some court payment-processing employee knew. I bit my nails, something I had not done since my divorce. As

I got closer to inheriting the vineyard the increased worry of being caught for my transgressions weighed on my psyche.

Stumpy hadn't heard the gist of my phone conversation. He and Isabelle had ignored me and were talking pleasantly together. "The '07 St. Sebastian was a spectacular year. The full bodied velvety texture and deep earthy aromas could stand up to the finest Bordeaux wines."

Isabelle listened to Stumpy with interest, clearly intrigued. "I've heard it's excellent."

I listened, amazed. An improbability a month ago, Stumpy had now become somewhat of a wine expert.

"We have a large vineyard, but our own wine production is small and we are relatively unknown outside of Duras." Stumpy smiled and nodded at me. "Jason is going to change all that."

I put my hands on the desk. "But we need your wire, Ms. Isabelle."

Isabelle smiled and stood up, ready to end our meeting. "Tomorrow at ten. I will be here waiting to help you."

We shook hands and said goodbye.

Stumpy and I walked out of BNP Paribas satisfied with the successful completion of our cup-selling mission. We had the cash! All we had to do was wire it, which seemed easy enough, yet I worried.

We walked to our car and I was about to press the key to unlock the doors when I stopped. Aceau's office was around the corner off the square. I just had to give it a quick check.

I led Stumpy down the block. I peered around the corner to the town square. My intuition had reason. "There, look."

"At the woman in the Chanel dress?"

I looked at Stumpy dumbfounded. "Wine and now fashion. How did you become such a cultural connoisseur?"

"What?" He shrugged his shoulders. "I've been reading French fashion magazines."

I pointed past the woman in the Chanel dress down to the next street. "Do you see the man pacing in front of Aceau's building?"

"Eustace."

"Exactly. He must be waiting for Aceau. Let's head him off."

"How?"

I started walking back to the car. "He's waiting for Aceau and we are going to give him Aceau."

"I'm tired of being the asshole."

"You can get used to it, trust me." We reached the car and I opened the trunk. "I brought our costumes just in case."

"In case what?"

"Jesus, Stumpy. Don't be so dense." I opened the back door and shepherded Stumpy inside and tossed the costume to him.

"Don't be so mean, Jason. What am I supposed to do?"

I tended to get impatient with Stumpy when I got nervous. I tried to relax. Stumpy needed to be in the right frame of mind to play Aceau. "I'm sorry, Stumpy. I'm worried. You know that. Can you change into the costume?"

"In the back seat? People will see."

"No one's going to see. And we're in France. Being naked is no big deal."

Stumpy rolled around in the back seat like a cold walrus trying to squirm his way into the middle of the warm herd. He stepped out and put on his hat. I straightened him up and fixed his beard.

I slapped Stumpy's cheek ever so lightly. "Look at me. You are Aceau. You are irritable. You have no time for this American's paltry complaints. Got it?"

Stumpy furled his eyebrows and looked intense. "*Oui.*"

I pushed Stumpy around the corner and proudly watched him walk through the square on his own. I felt like a father looking after his child marching off to school for the first time.

Stumpy walked calmly and confidently. Eustace continued to pace and when he saw Stumpy he approached him excitedly, his hands animated.

Stumpy recounted the conversation to me later and it went something like this:

Eustace runs up to Stumpy. "Monsieur Aceau, I've been waiting to see you."

Stumpy frowns condescendingly. "Our appointment is not until tomorrow afternoon. I am still on holiday." (I had forgotten about that. I had to hand it to Stumpy, he was in prime Aceau form.)

"I know, I'm sorry, but someone said they saw you working today. And this can't wait. I've information that Jason Barnes is in the country."

"But of course he is. I have seen him myself."

"You know, then?"

"Know what?"

"He is in the country illegally."

"That is a wild accusation, Monsieur Puny."

"My name is Small. Eustace Small."

Stumpy tries to walk up the building steps, but Eustace keeps getting in his way.

Stumpy says, "Can this not wait until tomorrow? I am a very busy man."

"You must help me contact the authorities."

"Monsieur Tiny, I understand your concern with upholding French laws, especially against the likes of Jason Barnes . . ."

"So you think he's a rascal, too. Will you help me?"

"Good sir. The French Customs Service is extremely capable. If Monsieur Barnes is good enough to pass their rigorous examination, then he must be legal. It is not up to me to administer justice." (Stumpy claims to have seen every episode of *Law and Order* and for once his television-watching had come in handy.)

Eustace becomes even more excited. "He must have snuck into the country. I can get proof."

"Then bring your proof to our meeting tomorrow. Until then I can take no action."

"But you agree that if Jason Barnes has committed a serious crime like this that it will be a Good Character Clause violation and the Barnes' estate shall pass to me?"

"I will have to research the caveats of the will again, Monsieur Youass Small, and I will have to investigate this proof you have. Until tomorrow, then."

"It's Eustace Small. And I'll have that proof tomorrow. By then that slacker will be considered a criminal in both the United States and France."

Stumpy walked into Aceau's building like the man in charge. After Eustace disappeared toward the hotel, Stumpy emerged and strutted back to me.

"Good job, Stumpy. That gives us a day, anyway."

We drove back to St. Sebastian.

"I'm hungry," Stumpy said.

"It's been a long day. Should we make spaghetti?"

We parked at the house. I could hear voices. "Change back to Stumpy, Stumpy."

"I'm Aceau."

"Yes, yes. I know. Just change back."

Stumpy rolled around in the back seat again and changed back into himself.

We walked around to the back and stopped. A long table had been set, overflowing with food and wine. I could see duck salad, roasted chicken, and buttered potatoes.

Sister Claudette, Sister Lucia, Laura, Betsy, Melanie, Jacqueline and her mom, Marjette, all sat at the table, talking, eating, and passing platters around. The sun glowed from behind horizon-hugging clouds. Dark would be upon us soon. A brisk breeze ruffled the tablecloth. The scent of roasted chicken made my mouth water. Neither of us had eaten since breakfast.

Two seats remained empty, one between the sisters and one between Jacqueline and Laura.

Stumpy and I walked onto the patio and the conversation stopped. I waved. "Hello, ladies."

Stumpy rubbed his belly. "Looks better than spaghetti."

Disgruntled looks rotated our way. We were late, and they were not happy.

Sister Claudette, Laura, and Jacqueline all spoke at once. "Where have you been?"

"Well, I, er, I—"

"Please, have a seat," Sister Lucia said, "And we can talk civilized."

Stumpy and I sat down. I sat between the good Sisters while Stumpy sat between Laura and Jacqueline.

"We had some serious business to take care of."

Silence.

"We had to go to Bordeaux," Stumpy said. My stomach sank. What was the idiot doing? He was going to divulge our cup-selling caper. "Jason had to fill out paperwork for his replacement passport."

I exhaled and relaxed. Stumpy's brainpower had increased over the past few weeks. Perhaps it was the wine. Anyway, the ladies nodded, satisfied with Stumpy's explanation.

"How was the vineyard tour?" I asked.

"Lonely without the vintners," Laura said.

Jacqueline shot her an angry look. My hopes that they would get along looked futile.

"It was lovely," Marjette said. She gave a warm smile, and I smiled back. "But we didn't get to see the chapel on the hill."

I gulped. I wanted to stay far away from the scene of my crime.

"And we didn't get to see your family cemetery," Jacqueline said. She addressed me rather crossly, I thought, like women do the longer they know me. "Do you have a big family, Jason?" Her head turned toward Laura. "I've been learning many things about you today."

Great. Just great. Laura could really talk, especially after sucking down the fermented stuff. God knows what she told Jacqueline. "Well, no. My Aunt Clara just died and that leaves me the last Barnes a-kicking. Is that right, Sisters? Are there any other Barneses still walking on top of the soil?"

Sister Claudette and Sister Lucia looked deadpan at me, and then at each other. "Barneses? Yes. I think there are still some in the area," Sister Claudette said. "I know there is a very distant cousin of yours in the Marseille prison."

Stumpy smacked his lips as he chewed. "Sounds about right."

I tried to kick him under the table and mistakenly kicked Jacqueline.

"Ow!" Jacqueline's eyes widened and she gave a look that made me feel like I did when a teacher would write "see me" on my homework.

"Sorry, so sorry! Leg cramp. It was an involuntary muscle reflex."

Jacqueline raised an eyebrow. "Like your heart?"

I stared at her. "Yes. Exactly. Like my heart."

"Pass the wine, please." Melanie cleared her throat. "How's your heart, Stumpy?"

"My heart?" Stumpy looked around. "My heart's good. I have a big heart."

"Big enough to lead two women on?" Melanie said.

Everyone stopped what they were doing and the table became quiet.

"I, I, I'm not sure how, what?" Stumpy looked at me for help. I raised my glass to him and smiled.

Betsy threw down her napkin. "Melanie is right. Make a decision, Neil. Tell her we are meant to be."

Stumpy looked back and forth between Melanie and Betsy, and then settled on Betsy. "Well, you see. I really don't know you as well."

"But we're a perfect match. The online form is never wrong."

"It's just that. Melanie and I met here, and we share the vineyard, and—"

"I love you, Stumpy," Melanie said.

Betsy stood up. "Fine. I wish you all the best. I believe I can catch the red-eye out of Bordeaux." She shook her head and rolled her eyes at Stumpy and then walked off toward the abbey.

I raised a glass. "To Stumpy and Melanie." Nobody joined me. I guess it was too early to celebrate, as everyone seemed to be feeling Betsy's sorrow. I drank a big gulp of wine. "So where were we?"

"I'd still love to see the cemetery and chapel," Marjette said. "I leave tomorrow evening. Could you show us in the afternoon?"

Traipsing through the cemetery and chapel was the last thing I wanted to do. Tomorrow was the big due date. I thought about all I had to do, but I didn't want to disappoint Jacqueline's mother. "Yeah, sure, no problem. Tomorrow afternoon. I look forward to it."

"Many tourists and pilgrims like to see our relics in the chapel," Sister Lucia said. "Jason can show you those, too."

I was swallowing a potato as Sister Lucia said this and I gasped. The sudden inhalation/exhalation whipped the round little spud snug into the old blowpipe. I tried to breathe and ask for help, but I could do neither. Everything became bright and the pressure behind my eyeballs threatened to expel them from my head. I hit myself in the stomach to no avail and then stood up and gave the old "I'm choking" signal with my hand around my neck.

Panic ensued.

A few of the ladies screamed.

"He's choking," Laura barked.

Stumpy flew around the table, nimble as a pro wrestler. He wrapped his meaty paws around me and squeezed me vice-like as if I was an evil foe, and thudded me with the trusty Heimlich. Pain shot into my ribs and the air in my lungs blew through my windpipe and dislodged the wedged potato like an exploding champagne cork. The potato piece, soaked with red wine, flew through the air and landed in Jacqueline's cleavage, which I had oddly been staring at as I struggled for life. Maybe I thought her breasts could save me.

Laura laughed.

"*Oh, mon Dieu*," Marjette said.

I tried to talk, but Stumpy didn't know he had saved me. He repeated the Heimlich, thrusting his fists into my solar plexus and lifting me off the ground. The jerking/lifting motion caused him to thrust his hips into my backside. He was frantic and did this over and over.

"Get a room," Laura said.

Stumpy gave up on the Heimlich and slapped me hard in the back. I slumped over and ran around the table gasping, trying to get away from him. Matthew and Mark appeared and jumped at my legs, trying to help Stumpy. Despite the protests of the others, Stumpy continued to chase me, like a man with a crazy-focused mind.

Eventually the Stumpy-gorilla and Jason-chimp chase ended. Stumpy looked confused and hurt as everyone laughed. He shooed the dogs away.

I breathed deep. I tried to console Stumpy and show my appreciation. "Hallelujah, brother. You saved me. A murderous save, but a save nonetheless."

Jacqueline looked at me as one would a broken horse that had to be put down. I suppose it would be rude to dislike someone because they were choking, but Jacqueline was appalled and unable to hide it— she had had enough of me.

Her mother blotted her blouse with a napkin as Jacqueline began to leave. "Goodbye, everyone. It's been quite a day." She walked down the drive toward their car, her mother attentively hovering around her.

I ran down the drive after them. "Jacqueline, please. I'm sorry. I'm a fool—an idiot—a total idiot. I'll never spit a potato on you again."

"Your wife told me how devastated you were after she left you."

It was true. I moped and cried like an abandoned puppy and I don't think I truly ever got over it until I met Jacqueline. "That's nothing unusual. I was upset, I admit."

"And she told me how you begged her to return to you. How you told her she was your one and only soul mate."

This was all true, too, but time changes things. What the hell was Laura doing telling Jacqueline all this old bottom-of-the-lake crud? "That was a long time ago."

"And she told me how she would now like nothing better than to get back together with you."

"She what?" I stopped moving my feet. I had spent years wishing Laura would take me back. I had longed to hear those words. And even though I no longer felt the same, the news had an effect on me that Jacqueline could clearly see.

Jacqueline stopped walking and stared at me. "No more words in that snap-happy mouth?"

"I, I . . ."

"I thought so." She turned and stomped off to her car.

Her mother lingered for a moment, feeling sorry for me, I think— I hoped.

"That was not fair. My ex-wife is crazy. Tell Jacqueline not to let the past ruin our present. Tell her I love her."

Marjette gave a look to size me up. I hope she could tell I was serious. "Jacqueline has good reason to be wary of your intentions. I think it best that you tell her." She smiled and whispered. "I will work on her. Come visit us in the morning."

I had never been good with parents and I don't know how I passed Marjette's motherly test, but thank God. "Thank you, Madame. I will see you in the morning."

I walked back to the house, shook-up from nearly dying and hearing that Laura wanted to get back with me, but mostly from Jacqueline not wanting anything more to do with me.

I walked into the kitchen. The Sisters stood side by side at the sink washing dishes. Laura was putting the dried dishes away. Melanie and Stumpy were placing the extra food into plastic containers. Sister Lucia hummed a tune.

I went straight for Laura, not caring that the others could hear. "I finally find someone, and you torpedo her the first chance you get?"

Laura held two plates in her hand and didn't say anything.

"For years you've been trying to set me up with other women. For what? So if I fell in love you could squash me again?"

She was strangely silent. What could she say? It was all true.

"And after years of groveling at your feet—once I inherit a vineyard you suddenly want me back?"

That got to her. "It's not like that."

"Oh, right it's not. I forgot. The asshole investment banker you jumped ship for is now underwater. You're a greedy pirate, Laura."

Her face turned red. She put the plates down and folded her arms across her chest. "And like you're not, Jason. That's why we got along so well in the first place, if I'm correct." She put her arms to her side. "But that doesn't mean I don't have feelings for you." She took a step toward me. "Real feelings."

I took a step back. "Stop it, Laura. You show up uninvited and thought I'd be all rockin' to take you back, but all you've done is cause a big mess. I'm sorry, but you have to leave, like ASAP."

Sister Lucia was nervous. She didn't like conflict. Stumpy and Sister Claudette, on the other hand, were looking on with a sort of pride, like they had been waiting for me to tell Laura off and approved.

Laura dropped her head and started to cry. "My life sucks. I've got nothing but two failed marriages. What am I going to do?"

Normally Laura's display of heart-wrenching emotions like this would have weakened all my defenses, but this time I remained tough, Rock of Gibraltar tough, something I should have learned how to do long ago. I hid behind my rock and lobbed my final words over. "I'm sorry, Laura. You know you'll always have a warm spot inside the J-man's heart, but I want you to leave. Stay the night in the abbey, but please leave tomorrow. If I don't see you, goodbye."

CHAPTER 22

I lay on my bed in my room, emotionally spent from my arguments with Laura and Jacqueline. I stared at a spot on the ceiling and tried to meditate. Jacqueline had every right to be angry with me. After being burned by a married man I wouldn't blame her for being nervous, or pulling back a little, or hell—even dropping me right then and there. But I wasn't married! Damn Laura for showing up. Calm down. Concentrate.

I stared at the spot. Relax. This is what it would be like if I were a monk; I'd be confined in a room and stare all day. I sat up. Or if I was in prison!

There was a knock on my door. Stumpy entered.

"Everyone gone?" I asked.

"That was tough, but you did the right thing." Stumpy fiddled with an old alarm clock on the dresser. "Melanie and I were wondering if you and Jacqueline would like to double-date for lunch tomorrow?"

"A double-date? Have we ever gone on a double-date before?"

"No," Stumpy said definitively. "We never had girlfriends at the same time."

I thought about our old days in high school. Stumpy was quiet and kind. The girls liked him as a friend, but few would go out with him. I don't know if any of the girls liked me, but I was able to whip up the dates through bravado and persistence. I guess Stumpy and I were an odd pair. "It would have been tough to find two girls who would appear in public with the both of us."

Stumpy laughed, but looked at me waiting for an answer to his question. I could tell all of us going out to lunch together was important to Stumpy, but I didn't see how it could work. "We have to wire the cash tomorrow. We can't be fooling around."

"That's in the morning. We'll be free for lunch."

"It's not that easy. Jacqueline doesn't even want to see me."

Stumpy looked at me like I was making stuff up even though he knew it was true. "Come on, J-man, you know you can patch that up. Now that you've gotten rid of Laura it shouldn't be too hard."

I felt flattered and grinned. "Jacqueline's a cosmopolitan woman. She sees right through my charades. And she's stubborn. I say again, it won't be easy."

"Oh you're killing me, Jason. The J-man's unstoppable." He danced around like a TV chef. "Talk her clean, mash and dash, whip the potatoes, and spread the butter . . ." I loved when he made up crazy shit like this. Stumpy waved his arms wildly. ". . . Pour on the gravy and it's Jason and Jacqueline Thanksgiving time." He slapped his hands together and pointed at me.

I cracked up. "They don't have Thanksgiving here."

He threw a pillow at me. "They will tomorrow."

"Okay, okay, but what about Eustace? He thinks he has that big meeting with Aceau."

Stumpy rolled his eyes. "So. He can have that meeting."

"How? I don't know how we can swing it. We would have to get rid of the real Aceau again."

"There's plenty of time. We'll figure it out."

I lay back on my bed and stared at the ceiling.

"We have to get rid of Aceau regardless of the girls. Come on, Jason, Melanie's leaving tomorrow night, and it's my last chance to see her. It would be great if we could all get along."

I could tell Stumpy was thinking about the future and the four of us doing stuff together—and that was nice, and I wanted the same thing—but I worried more about getting along with Jacqueline at the moment. He was right, though, we needed an Aceau plan, lunch with girls or not. "Okay. We can double-date."

Stumpy twirled around.

"Wait." I held up my finger. "Under one condition."

He stopped twirling. "I'm not dancing."

"No. God, no. But we have to be prepared at all times. We can meet the girls only if you dress in your Aceau costume."

"For the whole day?"

I started laughing to myself at his discomfort and the thought of him in the Aceau disguise for the whole day. "Yes, the whole day. We're not taking any chances tomorrow."

He closed one eye and looked at the ceiling with the other. "The disguise might make for interesting table conversation."

"I'm sure it will."

"I'll do it." Stumpy hopped up and did a pro wrestler's slam into the end of my bed.

The next morning I drove to town early, well, not early for the normal working person, but early considering I was visiting two women in a hotel. I wanted to try and see Jacqueline around nine so I would have time to return to the house to pick up Stumpy. At least Marjette had invited me. I hoped that she and Jacqueline were awake.

I dressed in my typical Jason Barnes costume and walked into the Hotel Duras proudly as myself. The café was busy with people drinking coffee and eating breakfast. A few kindred souls even drank wine.

I rested my elbow on the front desk and looked around the small empty lobby. Old black and white photographs were framed on the dark green-papered wall. One photograph showed a priest standing with many nuns, and another showed dignitary-like folks in front of St. Sebastian.

I took a step closer to have a better look.

"Monsieur Barnes, may I be of service?" It was Peter, the front desk manager. He had wavy blond hair and round, wire rimmed glasses. He treated his job like he was managing a luxury hotel in Paris.

"*Bonjour*, Peter." I was playing it by the rules today and going straight in. "Have the ladies in room twenty-three breakfasted this morning?"

"*Un moment.*" Peter rounded the front desk and went down the hall into the back kitchen. "Not, yet," he said as he walked back toward me. "Their cart is about ready to go up."

"Excuse me, Peter." I stopped him before he could return behind the counter and become more officious. "Do you think it would be possible that I could deliver the breakfast to the ladies in room twenty-three?"

Peter took off his glasses, and bit on an end with uncertainty, like he was calculating the pros and cons and how much trouble he could get into. I handed him some Euros. "I won't cause any problems. You know I'm good friends with Mademoiselle Thibodaux."

The old lanky waiter wheeled a cart out from the kitchen door.

Peter nodded toward the cart and waiter. "You may deliver the breakfast, but you must be accompanied. And he must serve."

Peter spoke to the waiter. "Monsieur Barnes will help you deliver the cart to room twenty-three." Peter touched my shoulder. "No tips for you, though."

I laughed and winked at him. "We shall see."

I took the cart and pushed it into the elevator. The waiter joined me.

"Shall I retrieve a third place setting, sir?"

"*Non, merci.* I'm talking, not eating."

He patted my back. "You should sing. The young lady likes your singing."

I looked at the old waiter. He was smiling. Clearly he had enjoyed watching my courting exploits.

I knocked on the door. Marjette answered. She wore a neat pantsuit and looked ready for a day of shopping and sightseeing. Shit. I was supposed to give her a tour of the chapel and cemetery. I'd have to figure that out later.

Marjette smiled at me. I waved my hand over the cart in a grand presentation. "*Voila.*"

She silently waved me in, excited. The waiter and I entered and Marjette pointed to the closed bathroom door indicating Jacqueline was inside getting ready. She signed the room service check. The waiter gave me a wink and left.

Marjette motioned me to sit down in front of a plate, but I protested. She insisted, and I had no choice but to take a seat at the table.

"Thank you, Marjette. I really—this is too much. Thank you for inviting me."

"Relax," Marjette said. "I had a quick chat with your friend Stumpy last night. He told me about your divorce, and other things."

I must have looked surprised.

"It's okay. He told me what a loyal person you were. How you stuck by him when no one else would be his friend. He also told me how you are giving him part of the vineyard. That is very noble of you."

"You can believe Stumpy," I said.

Marjette laughed. "And Sister Claudette and Sister Lucia spoke highly of you, too." She then looked at me with a serious, you might say threatening, look. "Jacqueline needs a loyal man. She doesn't need any shenanigans."

Now I must have looked worried.

"I know you are a funny, surfer-like man."

Surfer?

"Jacqueline needs a free spirit like you, but . . ."

Oh, boy, always the but . . .

". . . You need to be honest. You must be true to her."

"Yes, Madame. Thank you, Madame. I promise you. I will always be loyal and true to Jacqueline."

"I have some shopping to do." She turned and walked toward the door. "Good luck." She opened the door and left the room.

After another minute the bathroom door opened. Jacqueline walked out in a jumper dress. Her head tilted as she fastened an earring.

"*Bonjour,*" I said with as much good morning cheer as I could muster. "*Comment allez-vous?*"

She made a startled sound and then composed herself. "What is it with these breakfast surprise tactics? Is that what you American men do—scare the sanity out of your women before they can have a proper meal and think clearly?"

I picked up a petite baguette and put it on my plate. "I just love this breakfast spread. You're to blame, you know. You made me try it."

"I made you do nothing."

"Nothing?" I winked at her. "I remember doing some high stepping in this room."

She walked toward me, aggravated. "Oh, shut up, you bad, bad man." She was irritated, but I couldn't help notice that a slight smirk betrayed her for a fleeting moment.

I motioned to the other seat. "Please join me."

"Very funny. You are inviting me to my own breakfast." She looked around. "Where is mother? What have you done with *ma mère?*"

"Nothing. She went shopping. And to be truthful, she invited me to breakfast."

I could tell by the look on Jacqueline's face that she believed her mother had done such a thing. "Where's the monk costume? I thought you liked dressing up for breakfast?"

"I do. And I had this nun outfit on, but Sister Claudette chased me down and collared me by the habit."

She laughed, but then remembered she was angry with me.

"I told Laura she had to leave."

"No?"

"Yep. I told her to pack up and get the hell out today."

"You really did? Oh the poor thing." Jacqueline took a seat across from me at the table. "What did Laura say?"

I poured Jacqueline some coffee. "She cried and carried on like a spoiled two-year-old."

Jacqueline tore her croissant in two and took a bite. "And you still made her leave?"

"But of course. She was not invited, and she caused me too many problems."

Jacqueline's face betrayed her words. "Oh, that is simply horrible. You are such a brute."

I took a bite of some quiche Lorraine. "This is wonderful." I paused to chew. "I had to make her go. And she wasn't so nice herself—pretending to like me again after I inherit a vineyard. I'm not so stupid. I have to watch out for women like her going after the cash." I took a sip of coffee.

Jacqueline looked taken-aback. I couldn't believe she could be so concerned about Laura's welfare, but I quickly learned she had taken my words personally.

"Is that what you think about me, too? I mean, really! Mother seems to like you. Why? I have no idea. She thinks you're fun and have ideas or something, but if the rest of my family and friends knew I'd fallen for a farmer, an American farmer, oh la la the scandal!"

Scandal? Jeez o-mighty. The way Jacqueline talked it sounded like she was from some well-to-do family. Wow! Jacqueline might be loaded up with the berries. A rich girl! If that were true she might like me just for me. That would put her in a special category right there.

I smiled at her. "So what I'm hearing is . . ." I reached out and held her hand. ". . . You've fallen for me."

She pulled her hand quickly away. "Oh, you are an impossible man."

"I'm sorry. I didn't mean to be so direct. I should have said I've fallen for you." I paused. "I have, you know. I've fallen for you, Jacqueline, can you not see that?"

"Hmph," she said somewhat conciliatory.

"I'm sorry. I didn't mean to be so serious. I just, I don't know, can we just take a step back and start where we were before you got fed up with me?"

Jacqueline closed her eyes and then opened them slowly. "You confuse me." She reached out and we held hands again. "But yes, okay. I think I know what you mean. Let's begin again."

I smiled and squeezed her hand and tried to contain my joy. "Say, would you like to have lunch with me here in the café today?"

She shrugged. "Breakfast, lunch. We can eat all day."

"Oh, good. Thank you. And would it be all right if Stumpy and Melanie join us?"

"*Oui, bien sur.*"

I downed the rest of my coffee. "Speaking of Stumpy, we have an important meeting." I gave Jacqueline a kiss on the cheek. "I have to go. Shall we meet around one?"

She agreed. I left the room and I felt like the ship had been righted and we were skimming the sea. It was going to be a good day.

I closed the door with an uncontrollable grin on my face. I took one step and couldn't breathe. A thin rope strangled my neck. I tried to pull it off, but everything went blank.

CHAPTER 23

When I came to, I was lying sideways on the blue carpeting. A wooden desk stood along the wall. I saw a man's shoes. I tried to speak, but duct tape sealed my mouth. I looked above the shoes to khaki pants, a pink polo, and Eustace's geek-like mug. He sat on top of a black and yellow flower-patterned bed. I was in a hotel room, a Hotel Duras hotel room. Eustace smiled maniacally and stared at me. "Bonjour, Jason."

I struggled, but I couldn't move. Duct tape wrapped around my whole body and I looked like a handyman mummy.

"Today is the last day, Jason, and as of yesterday you still hadn't paid the court my damages." Eustace pointed at me. "I've been watching you. You're up to something and I can't take any chances." He stood up and walked toward the door. "I'm sorry, but to make sure I inherit the vineyard I'm afraid you're going to have to stay here for the rest of the day."

He opened the door to the hallway and made a great show of putting the do not disturb sign on the knob. He closed the door and I was stuck. I struggled for a few minutes, but had to stop as I found it difficult to breathe out of only my nose.

I rested and then rolled. I had the idea of making it over to the door to kick it and make some noise. I rolled twice and got stuck. Eustace had tied a bed sheet around my ankles and connected it to the bed rail.

I rested again and tried to think. I had time; Illinois was seven hours behind. I just needed to get to the BNP Paribas bank before the wire room closed at three. I rolled and struggled and tried to break free. The muscles in my torso cramped. Damn Eustace. Damn duct tape.

I thought about Jacqueline and Stumpy. Would they worry about me? Would they come looking for me? I tried to send them telepathic messages. I knew it was futile, but I still tried. I tried sending messages to Sister Claudette and Sister Lucia—Laura even. Someone save me.

Stumpy would have to figure out something was wrong soon. God, he was probably sitting in his stupid Aceau costume playing Gameboy waiting for me to pick him up. He could keep that up all day before realizing something was amiss.

And then, I admit it, I prayed. I prayed the most selfish prayer of all time: *Help me God to get out of here and inherit the ten million dollar vineyard and I promise to go to church every Sunday.* Like God hadn't heard that one before. But still, I prayed. I prayed the same prayer over and over and was unashamed.

The hours went by as I struggled, prayed, and tried to send telepathic messages. My constant saliva worked against the duct tape and eventually freed my lips. I was able to open them slightly. I stuck my tongue out and loosened the tape further. I worked my jaw and sucked the tape into my mouth and chewed. I chewed and chewed until a hole opened up and I freed my mouth. I could breathe, and the sensation energized me.

The ability to breathe regular helped my endurance, and I jack-knifed myself up and down until I jerked the bed over a couple of inches. I wouldn't be able to move the bed to the door, but I could conceivably move it closer to the window. I jackknifed and jerked repeatedly, and the bed moved a few more inches. As I moved closer to the window the sun's rays beat down through the glass, hot on my face, and I glistened with sweat. I struggled more until I had the bed about a foot from the window.

I arched my back and rocked back and forth like a seal. Once I got high enough, I landed my head on the bed. I buried my chin into the cushiony cover. I bit the covers and pressed down with my chin and pulled with my neck muscles until my torso was up onto the bed's edge. At that point I was able to move my legs underneath me, and I pushed myself up and rolled onto the soft pillow-covered mattress.

I wiggled close to the window and arched my head off the bed and rested it on the windowsill. I had a sideways view into the courtyard and café below. I tried tapping on the window with my head and gave a couple cries for help. This proved too difficult to keep up so I rolled back onto the bed and pressed my feet against the window. I pushed up and the double hung opened wide. A fresh breeze blew in. It felt cool and wonderful.

I rested a moment and then turned back around and planked myself so my shoulders were on the sill and my head stuck out the window. "Help! Help!"

People were eating and talking and waiters bustled back and forth. A couple people looked up but ignored me as a madman or else assumed someone else would take care of the annoyance. At least that's what it looked like to me as I could see no one interested in my predicament.

I heard the key in the door and felt instant relief; someone had come to the rescue. The door opened and shut. It was Eustace.

"Shut up!" Eustace grabbed at my legs and tried to pull me out of the window.

I wiggled free and kicked. He jumped on the bed and tried to put his body and arms around my legs.

I flipped out. Literally. In an adrenalin rush I made a spasmodic, chaotic jerk, pushed my feet against Eustace with all my might, and unintentionally vaulted myself out the window.

For a second I thought I was going to die, but then my feet jolted, and Eustace's leg rope held. I hung down the stone wall held by the bed sheet around my ankles. The bed was pulled up against the window and I prayed Eustace had tied good knots.

I swung upside down like a pendulum two stories above the ground and screamed. My shoulders and head bumped against the building until I stopped moving and the side of my nose and face stayed mashed against the stone.

Out of my one eye I could see Sister Claudette and Sister Lucia sitting at a table looking at me in horror. At another table there was Jacqueline, Melanie, and Stumpy. Stumpy, decked out in his Aceau costume, ran toward me in a blur. A trestle full of flowing vines rested against the building. Stumpy climbed up the vines like George of the Jungle, reached over, and wrapped an arm around my torso.

Eustace must have split as two waiters appeared in the hotel room window. They held on to the bed sheet and lowered me slowly.

Stumpy guided me down. His arms held strong around my stomach, but I was still inverted and my face bounced uncomfortably against his crotch.

"Not a word," he said. "One smartass comment and I'm dropping you."

"Not a word." Thank god for Stumpy. The good man had saved me again.

I saw Jacqueline running toward me, a frantic look on her face.

Stumpy worked me down as the men leaned out the window. I saw Sister Claudette standing below looking worried, her arms outstretched waiting to catch me. The old lanky waiter stood next to her.

They reached their arms up and cradled me, and with the help of some other waiters, gently lowered me to the ground.

Other waiters surrounded me and pulled on the duct tape and unwrapped me like a spinning top. The men pestered me with questions in French and English, but I didn't want the police involved so I remained silent.

"Careful," Sister Claudette said in a commanding voice. She kindly peeled duct tape off the side of my face. She looked at me with concern, like she really cared for me.

"Thank you, Sister. I'm okay now." I shook the lanky waiter's hand. "I'm fine. Thank you. Thank you." I motioned for everyone to leave me and to return to work.

Jacqueline stood at a distance with an incredulous look on her face. She shook her head slowly. I gave her a wink and a little salute. "Sorry I'm late—join you in a minute." I thought I saw the beginning of a smile, but then nothing. She simply nodded and returned to the table. Now that I was safe I think she was humored, but too embarrassed to be a part of it all.

Stumpy's beard was askew. I reached up, patted his cheek, and fixed the fake scruff. "Thank you, my friend."

"Jason, what—How?"

"Eustace." It was all the explanation he needed.

Stumpy helped me up, and we walked behind Sister Claudette through the café. My face had scratches. Duct tape fragments adorned my clothes.

Sister Claudette sat down at a table with Sister Lucia. I nodded to Sister Lucia. She nodded back, smiled, and shook her head.

I sat down and said hello to Melanie and Jacqueline. Melanie was going to catch a train and her suitcase sat ready to go next to her. I emptied my water in one gulp, refilled it from a carafe, and guzzled it down again. Jacqueline and Melanie stared blankly at me.

"Okay, then." Stumpy put his napkin on his lap. "Where were we?"

"We were wondering if Jason was ever going to show up," Melanie said. "And then he fell out of a window." She started giggling. Stumpy laughed.

Jacqueline remained stoic. "You realize as a French woman it is somewhat difficult, or embarrassing, to be associated with an American man who seems to have such a disastrous—"

I interrupted lest I have to hear a litany of my faults, "—A sense of freedom—a carefree love of life?"

Melanie lifted a glass. "As a French woman I recognize a man *qui sait profiter del la vie*. A man who really knows how to live!"

Stumpy lifted his glass. "Undoubtedly."

I held my glass up and we all looked to Jacqueline. Her lips curled up slightly. She put her hand to her forehead and rubbed her temples. "Dear God." She lifted her glass. "*C'est vrai.* To Jason. *Il sait profiter del la vie!*" She laughed.

If only Aunt Clara were here to hear this! I laughed, too, and the more we laughed the harder it was to stop.

Jacqueline finally spoke. "First Stumpy shows up dressed like Napoleon's banker and now this." She waved her hand at me. "You guys sure know how to put on a lunch."

I slapped my hand on the table. "Banker! Stumpy we have to go to the bank."

Stumpy leaned back and patted his protruding vest. "All taken care of Monsieur Barnes."

"Wait, what?"

Stumpy and I knocked heads and whispered.

"What do you mean it's all taken care of?"

"Just that. It's my bank account. I have your information. I took care of it."

"You wired sixty grand to the court for me?"

"That's what I just said. You didn't show up and I knew it had to be done—for both of us."

"And it worked?"

"It worked. I've a confirmation number and everything."

I looked at Stumpy. If the payment clerk notified Judge Crawford, that nasty conviction would be dropped and I could be considered an honest citizen again. Stumpy smiled proudly. Could it be true? Did he really wire the money? My shoulders relaxed and the tightness in my forehead disappeared. "You're the best, man."

Stumpy and I returned our attention to the lunch. "Sorry, ladies. We had some financial business."

Melanie and Jacqueline looked at each other and rolled their eyes. Melanie motioned toward the hotel. "Looked like you were into the business hanging on to each other over there."

Jacqueline's eyes went mockingly wide. "Big business."

The ladies looked at each other and laughed. Stumpy looked embarrassed, but still smiled, happy Jacqueline and Melanie were getting along. The food came. We ate and drank and had a good time.

Eustace walked out of the lobby. He saw me and then straightened when he saw Stumpy.

I gave Stumpy a kick under the table.

Eustace came toward us.

Stumpy licked his fingers as he told a story about throwing pepperonis onto a pizza. He needed to be in character. I kicked him again. He kicked me back.

"Mr. Aceau." Eustace stood before me, clearly rattled that Aceau and I were dining together.

Stumpy took the fingers out of his mouth and cleared his throat. "Ahem. Bonjour Monsieur Short."

"Bonjour. I wanted to make sure we were meeting this afternoon."

"Oh, I'm afraid I forgot." Stumpy looked at his cell phone, which impressed me because I knew he had no idea how to work the calendar. "Could we possibly reschedule to next week? I have a very important meeting at St. Sebastian with the Morceau sisters this afternoon."

Stumpy was brilliant. The longer we could stall Eustace the better.

"Perfect." Eustace nodded to the Sister's table. "I also have scheduled a meeting with the Morceau sisters this afternoon. We could all meet at once." Eustace stared at me menacingly. "I think there will be some interesting information from the United States justice system by then that will be very interesting to you and the sisters."

Eustace had thrown Stumpy in a box and he couldn't think his way to the outside. "Very well. If it so happens, we shall meet at St. Sebastian. But I am dining now, Monsieur . . ."

"Small, Eustace Small."

"That's right. Usedass Small."

Eustace's face turned red. "You're not getting away with it this time, Jason. Clara should have given me the vineyard straight out. I was always more of a son to her than you."

I stood up. "Aunt Clara raised me. We were flesh and blood." I saw Sister Claudette looking at me. I thought she would be angry with me for making another scene, but she looked concerned, sad even. "Six months, Eustace. That's all you lived with us and you think you deserve the world?"

"Six months, yes. But tell me. How many times did you see Clara this past year? The past five years?"

He had me there. "Maybe I wasn't so concerned about working the Last Will and Testament angle like you." He started to say something else and then stopped, probably deciding it wasn't worth it to have Aceau mad at him. He nodded to the table. "Monsieur Aceau. Ladies." He turned and walked away.

"Don't you guys ever get tired of those infantile ass jokes?" Melanie asked.

"No," Stumpy and I said at the same time.

Eustace walked through the café and stopped to speak with Sister Claudette and Sister Lucia. He waved his hand animatedly and they looked over at me. I looked away.

"That's your former stepbrother?" Jacqueline asked.

"My evil nemesis who is trying to steal the vineyard." I motioned to my scratched face. "He's the one who did this to me."

"You should tell the police. They're right there." Jacqueline quick nodded to her left. I looked over to the Sisters. Eustace was gone. Two gendarmes were now standing at their table.

"No. Stumpy and I will take care of Eustace in our own way."

"Is that why you're disguised as Aceau?" Melanie said.

"It's all part of the grand plan," I said.

Melanie looked at her phone. "I have to go."

We stood up. Jacqueline and I gave Melanie a hug. Stumpy walked her out to the sidewalk to a waiting taxi. They held each other and kissed. Stumpy looked overjoyed and sad at the same time.

The sisters paid for their lunch and came over to our table. Stumpy returned, nodded to the sisters and sat in his seat, downcast. I was curious and worried that the sisters had been talking to the police.

"Is everything all right, Sisters?"

They glanced at Stumpy and seemed unconcerned that he was in disguise.

Sister Lucia looked pale.

"No. Everything is not all right," Sister Claudette said. "Your former stepbrother Eustace is making wild allegations."

"He called the police?"

"No. That is another matter. Eustace wants to meet with us this afternoon. Will you be there to defend yourself, Jason?"

"I will be there." I nodded to Stumpy. "With my lawyer, too, of course."

CHAPTER 24

I sat in the abbey office with Sister Claudette and Sister Lucia, waiting for Stumpy and Eustace to arrive. I explained again how my stupidity and Eustace's malevolent actions had caused my legal troubles.

"Eustace wants to pinch the vineyard from me. He strangled me in the hotel hallway and mummified me up so I couldn't pay the court fine. Thankfully Stumpy came through for me."

Sister Lucia held her face in her hands.

Sister Claudette looked stern. She had her game face on and nothing was going to affect her.

"I've done some mean things to Eustace, and I admit, I overreacted when I wrecked his driving range, but we agreed about all that with Aunt Clara, and he, he,—he almost killed me. He'll do anything to get this vineyard."

Sister Lucia patted my hand. "We want to make sure the vineyard remains in the Barnes family."

I smiled at her. "Thanks, Sister." I appreciated their confidence in me, though I'm not sure I understood it. I guess it made sense—tradition was important to them.

"I don't understand why Stumpy still has to be Monsieur Aceau," Sister Claudette said.

"Eustace thinks he's Aceau."

Sister Claudette tapped her fingers on her ancient metal desk. "I know, but it doesn't matter any more now does it?"

She was right—as long as the payment had gone through, it made no difference if Eustace knew the real Aceau or not.

"It means a lot to Stumpy. He wants to see this through. And he's doing a great job acting; it's a treat to watch."

Sister Claudette looked at Sister Lucia. "I don't approve of deception."

"But like you said, Sister, what difference does it make?"

"I like Stumpy," Sister Lucia said. "And I like acting."

Sister Claudette considered. "Oh, all right. I don't care for this Eustace character anyway."

There was a knock on the door. Eustace and Stumpy walked in together chatting amicably.

I went on the attack. "That's him. He's the kidnapper. He tied me up and threw me out the window."

Eustace had walked in expecting to put on a show. My outburst took him off guard. I give him credit, though. He recovered quickly. His face calmed as he stared at me, calculating. I stared back at him, both of us waiting, wondering—who would be the first to draw.

"Monsieur Barnes has made some serious allegations about you, Monsieur Small," Stumpy said.

"Monsieur Barnes is a liar and a criminal. I've come here today to prove it."

"Go home, Eustace. You don't want me to invite the police in on this. I'll forget about the duct tape kidnapping and we'll call it even for that peanut butter shampoo Stumpy and I gave you in the fourth grade."

Stumpy coughed to stifle a laugh.

Okay, so reminding Eustace of the peanut butter shampoo was probably the wrong thing to do. Eustace's eyes narrowed as he recalled the famous peanut butter incident. "I was the laughing stock of the neighborhood."

"You took the biggest piece of cake. Aunt Clara was handing it to *me*."

Eustace charged at me. "It was my birthday!"

I lunged at him. "You tried to steal Aunt Clara from me."

Eustace and I locked in a standstill-wrestling match.

I heard a Bruce Lee type yell. Little Sister Lucia floated toward us and with a windmill of arms and spider-clenching fingers she separated Eustace and me.

Eustace straightened his shirt. "I'm sorry, Sister."

"I'm sorry, too. But he started it." I caught my breath.

Eustace looked more determined than ever. He chuckled viciously. "All right, Jason, but you're going down. Today is my day."

"Very well," Stumpy/Aceau said. "Monsieur Tiny, you have something to prove. Can we see this proof?"

"One simple phone call will reveal the truth about Jason Barnes. I assume you can help us out with the necessary communications, Sister Claudette? Do you have a fax machine or email?"

Stumpy looked around and walked behind the desk. "Here is a telephone." He touched the top of the receiver and searched the room. Sister Claudette cleared her throat. She nodded to a computer and all-in-one printer at the side window. "Yes, you can use the fax machine."

Eustace turned the telephone toward him and dialed some numbers. "Can we put it on speaker phone?"

"Of course." Stumpy pushed a button on the phone and disconnected the call. Eustace dialed again. Sister Lucia reached over and pressed a button. The speaker came to life.

"I had too much wine for lunch," Stumpy said.

A pleasant woman's voice answered. "Kankakee County Court—public notices and reports. This is Mary."

Sister Claudette sat behind her desk. Sister Lucia stood behind her. Eustace stood in front of the desk, breathing heavily trying to catch his breath. Stumpy and I stood together. We all stared at the phone.

Eustace spoke in a loudspeaker phone voice. "Hello, Mary. This is Eustace Small calling from France."

Mary's voice took on an exasperated tone. "Hello, Eustace. Making the daily call to check on the Barnes' case?"

"Today is the big day. I'm here with the French attorney, Monsieur Aceau, who is handling my late stepmother's will."

"Former stepmother," I said under my breath.

"*Bonjour, Madame*," Stumpy said.

"Would you be so kind, Mary, to fax over the automatic conviction notice that took effect today for Jason Barnes?"

Eustace smiled and looked around at us.

Stumpy said he had wired the money and even had a receipt, but still, I worried. I thought back to senior year in high school. Stumpy and I sat in a movie theater waiting to see *Star Wars: Episode I: The Phantom Menace*. I gave Stumpy money to go buy popcorn and he never came back. He mistakenly returned to the wrong theater and became so engrossed in *Notting Hill*, he didn't realize his mistake. I looked at Eustace. He was so confident I suddenly became terrified.

Why didn't I check the wire transfer? The odds of Stumpy messing it up were about the same as him ogling a short girl. I looked at the clock. Five minutes past three. The wire room was closed. Even if Stumpy wired the money correctly, what if the payment clerk notified the court I was in France? Could they put out an arrest for me for fleeing the country even though I had paid my fine? I chewed the inside of my cheek and ground my teeth.

Stumpy stared at the phone like he wanted to bite it. I kept forgetting he had a ton riding on this call, too.

We could hear papers stirring over the speaker all the way from Illinois like green beans in the hopper. "This is interesting."

"What?" Stumpy and Eustace said at once.

Mary's voice became chipper again. "There is no conviction notice for Jason Barnes, just the opposite. The conviction against him has been revoked. Mr. Barnes paid his obligation early this morning."

Eustace looked like he was choking down an ear of corn. His skin turned pale and his knees shook. He was about to crumble.

My insides screamed for joy.

Stumpy remained calm, ever the professional lawyer. "Ms. Mary could you fax me the payment notice and documentation of the revoked conviction? The fax number is . . ." He looked at Sister Claudette.

Sister Claudette said the number to Mary. Stumpy then ended the phone call.

"Thank you, Sister."

Sister Claudette put her hand on Stumpy's arm. "Thank you, Stumpy."

Eustace looked back and forth between Stumpy and Sister Claudette.

Stumpy ripped off his beard. "That's right. I'm not Aceau." He threw his beard at Eustace and hit him harmlessly in the chest. "Remember, me? Stumpy? The fat kid you used to make fun of?"

"Amen and Alleluia," I shouted. "The wine is mine and the good Lord can expect me on Sundays."

Sister Lucia clapped her hands.

Eustace's jaw opened and shut but no words came out.

Sister Claudette spoke with an authoritarian voice. "Jason, it appears this difficulty is behind you. You are now free and clear to inherit St. Sebastian." The fax machine made a click and a beep and pages began purring out. "We still need that passport. Any word from the consulate in Bordeaux?"

I hadn't told the Morceau sisters about the passport. It didn't seem relevant, and why add to my character flaws? "I should be receiving it early next week," I said confidently and truthfully. Since I couldn't find Hammersmith, I would have to call the court and have them send it to my apartment. I could have Lucky Mike pick it up and express it over to me. I'm sure he would be happy to get his own passport back.

"Passport!" Eustace regained his energy. "This isn't over yet." He pointed at me. "I know Jason entered this country illegally and I'm going to prove it. He must have a fake passport or something. Eustace looked at me sharply—and that is a Federal crime." He shook his finger at me. "And that is a Good Character Clause violation." He ran out the door. "And I'll inherit the vineyard!"

I shook Sister Claudette and Sister Lucia's hand. "Thank you."

"What's this passport business about?"

"Nothing you need to worry about, Sister."

CHAPTER 25

"We showed that bastard Eustace," I said.

"I wonder about him," Stumpy said.

Stumpy and I walked home immensely relieved after our meeting with Eustace and the sisters. What a wonderful feeling not to have the impending doom of prison hanging over your head. I picked up stones and flung them further down the dirt road. I picked up another one and threw it as far as I could. "Yes!" The blue sky, the green vines, the sandy colored road, they all looked so vivid. I was free.

"You better call the court first thing and see about getting your passport back."

We walked up the drive. "Number one on the list."

Jacqueline and her mother were waiting for us on the patio. We were supposed to give them a cemetery and chapel tour and we were late. I sighed. "Make that court call number two on the list."

Stumpy walked with Marjette, Jacqueline, and me into the vines toward the chapel on the hill. The vine colors were crisp in the late afternoon sun. Their leaves were a vivid bright green on their sunny side and a deep cool green on their shady side. The afternoon breeze had settled into wafts and the earth and air were blanketing us with soothing warmth.

When we reached the cemetery I couldn't contain my excitement. I showed Jacqueline all the pictures and told her the names of my ancestors that I could remember.

"Our family tomb is in the Père Lachaise cemetery in Paris," Marjette said.

"It is so crowded and dreary there." Jacqueline looked down the ridge and to the grand view of the vineyard. A gust blew and the tree leaves softly rustled around us. "I would rather be buried here."

Marjette frowned. "Let's go see the chapel. I really don't like cemeteries. Your live family members are what's most important."

"I don't have any live family members." I ran my hands over the vault and photographs. "This is my family."

Marjette turned red, embarrassed. "I didn't mean to be rude."

Jacqueline put her hand on my shoulder. She looked at me with empathy, or pity, but she seemed concerned. "You have Stumpy."

Stumpy punched me in the arm. "Yeah, bro."

"And Sister Claudette and Sister Lucia," Marjette said.

"And Jacqueline," Stumpy said practically shouting, his eyes open wide, the expression on his face implying it was all so obvious.

Jacqueline looked to the ground and spoke softly. "Yes, and me, too."

I could have hugged them all, but I felt too awkward. "Thank you. You all are very kind."

We walked up the rocky road to the chapel. The black Citroen and two police cars were parked on the side. One belonged to the local police. The other was a French National Police car.

Sister Claudette and Sister Lucia were speaking to the officers.

The two national police officers were serious and official-looking. They wore black SWAT-like jumpsuits and commando boots. They had a pistol holstered on the belts around their waists. The oldest one had award badges pinned to his left breast and gold epaulets on his shoulders.

The national officers spoke to the local gendarmes and looked like they had assumed control. They gave orders to the local officers who then left.

The award-decorated officer spoke with Sister Claudette and then spoke into his radio. He and the other national officer then left too.

We stood to the side and politely didn't ask either of the sisters anything about the police, but I presumed everyone wondered what the hell was going on.

Sister Claudette walked over to us. "Does anybody know of anyone who may have borrowed a gold chalice from this chapel?"

My knees felt week. "Borrow? What do you mean, Sister?"

A television news helicopter hovered over us for a minute and then headed in the abbey's direction.

"I was afraid of that," Sister Claudette said.

"Afraid of what?"

"A gold chalice is missing from the chapel. I reported it stolen this morning and word is starting to get out."

"Out of all those relics and cups someone only took one?" I rubbed my chin and couldn't help but bite a nail. "That's strange."

"The thieves were experts. They took the one thing of real value." Sister Claudette looked away to compose herself. "The Joan of Arc chalice has been stolen."

Jacqueline and her mother both gasped. "The Joan of Arc chalice. Oh, no!"

Sister Claudette shook her head and looked to the ground. "I know. I feel terrible. Only a few people knew St. Sebastian had it. I figured that if we kept a low profile and didn't surround it with guards and electronic contraptions it would be less likely to be stolen. And never did I expect someone to steal from a church."

Saliva was accumulating in my mouth and I found it hard to swallow. "Joan of Arc chalice? Is that a big deal?"

"The Joan of Arc chalice is a national treasure," Marjette said.

"It's priceless," Jacqueline said.

"Priceless," I said, softly. I looked to Stumpy. He avoided my gaze and looked to the sky.

Stumpy and I were silent as we entered the chapel. We stopped and looked at the relic shelf. Before I had thought one missing cup would be hard to notice, but as we all stared and talked about the Joan of Arc chalice, there now seemed a huge void at the end of the row. An intense pressure weighed on my chest. My stomach turned and I felt sick. I thought I might faint.

Stumpy looked to be having the same symptoms.

"The thief must be a godless, sinful person," Sister Claudette said.

Jacqueline shook her head. "An enemy of France. I shudder to think this type of person could be in our midst."

Stumpy wiped his eye. "It's just terrible."

"It was obviously the act of a desperate person," I said. "May God forgive them. But let's remain positive. Such a high profile treasure is bound to turn up."

Damn it. I was counting on nobody noticing one small chalice missing. I was going to replace it, eventually, honest I was, but nobody would believe that. The authorities would be able to track down the eBay transaction. It was only a matter of time before I was found out.

Sister Claudette looked at me proudly, which made me feel terrible. "Jason is right. We must pray for this troubled individual and for the safe return of the chalice."

"We should eat," Sister Lucia said. "That will make us feel better."

Stumpy perked up. "We can eat at the vintner's house."

"Wonderful," Marjette said. "Jacqueline and I would love to cook."

"The abbey pantry has Cornish hens," Sister Lucia said. "I'll bring some over."

I grabbed Stumpy's arm and we walked ahead. "Stumpy and I will go to town to buy dessert. Use whatever you want in our kitchen. We will see you soon."

We said goodbye and quickened our pace. Once far enough ahead and out of the ladies' sight, we broke into a run. When we arrived at the house, we jumped in the car and headed straight for Aceau's office.

Stumpy and I stood outside Aceau's office door. A man and woman came out of another office. They looked at us suspiciously and exited the building. Stumpy had his costume on. He adjusted his beard.

"This confirms you're an idiot," I said.

"I want to go up against the real Aceau."

"How can you be more realistic than the person you are portraying?"

"Acting! You be the judge."

Stumpy knocked on the door and we entered.

Aceau stood up when he saw us. "You, Barnes! We have a serious problem."

"I know. That cup your client bought—"

"Is the Joan of Arc chalice! You stole it from St. Sebastian."

I was walking a fine line here with Aceau. I would have to be careful not to risk my inheritance. "Someone allegedly stole it." I spoke slowly. "Your client has it. That would make him a prime suspect."

Stumpy assumed his Aceau persona, which I had to admit, was more dignified than Aceau himself. "We propose to reverse the transaction and return the chalice to its rightful owner." Stumpy stroked his beard. "We, unfortunately, must request a payment plan to return the thirteen thousand one hundred Euros."

"Who are you? I've seen you before."

"I'm Monsieur Barnes's attorney."

Aceau snapped his fingers. "The limousine in Bordeaux. That's where I saw you, but you didn't have a beard."

"He's in disguise," I said.

Aceau looked back and forth at us like we were nuts.

"You want the Joan of Arc chalice back for thirteen thousand one hundred Euros on credit? My client estimates the value at between three and five million Euros."

I sat down on the sofa, dizzy. I slapped my forehead. "Three to five million? Your client is a shark. He knew what that cup really was."

Aceau looked unconcerned. "You initiated the transaction. There is nothing you can do. My client is not interested in an exchange."

My eye twitched and I jumped up. I had to fight the urge to strangle him. "We could make this all public. You'd go down, too, Aceau."

"You'd risk being convicted and forfeit your claim to the vineyard?"

I sat back down and pulled at my hair.

"I didn't think so."

He had me. "Okay. I'll keep this quiet for now. But I must tell you something. My former stepbrother Eustace has been in town all week and will probably be contacting you to accuse me of passport fraud."

"I haven't seen him."

"Yes you have." I pointed to Stumpy. "That's why he's dressed up. We've been fooling Eustace. He's pretending to be you."

"Pretending to be me?" Aceau pointed at Stumpy. "He's me?"

Stumpy looked offended. "Why yes. I am Monsieur Aceau."

"He's a horrible me." Aceau pointed at me. "The car wreck! I thought that was suspicious. You were the monk. That's why you're bald."

I nodded. It didn't matter if Aceau knew the truth now or not.

"You're nothing but one deceitful wreck after another. Why would the nuns have anything to do with you?"

It was a good question, and I guess he was right, but I had to push my guilty feelings aside. "We will keep quiet on this chalice thing if you're good on Stumpy impersonating you."

"What about the passport allegations?"

"I will have a passport in a couple of days and we can notarize the inheritance and all this will be over."

Aceau rubbed his forehead. "I hope so. Is there anything else you've done?"

"No."

Aceau looked over at Stumpy. "He was me?"

"Better," Stumpy said.

CHAPTER 26

Stumpy and I walked around the house and onto the patio. The recently buried sun cast warm embers across the western sky. Jacqueline and Marjette sat at the table. Empty dishes and two burning candles were before them.

"Where's the dessert?" Jacqueline asked.

Stumpy and I looked at each other accusingly. We had left over two hours before on the precept that we were going to buy dessert.

Jacqueline looked at us suspiciously. "You missed supper. Mother and I made Cornish hens. We ate without you and then Sister Claudette and Sister Lucia left. Reporters wanted to talk to them about the missing Joan of Arc chalice."

My stomach churned. "We got sidetracked. I had to talk to Aceau about the inheritance." It was the truth, but not all of it. I hated not telling the whole truth to Jacqueline, but would she understand? Would anybody?

"I had a great performance," Stumpy said. "But I must admit there is only one true Aceau." He walked inside. "I'm going to change back into Stumpy."

"What's he talking about?" Jacqueline asked.

"His acting. I've created a monster, though I do say he has talent."

Stumpy called from inside. "We have to make that phone call about the passport."

I don't know why I kept forgetting about it. "I have to make this call," I said. "We'll be just a minute."

Jacqueline closed her eyes. "Mother and I are getting used to waiting."

"I'll hurry." I went inside and made the phone call to Illinois.

"Kankakee County Court—Public Notices and Records. This is Mary."

"Hello, Mary. This is—"

"I know, Eustace. You're my daily European call."

"No, this is not Eustace. This is Jason Barnes."

"Oh—the famous Jason Barnes."

"Yes, well. I've been informed my conviction has been revoked and I'm calling to see if you could mail my passport to my apartment."

Mary talked crisply. "Mr. Barnes, how are you in Europe without a passport?"

Stumpy came down the stairs. Holy shit. I covered the phone. I whispered to Stumpy. "I'm busted. She knows I'm in Europe because of the caller ID. What do I do?"

Stumpy's eyes went back and forth rapidly and then stopped as he hopped on an idea. "A solar flare has disrupted and scrambled all cell numbers." Stumpy nodded and looked proud.

I uncovered the phone and took on a calm deep voice befitting an international vineyard owner. "Ms. Mary. I travel extensively and I am using an international cell phone with an international number. I am currently at my Illinois estate and I am in need of my passport. Could you kindly mail it to me?"

I heard a giggle. "I see you live in Glenview apartments. That's right next to the Sunnyside trailer park, right?"

"Um, yes. It's very nice. I'm in the executive row."

"Mr. Barnes. I don't really care where you live or where you're calling from. I'm not mailing you a passport."

"Not, what?"

"We don't have your passport."

"I had to turn in my passport to the court. I couldn't leave the country."

"Not in this case. You weren't a flight risk. We didn't ask for your passport."

"Wait, what?"

"Whom did you give your passport to Mr. Barnes?"

I slapped my fist on the counter. "Hammersmith!"

"That lawyer who skipped town?"

"Yes. Thank you. Goodbye." I slammed the phone down. "Jesus Christ."

Stumpy put his fingers in his mouth. "What's wrong?"

I walked out to the patio and paced. Stumpy followed close behind, flustered. We ran into each other when I turned.

Jacqueline walked up and handed me a glass of St. Sebastian wine. "Have some wine. Goodness you are stressed. Is everything all right?" Darkness had almost set in. The crickets had begun their nightly symphony.

"Inheriting a vineyard is tougher than you think."

Headlights came up the drive. It was Laura's rental. Shit. I thought she had left.

Laura stepped out of the car.

I looked to Jacqueline and her mother. They were both alert, somewhat shocked.

"I thought she was gone, honest," I said.

"So did we," Marjette said.

Jacqueline and her mother glared at Laura. I could see their capacity for politeness toward her was over. "She'll never be gone," Jacqueline said.

I stood up. "Yes, yes. She will," I said with confidence. "She'll be gone and forgotten, soon. I promise."

Jacqueline seemed somewhat mollified with my determination.

I walked off the patio toward the drive, meeting Laura in the front of the house. She could see that I was angry.

"Relax, Jason. I just came to say goodbye."

I suddenly remembered. "Laura! You told me about Hammersmith splitting. Where do you think he could have gone?"

Laura shrugged.

"But Sheila worked for him, right? We could ask her?" I started ushering Laura into the house. "You have to call Sheila. We have to find Hammersmith."

Laura looked skeptical.

"Please. Just try."

We walked into the kitchen. Stumpy stood washing dishes while Laura used the old wall phone. She connected with Sheila and small-talked for a while before asking about Hammersmith. She then mostly listened. She hung up and looked in no hurry to tell me about the conversation.

I could hardly stand it. "Well? What did Sheila say?"

Laura savored her newfound knowledge. "I talked to her."

I opened my arms wide. "And?"

"And Sheila is not supposed to say anything."

"Say what? Come on, Laura. She told you something."

"All right. Sheila has been secretly reporting on Hammersmith to the District Attorney's office. She might have to go before a grand jury."

My eye twitched. "Okay, okay. And?"

"Hammersmith has been doing some shady things for years."

"I never liked that guy."

"Sheila says Hammersmith and Eustace convinced your aunt to put that Good Character Clause in the will. They were working together to scam this vineyard. You getting arrested right before your aunt died was the best thing that could have happened for them."

"The grapes were cooked!"

"Does Sheila know where Hammersmith is?" Stumpy asked.

"She doesn't have a clue."

I pounded my fist into my hand. "Damnit!"

Stumpy pounded his fist into his hand. "Damnit!"

"But . . ." Laura said.

"But what?" I said.

"But what?" Stumpy said.

I looked at Stumpy to let him know he was annoying me. He looked at me the same way.

Laura was driving me crazy, too. She loved watching us dance like fools while she parceled out morsels of information.

"But, she knows where your passport is."

Stumpy and I put our hands on each other's shoulders and jumped up and down. "She knows where the passport is," we both said. We looked at Laura salivating like ravenous bloodhounds.

She smiled at us.

I could have bitten her.

Finally she spoke. "Eustace has your passport."

"Eustace!"

"He took it with him to ensure you couldn't leave the country. Obviously he had no idea you had already left."

Stumpy and I let go of each other. A determined look rocked his face.

I felt the same. A fury of Eustace-hate bubbled inside me. "We have to make a plan."

We rattled back and forth recapping some of our more famous pranks.

"The snow cone blizzard."

"The corn cob crunch."

"The right field fence smackdown."

"The mac 'n' cheese slingshot attack."

Stumpy grabbed me by the shoulders. "The pillow. The pillow—" I grabbed his shoulders and we shook each other and shouted together. "The pillow corpse coffin stuff!" We slapped and bumped each other as we bumbled up the stairs quick as we could.

"Pillows. All the pillows."

"Scissors, tape, and belts—what else?"

I stopped. What were we doing? I wanted to be a vineyard owner and I was planning to attack someone with pillows and duct tape? There had to be a better way. I tried to think, but the bedroom wall suddenly twirled with red and blue light. I looked outside and saw three, four, or more police cars. Officers surrounded the house. The doorbell chimed.

Stumpy's head was buried in a closet.

"Keep working. I'll take care of this."

He stood up and bumped his head. "Ow. What?"

"Just stay up here." I walked into the hall and down the stairs. This was it. The cops were here to bust me for stealing the cup. I felt shame. The sisters would be devastated. I didn't deserve the vineyard; perhaps Eustace would be a better partner for the nuns, after all.

I walked down to face my fate when the gendarmes entered the house from all entry points. The national police force captain walked in and nodded to me with authority.

I was scared to death inside. This was it. Everything was going to come to an end. Still, I was good at this sort of thing, so I calmed my nerves and prepared for evasiveness. *"Bonsoir, Capitaine,"* I said, feigning innocence.

The captain walked right by me.

It all happened so fast.

"Get your hands off me," Laura yelled.

The gendarmes had Laura in a tangle and handcuffed her.

I ran to the captain. "What is going on?"

"After obtaining fingerprints from around the convent, we've determined that this lady's fingerprints are on the relic cabinet."

"I didn't steal anything," Laura said.

"Lots of people's fingerprints must be on the relic cabinet," I said.

"Yes, but hers were everywhere inside."

I thought back to how I had just grabbed the gold chalice and shut the door.

The captain looked at Laura with a mystery-solving eye. "Particularly the chalices. Her hands were all over the them. She must have inspected them searching for the Joan of Arc chalice."

"She can't keep her hands off anything." Jacqueline stood inside the patio door. She looked at Laura angrily. "You're the enemy of France."

Laura looked crazed. "I'm not the enemy, you Paris bitch. You're the one trying to get your hands all over this vineyard, pretending to like this country bumpkin from Illinois."

"Hey." I looked at Laura, but she was in cuffs because of me, so I didn't say anything else.

"Pretending?" Jacqueline said in a calm voice. "I like the vineyard. And I like Jason. The vineyard is good for Jason, and I believe he will be good for it, but money is not my goal. Money will never be my objective."

"Blah, blah, blah," Laura spat. "Aren't you high-and-mighty? Don't believe her, Jason. I know her type. Don't fall for that fake righteousness."

"Enough!" The Captain walked in front of Laura. "You talk a lot. Are you ready to confess? Tell me how you stole the Joan of Arc chalice."

Laura looked steadfast at the police captain. "I admit—"

The room became silent.

I waved my hands. "Don't admit anything, Laura."

Jacqueline looked at me shocked that I had defended Laura. I shut up.

Laura's eyes filled with greed. "I touched them all. I admit that. I couldn't keep my hands off them, but I didn't know anything about no Joan of Arc chalice, and I certainly didn't steal it. I mean the case was unlocked. Anyone could have taken it."

"We're taking you in for further questioning." The captain gestured to his men and they started to leave, taking Laura with them.

Laura looked at me pleadingly. I wanted to scream, *Stop. I did it.* I really did—but I couldn't. I couldn't give it all up. I still had hope, and besides, a part of me enjoyed seeing Laura hauled off by the police. God knows I went through enough pain because of her.

I spread my hands and shook my head. "I'll go to Aceau. Don't worry, we'll get you out."

Jacqueline shook her head. "You certainly stick up for your former wife, the thief."

"I really don't think she did it," I said.

The police left with Laura and all was quiet.

Jacqueline looked hurt. "I'm leaving."

"Leaving? Please, no. Don't let this bother you."

"It's been a long, strange day, Jason."

"No, no. Please stay. Let's talk. Stumpy and I will be outside in a second. We'll entertain you."

"Uh, no thank you." Jacqueline looked out to the patio. "Mother is tired—to say the least. We have to go." She turned and walked out without a kiss, a handshake, or a goodbye.

Stumpy stood at the top of the stairs.

"They arrested Laura for stealing the chalice."

"I saw. You just let them take her?"

"What could I do? Jacqueline was here. I thought they were going to arrest me. It was kind of convenient, actually."

Stumpy walked down the stairs. "*Convenient for you.* That should be your motto."

"Laura's my ex-wife and she put me through hell. She can handle a little questioning."

Stumpy sat on the couch, defeated. "I'm done. I'm going to confess. I'm sick of harming innocent people—the Sisters, Laura, the insurance company."

"The insurance company!"

"We wrecked that car on purpose. We robbed them!"

I put my head close to Stumpy and moved my face back and forth in front of his face looking into his eyes like I was searching for a sane person. "Stumpy! We're so close to packaging up this place. Come on, Stumpy, don't get all fucking philosophical on me now." I paused to let him think. "Let's go get Eustace."

Nothing.

I slapped him on the shoulder. "Come on, man, let's go."

"Go yourself."

"You're abandoning me now?"

"You're abandoning me."

"Fuck you, Stumpy, and all your honorable shit."

Stumpy looked hurt and sat down. I'd never been so mean to him.

"Fine. I'll go it alone." I walked out of the house and slammed the door. I'd do this my way.

CHAPTER 27

I parked the rental car in the alley and walked with determination around to the front of the Hotel Duras. The night was chilly, and the outdoor café was empty. Mounted iron and glass lamps burned a gas flame on each side of the castle-esque wooden entrance door.

I burst into the hotel lobby. An old man sat on the couch. Peter stood behind the registration counter. "*Bonsoir*, Peter."

Peter looked worried. "*Bonsoir, Monsieur Barnes.*" He came around front.

"Don't worry. I'm not delivering room service today."

"No trouble, Monsieur Barnes."

Peter looked to be trying to head me off but I was halfway up the stairs before he could get close. "No trouble," I called.

I walked down the second floor hallway and paused at Jacqueline's room. I had to fight the urge to knock. I had to stay focused. I had to find Eustace. I walked to Eustace's door and knocked. "Open up, Eustace. It's Jason." I didn't have a plan. I would just have to take him man-to-man.

No one answered. I knocked again and waited. I tried to think where Eustace would have gone. I decided to get back in the car and drive slowly around the town to look for him. To save time I walked down the back stairwell and cracked open the alley door.

There sat Eustace in our Toyota rental car. He was rifling through the glove box, most likely looking for evidence of my illegal entry into France. That grape rustler was watching my every move. He probably watched me enter the hotel and figured I'd be spending time with Jacqueline. Thankfully my Mike McCreedy passport was back in my room at the house.

The car trunk popped and Eustace got out to open it.

I slowly opened the door and stepped quietly onto the square stone alley. Eustace had his head in the trunk searching, moving his hands through empty wine bottles and vineyard tools.

I put a finger in his ear and grabbed the back of his pants.

"Ah!"

I shoved his head down and pushed his body against the car's open trunk. I lifted him up, knocked him into the trunk, and slammed down the lid.

"Help. Help!" he screamed.

I got in the car and blasted the stereo and drove. I drove back to the vineyard, past the house and into the vines. I followed the gravel road and rounded the ridge and climbed the chapel hill until I reached the cemetery.

I got out of the car. The cloud-covered night cast a darkness heavy and complete. The still air created an eerie silence. I could only imagine the gravestones and my family tomb in the blackness. I walked around to the back of the car and popped the trunk. I reached in and grabbed Eustace. He was trying to jump out so I used his momentum to pull him onto the ground.

I jumped on top of his back and shoved his face into the moist grass. We struggled, but I had the advantage. Eustace was wiry tough and stronger than I remembered, and I was out of shape, but I still handled him.

Eustace's cell phone had fallen out of his pocket. I grabbed it and pressed it into his back. "Don't move or I'll shoot, and don't think that I won't."

"We were brothers, once."

"Shut up!" I grabbed him by the hair and pulled him up until we were both standing. I still held the phone pressed to his back.

I pushed him over to the vault and knocked him down on top of it. I held his face against the copper plaque. "You see all those names. That's my family. Not yours! You were trying to steal my family, and this time I'm not going to let you."

"Clara put me in the will."

"Shut up. You pressured her. I know all about you and Hammersmith and your scam."

Eustace wasn't expecting that I would know this. He gasped and his body relaxed.

"You're going down, Eustace."

"What are you going to do?"

"I'm going to let my ancestors take care of you." Eustace had always been afraid of ghosts as a kid. "I'll bury you right in the back of this cemetery and you can plead your case to four hundred years of Barnes's souls."

Eustace flexed. I pressed down on him harder and pushed the cell phone against him. "Or maybe I'll let you go after you give me my passport."

He relaxed again, and I could tell he was thinking. "Give it to me now or tell me where it is. I'll have to tie you up, though, until I find it."

I heard music. The Star Trek theme song played from my hand. Eustace figured out the gun was really his phone before I realized it. His arms swung out and he rolled, catching me in the jaw with the back of his hand. I fell off the vault onto the ground. I pushed up and was halfway standing when Eustace kicked me in the balls. I bent over and he cross-hooked me in the jaw. I fell. Eustace ran.

Eustace ran to the car, but I still had the keys. I rolled to my side and pressed the small red panic button under the door lock. The car alarm blared and the headlights flashed. Eustace backed away from the car and ran down the hill into the vines toward the vintner's house.

I sat up and gathered my bearings. My jaw hurt and I felt dazed. I pushed up on the vault and tried to gather strength from my family.

I jumped in the car and drove down the hill. When I reached the grassy lane that cut through the vineyard, I stopped the car, got out and ran, thinking I could head Eustace off. I ran straight down the lane across the vine rows. My jaw throbbed. Sweat dripped down my cheek, and my side began to ache. The vines were rustling down a row on the side of the vintner's house. I stopped. I had missed him. Damn Eustace. I used to be the athlete. He was the geek. What happened?

I walked for a second to recover and then ran again, not as fast, but at a determined, manageable pace.

I saw the lights from the house. I attacked the last hill hard, fueled on by Eustace-hate. I'd wake up Stumpy and we could use the tandem to chase Eustace down.

Whack! A board hit my shins and I fell hard into the patio's edge. I screamed in pain.

Eustace stood over me with an old rusty nail-lined fence post. His face twitched with disgust. He swung the post high into the air and brought it down straight for my head.

Woosh! Thud! Eustace went down. Stumpy pummeled him with pillows and belts like an angry Stay Puft Marshmallow Man. Matthew and Mark leapt out of the dark and tore into Eustace.

I rolled over and grabbed Eustace by the legs to help Stumpy and his team. Eustace screamed, and then I heard the snap-ripping sound of duct tape and the shouts muffled. Stumpy wrapped an extension cord around Eustace's ankles, and I let go. Eustace was immobilized.

Stumpy and I stood up.

"Thanks."

Stumpy shook his head. "It was a difficult choice between two evils."

"Oh, come on."

"I'm still pissed, man."

Eustace moaned. He had pillows around his whole body secured by belts. Duct tape held a pillow over his head.

"Why so many pillows?"

Stumpy shrugged. "That was the plan, and it seems friendlier."

It was all a kids' game to Stumpy.

I put my knee into Eustace's back. "Where's the passport?"

Eustace garbled up some hostile sounds.

"Go get the plunger, Stumpy, and some spicy mustard."

The dogs stood over Eustace and growled.

Stumpy just looked at me. He wasn't going anywhere, but Eustace didn't know that.

"It's going to be a long night, Eustace. And, Stumpy, get the electric toothbrush and toenail clippers."

Eustace mumbled something.

"What?"

"S-pans."

"It's inside his pants," Stumpy said.

I started yanking down Eustace's khakis.

"Sxers."

"It's in his sox."

"Butsrs."

"Holy crap, it's in his butt."

Eustace struggled and yelled gibberish.

"I was right. Pull his boxers down."

Stumpy looked at me scared.

"Come on, together." I grabbed one side of Eustace's boxers and Stumpy grabbed the other. "One, two, three!" We yanked and pulled the boxers down. Eustace's white, hairy ass mooned the sky.

"Sbasser!"

"You see. Its in his ass."

"The whole passport?"

"It'd be just like him. He jammed it up there. Go ahead, check him, Stumpy."

"No way."

"Go on. Pretend you're a doctor or airport security. This could look good on your resume."

"No."

"Come on. How bad do you want this vineyard?"

Stumpy closed one eye and looked to the sky with the other. "Not that bad."

"Okay. Christ almighty. I'll do it." I stood straddled over Eustace and pointed my index finger. "Just a quick probe."

I bent over, grimaced, and lowered my finger toward Eustace's ass.

"There it is." Stumpy pointed. The top of a passport protruded out a pocket on the inside of Eustace's pants.

"Is it mine?"

"You check." Stumpy grabbed the passport and tossed it to me. It hit me in the chest and I bumbled it with my hands until grabbing it with my thumb and forefinger.

I opened the passport. It was mine, all right. In the picture I had messed-up hair with a sardonic grin, excited to go nowhere. I slapped the passport in my palm. "All right. Let's find Aceau and bag this mission."

"Are you going to confess?"

"Well, I, er. Are you?"

Stumpy looked determined. "I want to, but I'll leave the decision for you."

If the sisters found out I stole the cup our relationship could be damaged for the ages. And who knew what nasty punishment lay in store for stealing a French national treasure? Stumpy and I could be staring down years in a French prison. If only there was a way to absolve your sins without confessing. "I don't know what I'm going to do until I get there. You know that's how we play the rumble."

Stumpy smirked and wobbled his head back and forth in reluctant agreement. "What about Eustace?"

"I guess we should pull his pants back up." Stumpy and I reached down and grabbed Eustace's khakis. "One, two, three." We yanked the pants over his ass.

I grabbed his feet, Stumpy lifted his shoulders, and we hauled him up into my room. We threw him on my bed and tied him down with the extension cord.

Stumpy took the pillow off Eustace's head.

I grabbed the tape on his mouth and ripped.

"Ow."

"Duct tape don't feel so good, huh?"

"I'll get you for this, Jason." Eustace started screaming. "Help. Help."

I duct taped his mouth shut again. "Sorry, but I can see you will not be civilized." Eustace shook and mumbled.

"I have a vineyard to inherit. We'll release you when we get back."

CHAPTER 28

We drove to Aceau's house and knocked on the door. An older woman answered. She had on a flowered dress and black shoes. Her gray hair was cut short above her ears.

"*Bonsoir, Madame. Monsieur Aceau?* Is he here?"

She smiled warmly. "*Oui, Oui.*" She motioned us in.

We could hear Aceau's voice speaking French. He rounded a corner and stopped when he saw us. "Oh, no."

The woman ushered us into the kitchen.

"*Non, ma mère,*" Aceau said.

A rectangular white table was set for two. A pot steamed on the stove. It was ten o'clock and they were eating late like traditional Europeans. The room smelled rich and buttery. A small radio on the counter played classical music.

"Mother thinks you are my friends."

Stumpy grinned his stupid friendly grin that, I had to admit, sometimes worked on parents and such. He slapped Aceau on the back. "We are good friends."

Aceau sat down, neatly unfolded his napkin, and placed it in his lap, ignoring Stumpy.

Stumpy continued to speak good-naturedly. "You were my muse. I feel like I know you. I'm indebted to you for refining my acting ability."

Aceau's mother pulled out chairs. She fussed over Stumpy and me and sat us down. She set two more place settings out and despite our protestations served us sliced pork in a rich brown sauce.

Aceau's mother looked happy. She spoke in rapid French and smiled at us.

Aceau looked at us apologetically, embarrassed-like. "Mother is excited. I don't get many visitors."

"No?" I said.

Stumpy frowned at me.

"We want to confess to stealing the chalice," I said.

Aceau sat back and his eyes widened. "No." He wiped his mouth and slapped his napkin on the table. "My client would not be pleased."

"Tell him to return the cup, then," Stumpy said.

Aceau lowered his eyes and considered. "I don't know. It's not my decision. Please, though, no confessions just yet. Give me a chance to warn my client."

"Is that okay, Stumpy?"

Stumpy savored the pork, grinding his teeth as he methodically chewed. He swallowed and said, "Okay. But I think we should try and bail Laura out."

"Say, what?"

Stumpy looked at me steadfast. "You may not like Laura, but she did not steal the chalice. She doesn't deserve to be in jail."

I didn't say anything.

"Come on, Jason. Laura's from our hometown. We grew up together."

Drats. As much as I liked the idea of Laura sitting in jail, Stumpy was right. She didn't deserve it. "Okay, okay." I told Aceau about the police arresting Laura.

"I might be able to pull some strings at the station," he said.

"Thank you," Stumpy said.

Aceau's mother watched proudly.

I put my passport on the table in front of Aceau. "And I have this."

Aceau picked the passport up and examined it carefully. He smiled. "This is good—very good. Let's go to the office, make a copy, and notarize your inheritance."

Aceau was more excited than me. I couldn't have asked for a better response. "Let's go."

We brought our plates to the sink and thanked Aceau's mother as politely as we knew how. She smiled and waved, thinking we were going out to socialize, good friends of her son.

Aceau rode in our car. "To the jail first," Stumpy said.

"No," Aceau said.

"Monsieur Aceau is right. We have to notarize the inheritance first. What if you mess up and confess to stealing the chalice at the station? We'll be arrested and never inherit the land."

"I don't care," Stumpy said. "Laura first. It's a matter of principle, and if you want my silence that's the way it's gotta be."

Stumpy and his principles. It didn't make logical sense, but I could tell Stumpy was adamant. And who could predict what crazy stunt he'd pull if I really pissed him off. I would just have to hope he'd keep his mouth shut at the police station. "Fine."

We parked in front of the station. Reporters and camera crews waited disinterestedly on the sidewalk.

A gendarme guarding the door nodded to Aceau and let us through. The tiny three-room police station teemed with local and national police and officials.

In the far corner Laura sat in front of a desk. Two gendarmes stood behind her. An official-looking, lawyerly type woman asked her questions. Laura looked sullen. She saw me and her eyes widened and then glared. This woman had divorced me and torn my existence to shreds. I had wished her ill plenty of times, and I wanted to hate her, but seeing her there, arrested because of me, I felt bad, and I looked at her with pity.

Aceau shouted loudly in French. The lawyer woman shouted back. He shouted some more. I think he basically said, "I'm her attorney; stop asking her questions."

The lawyerly woman stood up and motioned toward us. The gendarmes escorted Laura over. Aceau kept up a nonstop verbal assault. The prosecutor did not look pleased, but she did not argue. She led Laura over to a desk. A policeman stamped some forms, and it looked like she was free to go.

Laura looked disheveled. "It's about time."

"It took a while to find Aceau," I said. "He was eating dinner."

Aceau spoke to the prosecutor. He then spoke with Laura. "They've released you to Sister Claudette's custody for now. The facilities here for women are limited. Sometimes the convent will house female detainees for the jail."

"Sister Claudette?" Laura glared at me like it was my fault, and I suppose it was. I looked away from her and saw Stumpy. He looked feverish. He shook nervously and kept looking around at the police officers and then at the ceiling. Good God he looked like he wanted to confess.

"Let's go." I nudged Aceau and pointed at Stumpy. Aceau ascertained the danger. "Out the back." He started walking down the hall. "We can avoid the reporters and take the alley to my office."

The gendarmes agreed and led us out the back door.

We walked into Aceau's office building. Our voices and footsteps echoed in the silent hall. Aceau unlocked his door and we filed in. Aceau sat behind his desk. Laura and I sat in chairs before him. Stumpy walked around the office with an air of ownership, like he was returning to an old, familiar house. "It was my first performance. Mark my word, Jason. This room saw the beginnings of a great acting career."

"Sit down. You're making me nervous."

Stumpy ignored me and ran his fingers over the books stacked high in the floor-to-ceiling shelves.

"The passport," Aceau said.

I placed the passport on the desk in front of him. Aceau looked at it and started writing information down on some official-looking forms. "The last missing piece."

"What? This is about him?" Laura said. "What about me? How are we going to solve this? I can't be stuck in a convent forever."

I stifled a laugh. "Might do you good."

"F-you, Jason."

Aceau continued preparing the paperwork and ignored Laura.

"I have to check into the abbey within the hour," Laura said.

Aceau walked to the computer desk area behind him. He took a metal stamper off the shelf. "Some official notary stamps and that should do it." He walked back toward the desk.

Yip yap barking came from the hallway. The office door flew open. Eustace raced into the room. His pants were torn and his legs were bloody. Matthew and Mark were attacking him. Feathers stuck to his sweaty face and arms. Black grease streaks were on his skin and clothes. God knows what Eustace had to go through to get here.

Stumpy put his hand over his mouth and pointed. "He's rabid!"

I stood up and faced Eustace. He dodged left and right and I did basketball slides back and forth in defense.

Aceau stamped papers quickly and loudly. He held them up. "It's done. St. Sebastian Vineyard belongs to Jason Anthony Barnes!"

Eustace growled and charged at Aceau. I cut him off and we collided, collapsing on top of Aceau's desk. Laura covered her head and screamed. Aceau held the papers to his chest. He ran back to the computer desk and fed the papers into a scanner.

Eustace tried crawling over me but I held on to him like a needy lover. The dogs circled and barked.

Aceau typed away at the computer connected to the scanner.

Stumpy yelled, "Geronimo!" I have no idea why, other than it was pure Stumpy. He landed on Eustace's back, crushing me on the bottom. "Ugh." The wind sailed out of me like it used to when I was on the bottom of a Stumpy-topped dog pile in grade school.

Aceau held up his hands. "It's done. Officially sent off and filed with the land bureau in Paris."

Eustace struggled for a minute and then stopped. "Damn you, Jason." A tear formed in his eye and then he let loose. He cried and sobbed and moaned in a pathetic display.

And then I felt what I thought I'd never feel. I felt sorry for Eustace. We were former stepbrothers after all. Well step-step-brothers. Or step-cousins. Oh, whatever. We had shared the same room for half a year. Sure we didn't get along, but like Stumpy sometimes says, who else are you going to stick up for in life?

Stumpy and I walked Eustace to the door. He continued to cry. "Easy, Eustace. I won't turn you in."

He sniffled. "You won't?"

"No. I don't blame you for going off the rocker on me. I suppose I deserved some of it."

Eustace looked like a kid again. "I suppose so."

Stumpy handed him a tissue and he blew his nose into it.

Eustace stepped into the hallway and I started to close the door on him. "Go home, Eustace. Forget about all this and get back to normal."

Eustace nodded and left.

"Safe travels," Stumpy said and closed the door.

"Good riddance," I said.

Stumpy and I shook hands. Aceau shook our hands.

"I'd like to transfer a percentage ownership to Stumpy. Is that a problem?"

"No. No problem. Does he have a passport?"

Stumpy whipped his passport out.

Aceau took it. "I'll print out the standard documents."

Stumpy and I shook hands again, smiling like new homeowners. "To us. The proud vintners of St. Sebastian Vineyard."

"You boys went through a lot," Aceau said.

We sure had. And I found it hard to believe we had actually done it. But still, I thought I would feel different when I actually inherited the land. I thought I would be more elated like I had won the lottery or something. I immediately knew the problem. Sister Claudette and Sister Lucia weren't here. I needed their approval, their blessing— their joy.

And my chalice swiping indiscretion gnawed on me. I had to convince Aceau's client to give back the chalice. I liked Aceau's mom, but Stumpy and I might have to work our magic on him if he didn't help us out.

The phone rang.

Aceau answered it and spoke in clipped French. He looked concerned when he hung up the phone.

"There is a news story out about the Joan of Arc chalice."

CHAPTER 29

"What's the news story?" Laura said. "Did they find the thief? Am I free?"

"No, but evidently the chalice was sold on eBay." Aceau looked knowingly at me. "For exactly thirteen thousand one hundred Euros."

"The thief is an imbecile," Laura said. She looked at me with that old "Where'd you go last night" look. I had made no secret to Laura that I needed exactly thirteen thousand one hundred Euros.

"They can catch the thief now for sure," Stumpy said.

"Apparently eBay is protecting the parties' identities right now. It might take an order from a court to force them to relinquish their names." Aceau tapped his pen. "All of France is up in arms." He looked at me. "It might take some pressure and some time, but I have to believe that eventually the thief's name will be known."

The sisters. I had specifically asked Sister Claudette for thirteen thousand one hundred Euros. She would immediately know I was the chapel burglar. My heart felt heavy, and I couldn't tell if it was beating or not. My shoulders sagged with guilt. What could I do?

Laura was livid. "I have to go."

Stumpy scooped up Matthew and Mark. "We have to give Monsieur Aceau a ride home."

Aceau locked up his office and we walked out into the cool night air. Stumpy and Aceau walked ahead.

Laura grabbed my arm and stopped me. "You stole that chalice."

"I, er—"

She looked angrier than I had ever seen her. "You stole the chalice and watched me get arrested?"

"Are you going to turn me in?"

She laughed sarcastically. "All you're worried about is yourself. I should, but, no, I won't turn you in. It won't be long until the cops figure it out and I will watch with pleasure as they haul your despicable little life to the slammer."

"Despicable?"

"Despicable, low-life, lazy, white trash. I can't believe I ever married such a weasel."

"Oh, come on now, Laura."

"I'm serious. Divorcing you was the smartest thing I ever did."

"Two days ago you said you wanted to get back with me."

"I thought you were going to live on a vineyard." Laura turned and started walking toward Aceau and Stumpy who stood waiting. "Now you're going to go to jail. And you'd fuck the vineyard up anyway I'm sure."

We caught up to Stumpy and Aceau and walked as a group.

Laura's words stung. I really was a loser. Too many kernels were popping in my mind. I needed to be alone. I needed to think. "I want to walk a bit," I said. "Can you guys pick me up at the hotel on your way back from dropping Aceau off?"

Laura frowned at me.

"Say hello to Jacqueline for me," Stumpy said.

I started to say something like, *No, I was not searching for Jacqueline*, but the gray matter was wobbling and I didn't have the energy. I walked toward the Hotel Duras a new vineyard owner and Joan of Arc chalice thief. I had trouble concentrating and accidently bumped into a man. *"Pardon, Monsieur."* The tension from the last weeks was too much to bear. It felt like some strings were unraveling inside me.

Stumpy was right. Jacqueline. I needed to see Jacqueline. She was strong, with good business sense. Jacqueline could see me through.

I quickened my pace and tried to gather my wits. I stepped through the hotel doors. Peter, the manager, stopped me dead in my tracks.

"Non, Monsieur Barnes. No more carousing around our hotel. Guests only please."

"Peter, have I not been a regular guest at the café?"

"When someone else is paying, I have noticed, Monsieur Barnes." Peter had a smug look and upturned nose. "But of course you are welcome at the café."

I turned to walk out. "No respect." I walked along the outskirts of the café when I saw her—them! At the far end of the iron fence sat Jacqueline and a tall man with a movie star-like chiseled jaw, cleft chin, velvety black hair, and sex-hungry eyebrows. At least that was my first impression.

The happy couple sat across from each other at a small table next to the short iron fence that separated the café from the sidewalk. I looked at Jacqueline, smiling, happy without me, happy with another man. A few more strings unraveled and the world tilted around Jacqueline's face. I got closer and she saw me. Jacqueline sat up and reared back.

I leaned over the rail and spread my hands out, placing them on their table. I looked left, right, and smiled at Jacqueline and the princely man. "What have we here—a romantic dinner for two at the Café Duras? What a novel idea."

"Jason, please."

"From one man's arms to another." I looked around wildly to the church steeple that contained the town clock. "What's it been, a couple of hours?"

"Jason!"

Handsome man looked me over. He had a confident air about him. He acted unafraid and unconcerned with my hostile demeanor. "Is this him?"

"The prince speaks."

"I think you should leave, sir."

I pointed my finger at him. "That, my friend, is exactly what I am not going to do."

The lanky waiter walked by and glanced at me. Our eyes locked. He shook his head slightly as if he were admonishing me, or warning me, or willing me to move on to save myself.

"Has she told you about the room service breakfast yet?"

"Jason!"

"If she does . . ." I gave the stud a wink. ". . . It's a done deal. You're in. And the breakfast is good, too, I must admit."

A strong hand clasped my shirt at the neck. I gasped. The beautiful man was tough. His face pulsed with anger.

"Please, no, Francois," Jacqueline said.

"Please, no, Francois," I said in a mocking tone.

Francois. Of course he was the gallant Francois, the complete antithesis to Jason Barnes.

Francois remained seated and pulled me forcefully down toward him. I did not resist. I felt hollow and oddly wanted the punishment. Life didn't matter. I had lost Jacqueline and was going to prison. I let Francois pull me toward him. As my face lowered, I stared into his plate filled with deep red beef bourguignon. My favorite—beef bourguignon. Why not? I hated myself. I pushed my head down through Francois's hands and slammed my face into his beef bourguignon. I lifted my head and slammed my face down again. I repeatedly smashed my face into the rich meaty sauce.

Jacqueline screamed.

The other diners screamed.

Beef bourguignon splattered everywhere.

Francois grabbed me by the back of my hair and yanked me upright. My face dripped in a bloody beefy mess.

"I am the owner of St. Sebastian Vineyard," I yelled to the café. "I am a vintner. I am a vintner and I am nothing."

Francois punched me in the stomach and I doubled over and sat on the sidewalk. My back leaned against the iron fence.

Jacqueline stood up and leaned over the fence, concerned. "Are you okay, Jason?"

I heard a call from the street. "Jason." Our rental car lurched to a stop as Stumpy parked it along the curb. Stumpy and Laura ran from the car and kneeled by me. Matthew and Mark barked from the window

"Fabio attacked me," I mumbled.

Jacqueline looked at Laura. "The police let you go?"

Laura mustered all the smugness she was capable. "Turns out I'm not the thief." She nodded toward me. "Turns out someone was robbing his own cupboard."

"No." Jacqueline reached over and touched my head. "Jason, tell me you didn't steal the chalice?"

They lifted me off the ground. I stood with my hands on my knees. I bowed my head. "I'm sorry, Jacqueline."

Jacqueline looked at me with anger and pity. "You have serious problems, Jason." Her scolding was too much to suffer. I stood up straight and felt tired and dizzy. Jacqueline was writing me off forever. "I think you should talk to a psychiatrist," she said.

My knees wobbled and everything went black.

Someone held me, rocked me, and it felt so warm. I saw Stumpy as a kid chasing me on his bike with a water balloon. I felt Aunt Clara kiss me on my wedding day before I turned to Laura, her eyes sparkling. I saw Sister Lucia smiling and Sister Claudette proudly holding up a grape cluster. I saw Jacqueline; her long black hair fell loosely onto her shoulders, as she looked deep into my eyes. She leaned in and kissed me, a warm tender kiss, with lips full of love. I reached up and tenderly ran my hand over her stubbly, bearded face.

I opened my eyes. "Ah!" Francois was making out with me. "Ah!" I pushed him away and sat up.

"Relax, man," Stumpy said. "He was giving you mouth to mouth." I wiped my mouth and spit.

"*Mon frère*, Francois, is a doctor," Jacqueline said.

"Of course he is." Wait. *Frère*? "Say, what? Brother!"

Francois had meat sauce around his lips. He held my wrist, monitoring my pulse. "Only a fainting spell, but I took no chances. I was worried it might be your heart."

The lanky waiter stood over me. He had a towel and wiped my face.

I looked to Jacqueline. She looked at me with sad eyes. "You saved your wife? You stole the chalice from the church? From France? What about Sister Lucia and Sister Claudette? Do you not care one bit for them? Do you not care one bit for me? What I would think? How could I possibly be with a man like you?"

I looked down. I couldn't face her. Jacqueline was done with me for good. "It is my heart," I whispered.

Stumpy helped me up. "You've had a long day, buddy. Let's go home."

I sat in the back seat with Laura and we drove off. I owned the vineyard and I was worthless.

CHAPTER 30

I felt dead to the world when we reached St. Sebastian. Jacqueline was right. I was a low-life. How could she be with a man like me?

A lone figure stood under our porch light. "Melanie!" Stumpy shouted.

Melanie sat on her suitcase by the front door. Stumpy tumbled out of the car and ran toward her. They kissed and embraced. Laura and I got out of the car and looked on at the happy couple. Their innocence and love was hard not to appreciate and their joy at seeing each other again brought a smile to both of us.

"My schedule was changed. I've got three days." Stumpy opened the door and Melanie quickly entered the house. "I don't want the sisters to see me. I'm not spending the night in the abbey."

I arched my eyebrow at Stumpy in response to Melanie's planned sleeping arrangement.

He arched his eyebrow back at me.

I walked in and plopped down on the couch. Stumpy opened a bottle of wine. Melanie clung to him. Laura stood awkwardly in the entranceway. I think she was torn from despising me and wanting to help me. I couldn't care less.

The phone rang.

"Yes, Sister," Stumpy said. "I will send her over." He hung up and looked knowingly at Laura.

Laura stared at me accusingly. "Back to Catholic prison. I hope they catch the thief soon. I can't take Sister Claudette for long." She turned and walked out.

After Laura left, Stumpy, Melanie, and I drank wine and small-talked, but I could tell they wanted to be alone.

Stumpy went to open another bottle of wine and I followed him into the kitchen. "I'm sleeping in the shed, man."

"You are?"

I slapped him on the shoulder. "I am. I've an all night project to work on, so the house is all yours."

Stumpy looked excited but worried at the same time. "You shouldn't be alone, Jason. You've been acting strange."

"I'm fine." I slapped him again. "You're the man."

He smiled and nodded.

I walked out the back door and onto the patio. I stepped off the cement and scooted my way down the grassy slope to the vineyard. I passed the shed and kept going. The night was warm and sticky, the air silent, the vines asleep. I walked slowly, without direction, running my hands across the wet leaves, kicking an occasional vine post to make sure it was steady. The vineyard was mine and I was soon to be caught.

I rounded the ridge and I could no longer see the lights from the abbey or the house. The lackluster stars flitted around dull clouds.

Jacqueline had had it with me, and who could blame her? I walked up the hill and stopped at the cemetery. I sat on the family tomb and wondered how many guilty Barnes souls there were.

I stood up and looked out. I could only see a few feet ahead of me in the moonless night. The blackness further oppressed me. I clenched my fists and spread my arms. "Stella!" I shouted to the universe because it made no sense and felt right.

I walked up to the chapel and quietly opened the door. Dim lights illuminated the front altar area. I kneeled by the relic cabinet. There was a note on one of the glass doors: *Like the Kingdom of Heaven, the doors remain open. May the person who has our chalice find it in their heart to return it to its rightful place.* Ugh. I felt like shit. If only I could return it. I opened the cabinet and looked over the other cups. Why did I have to choose the Joan of Arc chalice?

I closed the cabinet and sat down in the last pew. It was dark and the glowing altar looked religious and holy and special, like it was meant to. I sat and stared and became mesmerized by the light and dark and silence.

My soul calmed. I knew what I had to do. I lay down on the cold wooden pew. The darkness was eerie and comforting at the same time. I closed my eyes and fell asleep.

CHAPTER 31

I awoke to a prayer.

A barely perceptible glow emanated from the chapel's east stained glass window as the rising sun's rays reached out, cheering me slightly. A heavy tension weighed on my shoulders and chest. I ached to rid myself of this oppressive guilt.

A nun knelt before the altar fervently speaking to God.

I sat up quietly and clasped my hands and bowed my head in sympathy. I would wait until the prayer was over before I announced my presence.

The nun spoke louder. It was Sister Claudette. "Please forgive me, Lord, for I have sinned." Sister Claudette paused and I could hear her crying. How could this be? Sister Claudette was the most sinless person I had ever known.

"I pray for the lost soul of Jason Anthony Barnes. Forgive me Lord for I have failed." She cried more, harder and longer.

I stood up. "Are you okay, Sister?"

Sister Claudette whipped around, startled at first, but she relaxed when she recognized me.

I walked gingerly toward the altar. "I'm sorry, Sister. I didn't mean to intrude, but I was sleeping in a pew."

She wiped her eyes and stared at me.

"I had some praying to do," I explained.

She smiled slightly. "Yes, I can imagine."

"You know then?"

She nodded. "Thirteen thousand one hundred Euros."

I looked to the ground. "I'm so sorry, Sister. I let you down."

"It is I who have let you down, Jason."

I laughed. "How can that be? You've nothing to do with my selfish behavior."

Sister Claudette looked to the ground and started to cry again.

Her crying was more than I could endure. "I've thought on it, Sister, and this is what I want to do. Monsieur Aceau notarized the will last night and I officially inherited the vineyard."

She nodded. "Yes, I heard."

"But I don't want it. I don't deserve it. I'm giving the vineyard to the church, to you and the abbey, and all the good nuns who have cared for the land."

She stared through me as if assessing my sincerity.

"I love this land, but I've messed up here. I want to pay the convent back for the chalice and return to my old life if possible. I was hoping you might not press charges and help me out with the police."

She continued to stare. "I don't want the land."

"Don't, what?"

"The land is yours. You keep it."

"But the church. How can you refuse? The church will want the land. And I have to atone for my sins."

"I will atone for your sins. Your sins are my sins. I'm sure the church does want the land, but I want you to have it. The land must stay with the family."

"You're confusing me, Sister."

Sister Claudette took my hands into hers. "I'm sorry, Jason. I haven't been forthcoming. For thirty-two years I have been a silent coward. Your parents did not die in a car crash. We have lied to you. You see, Jason, my son. I am your mother."

The right side of my body had a spasm. It was difficult to breathe.

Sister Claudette cried. She hugged me tight and buried her face in my chest and sobbed. I wrapped my arms around her tentatively, uncertain and shocked to the core. I felt love and happiness, but at the same time had questions, anger and resentment. I was conflicted and tormented and confused and . . . overjoyed.

I heard crying behind me. I turned around and saw Sister Lucia. I looked to her and Sister Claudette and immediately recognized Aunt Clara in them. How stupid of me not to have seen the resemblance before.

"And so you're my aunt?"

Sister Lucia wrapped her arms around me and cried. "I've so waited for this day."

I hugged Sister Lucia. She was always so good and kind, and she had not abandoned me. I had no misgivings toward Sister Lucia, only love. I hugged her tight and cried and felt her good soul.

The chapel warmed with the brightening sun. The three of us stood staring and smiling at each other, not knowing what to say.

"I have so many questions."

"I became pregnant with you when I was seventeen." Sister Claudette had a faraway look in her eye. "My father was furious and embarrassed and sent me off to live with my sister Clara in the United States to have the baby in secret." She paused. "To have you, that is."

I was thinking too many things at once. "So you two are Barneses too?"

"Yes," Sister Lucia said. "We three sisters grew up in the vintner's house." She clapped her hands, thrilled. "Clara and I shared Stumpy's room."

I thought of Stumpy and Melanie in that room right now and felt a twinge of guilt.

"We changed our name when we became nuns." Sister Lucia looked fondly at Sister Claudette. "But we chose the same last name because we still wished to feel like real sisters."

"I was supposed to put you up for adoption in the United States and return home, but—"

"But she loved you so much, she couldn't bear to do it and instead convinced Clara to keep you."

"Practically forced Clara," Sister Claudette said.

"That makes sense," I said.

"But I did love you. I have always loved you. Our father was—"

"Overbearing," Sister Lucia said. "It was impossible to go against him."

"Upon my return he made me enter the convent."

"And I followed soon after." Sister Lucia smiled. "But I wanted to. I always loved the nuns growing up and wanted to be just like them."

"And here we are," Sister Claudette said.

Sister Lucia clapped her hands again. "Yes, here we are. The last of the Barneses."

I sat down on a pew. It all felt right, but accepting the fact that my parents were not dead would take some time to get used to. "And my father?"

Sister Claudette sighed. "A local boy. His life went on. He came to the states for your birth, but he believes you were given up for adoption."

"And he is still here?"

Sister Claudette nodded. "One thing at a time."

I hadn't considered the ramifications for Sister Claudette. She was Mother Superior of a convent. What would happen if everyone found out she had had a love child? "We can still keep the secret,

Sister. You are the Mother Superior. It would not be strange for me to call you mother?"

Sister Claudette bowed her head. "It is up to you, but I would be honored and it would give me great joy."

My insides crumbled. The lost son was home. Tears flowed from my eyes. "Okay, sure. Thank you, Mother." I cried.

Sister Lucia cried.

My mother cried. We three embraced as one, the remaining Barnes family. I felt eternal.

"You see why I want you to keep the land," Sister Claudette said. "We are part of the church, but we are Barneses at heart, too."

"We want you to have a big family." Sister Lucia's tearful red eyes began to shine. "The vineyard needs the Barnes spirit now and in the future as well."

Wow. I'd just found my mother and I was already getting the marriage/family pressure.

Sister Claudette put her hand on my shoulder. "You can live as you want, Jason. I realize marriage and family might not be your style. I am happy just to be near you, finally."

I thought of Laura and Jacqueline and smashing my face into Francois's dinner. "I'm not sure what my style is. I might be too selfish and greedy to have a family."

"You have a good soul," Sister Lucia said.

"I take responsibility for your faults," Sister Claudette said. "Clara had her hands full with you. She loved you, yes, but I think she had her own regrets."

"I'm not sure what you're driving at, Sister, er Mother, but I've recently been told to see a psychiatrist. Maybe all I need to do is talk to you."

The sisters laughed.

"Of course," Sister Claudette said. "All humor aside, I would like that."

"I still need to pay the church back for the chalice. If I could have a living allowance I'd like to give the rest of my profits to the church until I repay the chalice's value."

"That will take some time."

"So be it. I don't need much."

The sun now beamed in at full strength. Dust particles floated contentedly in the warm rays. The wind blew outside causing the wood door to creak.

"Okay, Jason," Sister Claudette said. "I like your conviction. You shall repay the church."

I nodded and accepted the plan. It felt good and right. And then I thought of the police and felt anxious. "What about the French police? They will run me down soon enough."

Sister Claudette pursed her lips. "Hmm. We will have to think about that."

Sister Lucia looked ready to explode. She twittered excitedly and smiled. "I took care of the police. The case is closed."

Sister Claudette looked shocked.

"Say, what?"

Sister Lucia did a little hop and motioned toward the relic cabinet. "After all, the Joan of Arc chalice has been returned."

Sister Claudette and I did a quick jerk and extended our necks to see the cabinet. Sure enough the Joan of Arc chalice sat in its spot, basking in glorious sunshine.

"How? What? Where?"

Sister Lucia clapped her hands and laughed. "I had the chalice the whole time. I bought it on eBay for thirteen thousand—"

"One hundred Euros." I ran to the cabinet. Sister Lucia opened the door. I took out the chalice and held it up and inspected it. I clutched it to my chest and returned to the sisters. "We have to lock this up. There are thieves out there."

The sisters laughed.

"That is a good idea." Sister Claudette rubbed her chin in thought. "We can put the chalice in the abbey safe for now."

"We could make a high-tech secure cabinet and put the chalice on display. Think of the tourists it would draw to the vineyard. Think of the donations and wine sales. We'll put out a little cash donation box right next to the display."

The sisters smiled. We exited the chapel into the warm day and blue sky. I leaned up against the Citroen. "How'd you know to buy the chalice on eBay?"

Sister Lucia became serious. "I saw you, Jason. I saw you take the chalice."

I was surprised and must have looked so.

Sister Lucia looked at the chapel. "I like to sit in the back pew, too. The dark is calming."

"I'm sorry, Sister."

"I watched your place like a hawk the next day and when I saw Stumpy he could talk of nothing else but an eBay auction and I knew."

"Why didn't you stop me?"

Sister Lucia smiled. "Simple. I wanted you to own the vineyard."

Sister Claudette looked stern. She was a straight shooter and this scheme probably seemed wrong to her. She shook her head and then a slow smile worked across her face. She laughed. "I so wanted to give you the money. Maybe God wanted me to as well. He had to work around me, though." She chuckled some more. "But where did you get thirteen thousand Euros, Lucia?"

"Thirteen thousand one hundred Euros," I said.

"I had a little saved," Sister Lucia said.

Sister Claudette looked at her suspiciously because she knew Sister Lucia did not have that kind of money.

"And I have friends that loaned me the extra."

Sister Claudette again gave her the eye. "What friends?"

"Friend, actually." Sister Lucia blushed. "Monsieur Aceau and I were sweet on each other when we were young, if you remember?"

Sister Claudette nodded and said a knowing, "Ah." She smiled. "I remember."

Aceau! He knew the whole time. That's why he was so agreeable and wanted to file the inheritance papers quickly. I had new respect for the man.

The sisters offered me a ride, but I wanted to be alone for a while to ponder all that had happened. They understood and drove back to the abbey, Sister Lucia holding the chalice in her lap.

I started to walk back. I walked and then I ran. I ran down the hill and into the vineyard with my arms out. I sang, "*The hills are alive with the sound of music.*" The song felt right. The vines swayed in the breeze and applauded my victory run. They lifted up and then lazily fell in a forgiving wave. The vineyard was mine and I felt it was accepting me, blessing me. I was one with the land, one with the vines, one with my ancestors, and one with my new family. I had a mother and a friendly aunt. I had the best friend in the world.

The long joyous run made me feel content, like I had arrived to my fated place in life. I ran hard up the final hill to the patio and house. I was sweaty and spent.

I walked through the front door. I had been out the whole night. I was hung-over with emotion. I marched up the stairs elated.

I kicked open Stumpy's door euphoric to tell him the news. Holy Carnivale! I forgot Melanie was there. I saw what I shouldn't have seen. What I hope never to see again—a roller derby of twisting dough-like smashing flesh—Stumpy style.

Stumpy and Melanie dove under the covers. I pulled the door three quarters shut so I couldn't see them. "Sorry, campers."

"What are you so fired up about?"

"You're not going to believe it."

Melanie shouted. "You can come in. You ruined it anyway."

I burst through the door and pulled a desk chair over to the bed and sat on it. Stumpy and Melanie lay side by side with the covers pulled up to their chins.

I talked rapidly. "Sister Lucia bought the chalice from us on eBay. We have it back. Sister Claudette is my mother. Sister Lucia is my aunt. I own the vineyard free and clear."

They both looked at me with wide eyes.

"You too, of course, Stumpy—ten percent."

They continued to stare.

"Ain't it great? It's over. It's all over."

Stumpy looked dizzy. "Sister Claudette is your mother?"

"Yeah. It's a secret for now." I told them the whole story.

Stumpy cried.

CHAPTER 32

Stumpy and I sat in our booth at Lucky Mike's.

It felt strange being back in the United States. We kept saying "Bonjour" to everyone.

The night was early and the crowd was light. A decades-old stale beer smell floated up from the warped vinyl floor, something I had never noticed before. A red plastic basket filled with popcorn sat on the table between us.

"Well, well. What have we here? I thought you guys were gone for good." Lucky Mike stood over us with a tray full of bottled beers. I handed him his passport, and he put it in his cash pouch without comment.

"*Bonsoir.* I mean good evening, Mike," Stumpy said. Mike looked at him with a suspicious eye.

"I was wondering." Stumpy tapped his chin with his index finger. "Would you happen to have an '09 St. Emilion Bordeaux? Or an '07 Rothschild Mouton Cadet?" Mike glared at him. "Or better yet, what would really go well with a burger would be a fine Louis Jadot Beaujolais."

Mike looked at me. "You got cash?"

I nodded.

Mike slammed our two regular beers on the table. "Welcome back, assholes, and quit fucking with me, Stumpy."

Mike walked off, and Stumpy's eyes opened wide. His jaw dropped as if to say "What?"

I laughed. "Man, France has gotten into your blood."

"And yours. I keep seeing that dreamy look in your eye. You wish you were back there now."

Stumpy was right. I couldn't stop thinking about France. I couldn't stop thinking about Jacqueline or that Sister Claudette was my mother. "I do wish I was back there now. I admit it. I can't stop thinking about Jacqueline."

"I thought you two were great together. You should look her up when we go back."

I lifted my beer. "Cheers." We clinked and drank.

Stumpy's face puckered. "Oh, this is awful."

I had to agree. The beer was flat and weak and tasted like a frat house basement. "Yuck. What morons drink this stuff?"

Stumpy put his index finger to his chin like an aristocrat. He tilted his head in thought. "Maybe we should try that wine bar on the east side that just opened up."

"Probably more your style," I said. "More sophisticated clientele."

"I absolutely agree." Stumpy nodded and looked serious. "So are you going to call her?"

"Who?"

"Jacqueline! When we go back."

I sat back in the booth. I put my hands on my forehead and then flung them out toward Stumpy in frustration. "Did you not see and hear how upset she was? I messed it up. She deserves better than me, anyway."

Stumpy had a huge grin on his face. He could barely contain himself. I thought he was going to crack up laughing.

"Oh, sure. Rub it in. You found love, and I found out what a jerk I really was."

"I've been telling you that for years."

"Ha, ha."

Stumpy's eyes gazed over my shoulder and his face beamed. Singing came from behind me. *"Oh when you're smiling, when you're smiling."*

"Wait, what?" I spun around and there she was, walking toward me looking more beautiful than I could ever imagine. Everyone in the bar watched as Jacqueline continued to sing. *"Yes when you're laughing, when you're laughing."*

I reached across the table and grabbed Stumpy's head. I leaned over and kissed him on the forehead. I jumped up and faced Jacqueline. The joy I felt was overwhelming. Tears welled up in my eyes. Jacqueline had come for me. We sang together. *"Oh when you're smiling, when you're smiling. The whole world smiles with you."*

Everyone in the bar clapped. I saw Sheila at the far end giving Jacqueline an unfriendly look-over like only women can do. She immediately went to her phone and started texting.

Jacqueline smiled at me. "I hear this is the place for a good beer and brat."

"And free popcorn," I said.

Her eyes sparkled like a starry vineyard night. I knew we would be all right. We held hands and looked into each other's eyes.

"Jacqueline, I'm sorry about the chalice—"

She held her index finger over her lips. "Sh." She held my hands. "I know everything."

"Know what?"

"Sister Claudette and Sister Lucia came to see me."

"In Paris?"

"Marketing St. Sebastian wine they said. But I imagine it was mostly me and you they were concerned with."

My head spun. I didn't know what to say.

"They told me your confession, and I—I forgive you, too."

I was the luckiest man in the world. "I'll never let you or the sisters down again."

Jacqueline smiled a sweet, yet challenging smile. "Sister Claudette, that is—your mother—has promised me the same thing."

"I've no one better to vouch for me."

She laughed. "Stumpy emailed me quite a long essay defending your character as well."

I laughed. "Well, there you go." I hoped I wasn't being too cavalier, but she smiled and looked at me with affection. Without thought I blurted, "I love you, Jacqueline."

She gave me the look. "I love you, Jason."

We kissed.

CHAPTER 33

Two weeks later we were all back in France. It was time. It was time to have a party. Stumpy and I stirred up a celebration, a celebration for the harvest, for the vineyard, for the nuns, and for us. We invited all who wanted to come from the town, including the Hotel Duras's staff.

The sun set behind the ridge and the sky turned a Bordeaux red. A warm breeze cooled the skin, heightening the senses.

Jacqueline and I stood together, holding hands more often than not.

I shook Peter's hand. "I'm terribly sorry about all the incidents at the hotel." Peter, full of wine and feeling merry, shrugged. "Love does strange things to people."

The early evening glow cast a warm beauty over the vineyard. Nuns and town dignitaries and welcome party crashers stood close together and filled our patio. Wine flowed freely. Nuns worked the crowd with plates of food.

We made our way over to Monsieur Aceau and his mother. I shook his hand. "Thank you for everything."

He laughed. "It was fun."

I laughed. "And here I thought your client was a mobster-type from Bordeaux."

Aceau reached inside his suit jacket. "I have the papers ready."

"Oh, good." I called and waved to Stumpy. He and Melanie talked and laughed with a group around them. Stumpy beamed. Melanie stood by his side, softly clutching his hand.

"I understand I owe you some money, Monsieur Aceau," I said.

He shook his head. "It is Sister Lucia with whom I did business."

"Nonsense. You and I know it was all for me. I will pay you first thing after the wine sale profits."

Aceau nodded in acquiescence. "There is no hurry." He winked at me. "I have no worries about Sister Lucia's debt."

I laughed. "You have a good son, Madame Aceau. You both are welcome to our vineyard and to our wine whenever you desire."

Madame Aceau put her hand on her son's shoulder and her face burst with pride.

Stumpy broke into our group with Melanie clinging to his arm. "What's up?"

"Aceau's got the papers. Are you ready to own part of a vineyard?"

"I feel I've drank part of this vineyard. I might as well own it, too."

Aceau led us to a small table and spread the papers out. He handed me a pen and pointed to several places I was to sign. I signed and handed Stumpy the pen. He dropped the pen and when he bent over to pick it up his rear end knocked into Jacqueline and some of our guests, creating a domino-bumping ripple through the crowd.

Matthew and Mark darted through the party. They each barked once and then scooted off into the vineyard.

Stumpy followed Aceau's pointing finger and signed underneath my signatures. Aceau brought out his stamper and officiously whacked away at the documents. Stumpy and I clinked glasses and shook hands.

"To my new partner," I shouted.

Everyone cheered.

Stumpy set his glass down and gave me a gregarious hug. He lifted me off the ground and spun. I held my glass up high and tried not to spill. People laughed and ducked in fear.

Stumpy set me down. Jacqueline and I kissed. Sister Lucia and Sister Claudette stood next to us. They shook our hands. "Congratulations."

"Thank you, Sister." I just couldn't call her mother. Not yet. Not that I didn't want to, but "Sister" had become a habit.

The party continued. Strings of white lights around the patio lit up the ever-darkening night, complementing the emerging stars. The heat escaped into the night air and the conversations became more animated.

Sister Lucia hit a spoon against a wine glass stem and it clanked shrilly. Sister Claudette put her hand on Sister Lucia's shoulder and climbed onto a chair. She looked over the crowd. She spoke in French and then translated into English as she went. "Could I have everyone's attention?"

She lifted her wine glass. "A toast to the new Saint Sebastian vineyard owners and vintners. Jason Barnes and Neil, uh Stumpy, Hammond."

"*Santé. Très bon!*" People laughed, patted us on the back, and clinked glasses with Stumpy and me.

Sister Claudette spoke again. "On a more serious note." The party became countryside quiet. "My new friends, my dear fellow Sisters, and my life-long friends." Sister Claudette nodded to the older locals. "Some of you knew me before I became a nun. When I was, let's say, more of a free spirit." The folks Sister Claudette's age laughed and smiled to each other. "But to all my friends I have a confession to make."

Sister Lucia clasped her hands and silently prayed.

Sister Claudette continued. "Before I became a nun I made this same confession to the church as part of absolving my sins to become one with Jesus."

I wanted to hide. I knew what was coming and I felt like it was my fault. I was living proof of her sin.

"When I was a teenager I had a baby. And that baby grew into a fine boy, and became a wonderful man."

A collective gasp and murmurs rippled through the crowd. I stared at my shoes.

"My sin was not in having such a beautiful baby. My sin was keeping it a secret from him and you. I will forever regret not being a part of his life for thirty-two years. Jason, I'm sorry. I hope you can forgive me. I love you."

I continued to stare at my shoes. The next thing I knew Sister Claudette stood before me. She wrapped her arms around me. I melted. I felt like a small boy and had feelings I'd never had before. I felt warm and content like I would never have another worry. I had a mother and she would make everything all right. For the first time in my life, I felt loved. I hugged my mother back, and I cried.

Sister Claudette pulled away. She wiped her eyes. "I'm sorry." She turned and put her hands up in the air. "This is a joyous occasion. Please celebrate!"

The crowd clapped and smiled. The clapping grew louder and cheers erupted.

"Thank you, Sister. I mean Mother Superior. I mean Mother."

Sister Claudette gave me another hug. "Don't stress over it, Jason. Any name will do. Whatever you are comfortable with."

The old lanky waiter was standing near us, smiling.

"By the way," I said to him. "I wanted to thank you for helping me out, especially, you know, with the beef bourguignon fiasco."

The waiter shrugged. *"Pas de problème."*

"I'm Jason." I held out my hand. "Jason Barnes."

He shook my hand. "Anthony."

I laughed. "My middle name is Anthony."

He looked at Sister Claudette and smiled. "I know."